Although still appearing to be a man in his early twenties, Robert Rankin was, in fact, born during the first years of Queen Victoria's reign. A retired Tupperware salesman, he now divides his time between wearing old straw hats, collecting whales and commuting between the planets.

His wife is very tall. Very tall.

Robert Rankin is the author of *The Fandom of the Operator*, *Web Site Story*, *Waiting for Godalming*, *Sex and Drugs and Sausage Rolls*, *Snuff Fiction*, *Apocalypso*, *The Dance of the Voodoo Handbag*, *Sprout Mask Replica*, *Nostradamus Ate My Hamster*, *A Dog Called Demolition*, *The Garden of Unearthly Delights*, *The Most Amazing Man Who Ever Lived*, *The Greatest Show Off Earth*, *Raiders of the Lost Car Park*, *The Book of Ultimate Truths*, the *Armageddon* quartet (three books), and the *Brentford* trilogy (five books) which are all published by Corgi books.

For more information on Robert Rankin and his books, see his website at:
www.lostcarpark.com/sproutlore

Also by Robert Rankin

ARMAGEDDON THE MUSICAL
THEY CAME AND ATE US, ARMAGEDDON II: THE B-MOVIE
THE SUBURBAN BOOK OF THE DEAD, ARMAGEDDON III:
THE REMAKE
THE ANTIPOPE
EAST OF EALING
THE SPROUTS OF WRATH
THE BRENTFORD CHAINSTORE MASSACRE
THE BOOK OF ULTIMATE TRUTHS
RAIDERS OF THE LOST CAR PARK
THE GREATEST SHOW OFF EARTH
THE MOST AMAZING MAN WHO EVER LIVED
THE GARDEN OF UNEARTHLY DELIGHTS
A DOG CALLED DEMOLITION
NOSTRADAMUS ATE MY HAMSTER
SPROUT MASK REPLICA
THE DANCE OF THE VOODOO HANDBAG
APOCALYPSO
SNUFF FICTION
SEX AND DRUGS AND SAUSAGE ROLLS
WAITING FOR GODALMING
WEB SITE STORY
THE FANDOM OF THE OPERATOR

and published by Corgi Books

THE BRENTFORD TRIANGLE

Robert Rankin

CORGI BOOKS

THE BRENTFORD TRIANGLE
A CORGI BOOK : 9780552138420

Originally published in Great Britain by Pan Books Ltd

PRINTING HISTORY
Pan edition published 1982
Abacus edition published 1988
Corgi edition published 1992

31

Set in 10/11pt Plantin by
Chippendale Type Ltd, Otley, West Yorkshire.

Corgi Books are published by Transworld Publishers,
61–63 Uxbridge Road, London W5 5SA,
A Random House Group Company.

Addresses for Random House Group Ltd companies outside the UK
can be found at: www.randomhouse.co.uk
The Random House Group Ltd Reg. No. 954009.

Penguin Random House is committed to a sustainable future for
our business, our readers and our planet. This book is made from
Forest Stewardship Council® certified paper.

Printed and bound in Great Britain by Clays Ltd, Elcograf S.p.A.

*For my unfailingly
cheerful son, Alex*

Prologue

The solitary figure in the saffron robes shielded his eyes from the glare and squinted down the glacier to where the enormous black vessel lay, one-third submerged, in the floor of the valley. Allowing for the portion lost below the icy surface of the frozen lake it was easily some three hundred cubits long, at least fifty wide and another thirty high. It had, overall, the appearance of some fantastic barge with a kind of gabled house mounted upon its deck. Its gopherwood timbers were blackened by a heavy coating of pitch and hardened by the petrification of the glacier which had kept it virtually intact throughout the countless centuries. A great opening yawned in one side; several hundred yards away lay the door which had once filled it, resting upon two huge rocks like some kind of altarpiece.

The solitary figure dropped the butt of his Wild Woodbine, ground it into the snow with the heel of his naked left foot and raised his field glasses. His guides had long since deserted him, fearing in their superstition to set foot upon the ice pastures of the sacred mountain. Now he stood alone, the first man to breast the glacier and view a spectacle which many would gladly have given all to witness.

He whistled shrilly between closed teeth and a faint smile played about his lips. He slapped his hands together, and with his orange robes swirling about him in the bitter winds of the mountain peak, he girded up his loins and strode down the frozen escarpment to survey the ancient wreck at closer quarters.

I

Neville the part-time barman drew back the polished brass bolts and swung open the saloon-bar door of the Flying Swan. Framed in the famous portal, he stood yawning and scratching, a gaunt figure clad in Japanese silk dressing-gown, polka-dot cravat and soiled carpet-slippers. The sun was rising behind the gasometers, and in the distance, along the Ealing Road, the part-time barman could make out the diminutive form of Small Dave the postman beginning his morning rounds. No mail as usual for the Four Horsemen, more bills for Bob the bookie, a small brown parcel for Norman's corner shop, something suspicious in a large plain envelope for Uncle Ted at the greengrocer's, and, could it be—? Neville strained his good eye as Small Dave approached – tunelessly whistling the air to 'Orange Claw Hammer' – a postcard?

The wee postman trod nearer, grinning broadly. As he drew level with the part-time barman he winked lewdly and said, 'Another!' Neville extended a slim white hand to receive the card, but Small Dave held it below his reach. 'It's from Archroy,' announced the malicious postman, who greatly delighted in reading people's mail, 'and bears an Ararat postmark. It says that our lad has discovered . . . ' Neville leant hurriedly forward and tore the card from his hand ' . . . has discovered the remains of Noah's Ark upon the mountain's peak and is arranging to have it dismantled and brought back to England.'

9

Neville fixed the little postman with a bitter eye. 'And you could tell all that simply by reading the address?' he snarled.

Small Dave tapped at his nose and winked anew. 'I took the liberty of giving it the once-over,' he explained, 'in case it was bad news. One can never be too careful.'

'One certainly can't!' The part-time barman took a step backwards and slammed the Swan's door with deafening finality upon the dwarfish scrutineer of the Queen's mail. Neville took a deep breath to steady his nerves and turned away from the door. His long strides took him with haste across the threadbare carpet of the saloon-bar.

His first drew him past the pitted dartboard, the chalked scores of the previous night's play faintly aglow in the early light. His second brought him level with the aged shove-halfpenny table, and a third took him past the first of the Swan's eight polished Britannia pub tables. Two more soundless strides and Neville halted involuntarily in his tracks. Before him stood an object so detestable, so loathsome and so mind-stunningly vile that the postman's irritating habits paled into insignificance.

The Captain Laser Alien Attack Machine!

Its lights blinked eternally and a low and sinister hum arose from it, setting the part-time barman's ill-treated teeth on edge. Installed by one of the brewery's cringing catspaws the thing stood, occupying valuable drinking space, and as hated by the Swan's patrons as it was possible for any piece of microchipped circuitry to be hated.

Neville caught sight of his face reflected in the screen and surprised even himself with the ferocity of his expression. He addressed the machine with his regular morning curse, but the monster hummed on regardless, indifferent to the barman's invocation of the dark forces. Neville turned away in disgust and slouched off up the stairs to his rooms. Here in privacy he poured milk upon his corn-flakes and perused Archroy's postcard, propped against the marmalade pot.

A rooftop view of Brentford.

It was a great pity that Archroy, in the interests of economy, as he put it, had chosen to take a bundle of local postcards with him when he set off upon his globe-trotting. Rooftop views of Brentford were all very pleasant of course, but they did tend to become a little samey. After all, when one received a card postmarked 'The Potala, Lhasa', or 'The East Pier, Sri Lanka', it wouldn't hurt to see a bit of pictorial representation on the front once in a while. It did tend to take the edge off, having read the exotic details of a Singhalese temple dance, to turn over the card and view the splendours of two gasometers and a water tower.

Neville sighed deeply as he squinted over to the row of identical postcards which now lined his mantelpiece. Certainly, the one view was so commonplace as to be practically invisible, but each of these little cards had been despatched from some far-flung portion of the great globe. Each had travelled through strange lands, across foreign borders, over continents, finally to return, like little pictorial homing pigeons, to the town of their birth. Certainly there was romance here.

Neville plucked up the card and turned it between his fingers. 'Noah's Ark, eh?' That one took a bit of believing. Each of the postcards had boasted some fabulous deed or another, but this outdid them all.

Noah's Ark? To the pagan Neville it did seem a trifle unlikely. Even if it had existed at all, which Neville con-sidered a matter of grave doubt, the chances of it surviving, even partially intact, down through the long centuries on the peak of Mount Ararat did seem pretty slight. Such things were just silly-season space-fillers for the popular press. The barman recalled reading about that chap up north who claimed to have discovered the bottomless pit in his back garden. He would probably have come clean that it was all a hoax had he not stepped backwards down it while posing for the press photographer.

Noah's Ark indeed! Neville took the card and placed it with its eight identical brothers upon the mantelshelf. Noah's Ark indeed! It couldn't be true. Could it?

2

That same sun, having now risen from behind the gas-ometers, stretched down a tentative ray towards a rarely washed bedroom window at Number Six Abaddon Street. Passing with some difficulty through the murky pane, it displayed itself upon an inner wall as a pale lozenge of light surrounding a noseless statuette of Our Lady.

This mantelpiece beatification of the blessed Virgin was as usual lost upon the room's tenant. John Vincent Omally was what the textbooks are wont to describe as 'a late riser'. Usually the lozenge of light would move noiselessly across the mantelpiece wall until it reached the cracked mirror, and then reflect itself on to the face of the sleeper, thus awakening him from his restful slumbers. But today, as for some days past, it was to be denied its ritual.

Today it would find but an empty pillow, showing naught of a recumbent head but a slight indentation and a Brylcreem stain. The coverlet was tossed aside and a pair of ragged pyjama strides lay in an athletic splits posture upon the linoleum. A timeworn tweed jacket was missing from its appointed hook behind the door. It was not yet eight of the clock and John Omally was no longer at home to callers. For John Omally had important business elsewhere.

John Omally was gone a-golfing.

'Fore!' The cry echoed across the allotment, struck the wall of the Seamen's Mission and passed back over the head of a curly-headed son of Eire, clad in soiled Fair

Isle slipover and rolled-up tweeds. 'Fore and have a care!' Omally swung the aged club, the relic of a former and more refined age, with a vengeance and struck the little white pill a mighty blow. The ball soared some four feet into the clear morning air and fell to earth in the midst of Jim Pooley's radish patch.

Jim stifled a titter and read from a dog-eared exercise book entitled *The Now Official Handbook of Allotment Golf*: 'Unless rendered totally inextricable, by nature of being unreachable, i.e. under more than four feet of water or beyond climbing capability, the player will play the stroke. Should the player, however, endanger the growth of his opponent's radishes he will forfeit the hole.'

Omally scratched his head with a wooden tee and eyed Pooley with some suspicion. 'I don't recall that bit at the end, Jim,' said he. 'May I venture to ask whether the rule applies to runner beans, possibly of the variety which you uprooted from my plot yesterday whilst attempting that trick shot of yours on to the fourth?'

Pooley made a thoughtful face. 'Beans are not specifically mentioned,' he said, carefully examining the note he had so hastily scribbled. 'But if you are making an official request to have them included in the handbook then I think we might stretch a point and pencil them in.'

At this moment the two golfers suddenly threw themselves down commando-fashion into a clump of long grass. An explanation for this extraordinary behaviour was almost immediately forthcoming as the distinctive tuneless whistling of Small Dave signalled the approach of that midget as he took his regular morning short cut through to the Butts Estate.

Allotment Golf had not yet caught the eye either of the allotment holders or the general public, and both Pooley and Omally wished to keep it that way. They would have greatly preferred to golf upon one of the municipal courses but circumstances had decreed that their photographs now appeared upon every persona-non-grata board throughout the county.

It had all appeared so trivial at the time, the small disagreements, the occasional bout of fisticuffs; hardly police matters one would have thought. Golfers, however, are a clannish bunch with rather a conservative attitude towards sport. The two Brentonians' extraordinary conception of the game had not been appreciated. Their constant rule-bending and wild club-swinging, their numerous bogus claims to the course record, achieved for the most part by omitting to play the more difficult holes, their total disregard for other players' safety, refusing to shout 'Fore', before what Omally described as 'heavy putting', had been too much to bear. The secretary of one course had shown moments of rare tolerance: he had respected Pooley's request to play the holes in reverse order, he had suffered Omally playing in cycling cape and fisherman's waders one particularly wet day, but when Pooley relocated all the tee markers (in order to make the game more interesting) and Omally had dug a second hole upon the third green in order to sink a birdy four, stern measures had been taken. The two potential Ryder Cup winners had been given what the French refer to as 'La Rush de la Bum'.

Thus in a moment of rare inspiration, necessity being, like Frank Zappa, the mother of invention and Jim Pooley being a man of infinite resource when cornered, Allotment Golf had been born.

It had much to recommend it. There was no queuing up to be done, no green fees to pay, no teeing off in front of cynical observers to be suffered; above all, they could invent their own rules as the fancy took them. As originator, Jim took sole charge of the exercise book until every detail was clarified. This, he told Omally, was what is called 'a divine right'. A certain amount of

subterfuge was called for, of course; they had no wish
to alert any of the other allotment holders to the sport
for fear that it might catch on. It had been a moment of
rare inspiration indeed on Pooley's part, but one which
was to play its part in changing the face of Brentford
as we know it for good and all.

'Fore!' Small Dave had departed upon his round and
John Omally set to it once more to shift his ball from
Pooley's radish patch and belt it heartily towards the fourth
hole, which lay cunningly concealed between Old Pete's
wheelbarrow and his battered watering-can.

3

Norman was one of those early birds which catch the proverbial worm. Running the down-at-heel corner-tobacconist's at anything remotely resembling a profit was pretty much a full-time occupation. Norman went about it, as he did with everything else, with a will. 'One must remain constantly in the field if one wishes to ladle off the cream which is one's bread and butter,' he constantly explained to his customers. This remark generally met with enough thoughtful head-nodding to offer the shopkeeper the encouragement he needed.

Norman had been up since six, sorting through and numbering up the day's papers. It was Wednesday and the first crop of specialist journals had arrived. There was the *Psychic News* for Lily at the Plume Café. This Norman numbered in large red figures as the new paperboy had the irritating habit of confusing it with *Cycling News* and delivering it to Father Moity at St Joan's. There was the regular welter of sporting mags for Bob the bookie, and a selection of Danish glossies for Uncle Ted the greengrocer. Norman folded a copy of *Muscle Boys* into the widow Cartwright's *Daily Telegraph* and hummed softly to himself. There was a busy day ahead and he intended to take advantage of its each and every minute.

Nick, the big-nosed paperboy, sidled into the shop, chewing gum and smoking what the lads at the Yard refer to as the certain substances. 'Kudos, Norm,' he said.

Norman looked up from his doings and eyed the youth

with evident distaste. 'Good morning, Nicholas,' he said, giving his watch minute scrutiny and rattling it against his ear. 'Can that be the time already, or is the old Vacheron Constantine running fast again?'

The paperboy flicked idly through a copy of *Bra-Busting Beauties*. 'Look at those charlies,' he said, salivating about the gums, 'you'd think you'd gone deaf, eh?'

Norman thrust the bundle of folded papers into the worn canvas bag and pushed it across the worm-eaten counter. 'Away on your toes, lad,' he grunted. 'Time heals all wounds and absence makes the heart grow fonder.'

'Oh, it do,' the lad replied, sweeping up the bag in an eczema-coated fist and bearing it away through the door like the standard of a captured enemy. 'It do that!'

Norman watched him depart in sorrow. There was something decidedly shifty about that boy, but he couldn't quite put his finger on exactly what. The shopkeeper crossed the mottled linoleum floor and turned the CLOSED sign to OPEN. Soon they would arrive, he thought, as he peered through the grimy door-glass: the office girls for their cigarettes and chocolate bars, the revellers of the previous night for their aspirins, the school lads for their comics and penny toffees, the old dears for the pints of milk Reg the Milkman had neglected to leave upon their steps, Old Pete for his half-ounce of tobacco, Pooley and Omally for five Woodbines on their weekly accounts. The same old regular morning faces.

Norman shook his head thoughtfully. It wasn't a bad old life if you didn't weaken, was it? And a trouble shared was definitely a trouble halved, and you had to laugh didn't you?

Retracing his steps to the counter he selected one of the newer brands of bubblegum that the local rep had persuaded him into stocking. Stripping away the wrapper from the stick of Captain Laser Astrogum he thrust the gaudy piece of synthetic sweetmeat into his mouth.

Chewing distractedly he drifted about his shop, flicking without conviction at the dust-filled corners and blowing the falling residue from the faded coverings of the out-of-date chocolate boxes which lined his shelves. Here was the Queen smiling sweetly, if somewhat faintly, at her Coronation. Here two stuffed-looking Scotties peered through the rust from a shortbread biscuit tin, and here was the Pickwickian character still grinning idiotically at that uneatable coughsweet.

Norman drew a bespittled finger across the old tin's surface in an attempt to bring up the brand-name. Did people still eat sweeties like this? he wondered. Or had they ever? He couldn't recall ever having sold any. Out of sudden interest he picked up the old tin and gave it a shake. It was empty, of course. Probably evaporated, he thought.

Norman shrugged once more; he really ought to sling them all out, they served little purpose and could hardly be described as decorative. But he knew he would never part with them. They gave his shop character and were always good for inspiring conversation from the lonely pensioners who happened by, upon some pretext or another, only really wanting a bit of a chat.

Norman thrust his one-feather duster back into its appointed niche and flexed his shoulders as if in an attempt to free himself from the strange melancholia which filled him this morning. Things were going to change in Brentford and there was little good in crying over spilt milk or whistling down the wind.

Upon the counter lay the small brown package which Small Dave had delivered. Norman knew exactly what it contained; the American stamps and spidery Gothic lettering told him well enough. This was the last component he required, the final tiny missing piece of the jigsaw.

This was the make or break. Several years of planning

and many many months of hard and exacting work had gone into this, not to mention the small fortune spent upon research, preparation and final construction. This experiment was indeed 'The Big One'. It was a Nobel Prize job this time, and no mistake. Norman had named it 'The Ultimate Quest', and it was indeed a goody.

Certainly, in the past, Norman's little scientific diversions had not been altogether successful. In fact he had become something of a figure of fun because of them. But this time he was sure he had cracked it. The people of Brentford would certainly sit up and take notice of this one. If his calculations, combined with those of a certain Germanic physicist not altogether unknown for his theory of relativity, proved to be correct, then things were going to be very different indeed hereabouts.

Norman patted the tiny brown package. If all was present and correct he would begin the first practical working tests this very early-closing day, then we would see what we would see.

The shop bell rang in a customer. It was Old Pete with his half-terrier Chips as ever upon his heels. 'Morning, Norman,' said the ancient, cheerily, 'a half-ounce of Ships if you will.'

'Grmmph mmmph,' the shopkeeper replied, for the first time becoming aware that the Captain Laser Astrogum had suddenly set hard in his mouth, welding his upper plate to his lower set.

'Grmmph mmmph?' queried Old Pete, scratching at his snowy head. 'Now what would it be this time? Let me guess? Experimenting with some advanced form of Esperanto is it? Or having a try at ventriloquism?'

Norman clutched at his jaw and grew red about the jowls, his eyes began to roll.

'Ah,' said Old Pete, tapping at his nose. 'I think I am beginning to get the measure of it. Something in mime, isn't it? Now let's have a go, I'm quite good at this, give me a clue now, how many words in the title?'

Norman tore at his welded teeth and bashed at the counter-top with a clenched fist.

'Five words,' said Old Pete. 'No, six, seven? Is it a film or a book?'

Norman lurched from the counter in a most grotesque fashion, grunting and snorting. Old Pete stepped nimbly aside as he blundered past, while Young Chips sought a safe hideyhole.

'It's a poser,' said the Old One, as Norman threw himself about the shop, toppling the magazine stand and spilling out its contents. 'I have it, I have it!' he cried suddenly. 'It is the now legendary Charles Laughton in his famous portrayal of Victor Hugo's *Hunchback of Notre Dame.*'

In hearty congratulations for Norman's excellent impersonation the old man, who still retained a considerable amount of strength in his right arm despite his advancing years, slapped Norman upon the back. The blow loosened the cemented teeth, which flew from the shopkeeper's mouth, tumbled noisily across the linoleum, and finally came to rest in an impenetrable place beneath the counter, where they lay in the darkness grinning ruefully.

'Sanks yous,' spluttered Norman, 'sanks yous, Petes.'

'Credit where credit is due,' the elder replied. 'My tobacco now, if you please.'

Norman staggered to the counter and tore out a one-ounce packet from the tin. 'Ons a houses,' he whistled through his naked gums. 'Ons a houses.'

Old Pete, who was never a man to look a gift impersonator in the mouth, accepted his reward with a hasty display of gratitude and departed the shop at speed. Halfway up the Ealing Road Young Chips unearthed a pristine copy of *Bra-Busting Beauties* from its secret hiding place beneath a beer crate outside the Swan.

'This has all the makings of being a most profitable day,' said the ancient to his furry companion. Young Chips woofed noncommittally. Being naturally clairvoyant he sensed something rather to the contrary and therefore wished to reserve judgement for the present.

4

The allotment golfers had come to something of a critical stage in their game. They had by now reached the eighteenth 'green' and Omally had but to sink a nine-foot putt across Reg Watling's furrowed spinach patch to take the match. Betting had been growing steadily during the morning's play and with each increase in financial risk the two men had grown ever more tight-lipped, eagle-eyed, and alert to the slightest infringement of the rules.

Omally spat on his palms and rubbed them together. He stalked slowly about his ball and viewed it from a multiplicity of angles. He scrutinized the lie of the land, tossed a few straws into the air and nodded thoughtfully as they drifted to earth. He licked his finger and held it skyward, he threw himself to the ground and squinted along his putter sniper fashion. 'Right then,' said the broth of a boy. 'It looks like child's play.'

Pooley, who was employing what he referred to as 'the psychology', shook his head slowly. 'That would be at least a three to the sinking I would believe.'

Omally gestured over his shoulder to the water-butt wherein lay Pooley's ball. 'You would be phoning for Jacques Cousteau and his lads, I shouldn't wonder.'

Pooley shrugged. 'That is an easy shot compared to this.'

Omally sniggered. 'Keep your eye on the ball, Jim,' he advised.

Omally's putting technique bore an uncanny resemblance to that practised by seasoned Yorkshire batsmen at the Oval. The putter had a tendency to dig well in on such occasions, sometimes to a depth of some three inches or more, and once beyond digging range. There was generally a fair amount of lift on the ball, although the *Now Official Handbook of Allotment Golf* suggested that any balls putted above shoulder height should be considered as drives and the player penalized accordingly.

Omally squared up his ball whilst Pooley continued to employ 'the psychology'. He coughed repeatedly, rustled sweet papers in his pocket and scuffed his blakey'd heels in the dust. 'Is that a Lurcher or a Dane?' he asked, pointing towards some canine of his own creation.

Omally ignored him. There was big beer money on this shot. John suddenly swung the putter in a blurry arc and struck deeply behind his ball, raising a great clod of earth, which is referred to in golfing circles as a divot. The ball cannonaded across the allotment, with a whine like a doctored tom struck a section of corrugated iron fencing, bowled along Old Pete's herbaceous border, and skidded to a halt a mere inch from the eighteenth hole.

Omally swore briefly, but to the point, flung down his putter and turned his back upon the wanton pill.

'Bad luck,' said Pooley, amid an ill-concealed snigger. By way of consolation, he added, 'It was a brave try. But would you prefer that I pause a moment before sinking my ball, on the off chance that an earth tremor might secure you the match?'

Omally kicked his golf bag over.

'Steady on,' said Pooley.

John turned upon him bitterly, 'Go on then, Jimmy boy,' he sneered, 'let us see you take your shot.'

'You won't like it.'

'Won't I, though?'

Pooley tapped at his nose. 'Care to up the betting a trice?'

Omally stroked his chin. 'From the water-butt in one, that is what you are telling me?' Pooley nodded. 'Unless you, like the Dalai Lama, have mastered the techniques of levitation and telekinesis, which I do not believe, I do not rate your chances.'

'You will kick yourself afterwards.'

Omally spat on to his palm and slapped it into that of his companion. 'All bets are doubled, will that serve you?'

'Adequately.' Pooley strolled over to the water-butt. With the lie of the land, it certainly was in a perfect line for the hole. Just down a slight slope and into the depression where lay the eighteenth.

'I shall play it from here,' said Jim, turning his back upon the target.

Omally stuck his hands into his pockets. 'As you please,' said he.

'I will play it with a mashie if you have no objections.'

'None whatever.' Omally selected the club and handed it to his companion. Pooley leant forward and chalked a small cross at the base of the water-butt. Drawing back, he grasped the club hammerlike in his right fist and with a lewd wink struck the ancient zinc tank a murderous blow.

It was a sizeable hole and the water burst through it with great enthusiasm. Bearing down with the sudden torrent, and evidently much pleased to be free of its watery grave, Pooley's ball bobbed along prettily. It danced down the slight incline, pirouetted about the eighteenth hole, as if taking a final bow, then plunged into it with a sarcastic gurgle.

'My game,' said Pooley rubbing his hands together. 'Best we settle up now, I think.'

Omally struck his companion a devastating blow to the skull. Jim collapsed into a forest of bean poles but rose almost immediately with a great war cry. He leapt upon

Omally, catching him around the waist and bearing him towards the now muddy ground. 'Poor loser!' he shouted, grinding his thumb into Omally's right eye.

'Bloody damn cheat,' the other replied, going as ever for the groin.

The two men were more than equally matched, although Omally was by far the dirtier fighter. They bowled over and over in the mud, bringing into play a most extraordinary diversity of unsportsmanlike punches, low kicks and back elbows. They had been tumbling away in like fashion for some ten minutes, doing each other the very minimum amount of damage, yet expending a great deal of energy, when each man suddenly became aware that his antics were being observed.

Some twenty yards or so away, a solitary figure in a grey coverall suit stood silently watching. At the distance it was difficult to make out his features clearly, but they seemed wide and flat and had more than the suggestion of the Orient about them.

The two men rose from the ground, patting away at their clothes. The fight was over, the ref's decision being a draw. They beat a hasty retreat to the doubtful safety of Pooley's allotment shed. Through a knot-hole in the slatted side they squinted at the grey figure. He was as immobile as a shop-window dummy, and stared towards them unblinkingly in a manner which the sensitive Jim found quite upsetting. He was of average height with high cheek-bones and a slightly tanned complexion and bore a striking resemblance to a young Jack Palance.

Pooley sought about for his tobacco tin. 'I don't like the look of this,' he said.

Omally, who had liberated Pooley's tin from his pocket during the fight, was rolling a cigarette behind his back. 'He is probably some workman chappy,' he suggested, 'or possibly a bus conductor or site engineer from the gas works.' The hollow tone in Omally's voice was not lost upon his companion.

'He has more of the look of a municipal worker to me,' said Jim, shaking his head dismally. 'A park-keeper perhaps, or . . . '

'Don't say it,' said John. 'Some spy from the Council come to inspect the allotment?'

Pooley clenched his fists. 'This is all too much. Discriminated against and ostracized from the Council courses, now tracked down here for further discrimination and ostracization, hounded down because of our love of the game. It is all too much to bear. Let us kill him now and bury his body.'

Omally agreed that it was all too much to bear but thought Pooley's solution a little drastic. 'All may not be lost,' he said. 'He may have only just arrived and may only have witnessed our slight disagreement regarding the excellence of your trick shot. He may not suspect the cause.'

Pooley gestured through a broken window-pane to where his golf caddy, a converted supermarket trolley, stood bristling with its assortment of unmatched clubs.

Omally hung his head. 'The game is up,' said he in a leaden tone.

Pooley put his eye once more to the knot-hole. 'He is still there. Perhaps we could reason with him, or better still offer a bribe.'

Omally thought this sound enough, every man having his price. 'How much have you in your pockets?' he asked.

Pooley smiled grimly. 'We have not yet settled up over the game. I think that it is for you to approach him, John. Employ your silken tongue and feel free to invest a portion of my winnings if needs be. You can always owe me the difference. I consider you to be a man of honour.'

Omally licked the end of his captured roll-up. 'All right,'

he said nobly, 'I shall go. We shall consider your winnings to be an investment to secure a further season of uninterrupted play. During this period I have not the least doubt that if your game continues at its present standard you will have the opportunity to lighten my pockets continually.'

Pooley opened his mouth to speak but thought better of it. In such matters Omally generally held the verbal edge. 'Go then with my blessings,' he said, 'but kindly leave me my tobacco tin.'

Omally straightened up his regimental necktie, squared his broad and padded shoulders, threw open the hut door, and stepped out into the sunlight. The figure lurking amongst the bean poles watched the Irishman with an inscrutable expression. Omally thrust his hands into his trouser pockets and gazed about the allotment with extreme nonchalance. He yawned, stretched, and then, as if seeing the figure for the first time, flicked at his mop of curly black hair and bid the stranger a hearty 'Good morning there.'

The figure uttered not a word but merely stared on regardless.

'There'll be rain before the evening I shouldn't wonder,' said Omally, who was rarely rattled. 'Won't do the ground any harm though.' As he spoke he slowly strolled in the stranger's direction, covering his approach with the occasional sidestep to scrutinize some flowering bloom. But soon there was less than fifteen yards between them. 'Should get a rare old crop of beans up this year,' said John, stepping nimbly over Old Pete's watering can.

In order that he might reach the Council spy, for by this time Omally felt one hundred per cent certain that this was in fact the lurker's despicable calling, it was necessary for him to pass behind Soap Distant's heavily-bolted corrugated iron shed. Soap himself had vanished away from Brentford under most extraordinary circumstances, but his rental upon the shed was paid up until the turn of the following century and his hut remained untouched and inviolate.

Omally sneaked away behind it. He lost sight of the spy for but a moment, but when he emerged at the spot where the malcontent should have been standing, to John's amazement, not a soul was to be seen.

Pooley came ambling up. 'Where did he go?' he asked. 'I took my eyes off him for a moment and he was gone.'

Omally shook his head. 'There is something not altogether kosher about this, I am thinking.'

'He must have legged it, had it away on his toes.'

Omally scratched at the stubble of his chin. 'Perhaps,' said he, 'perhaps. There is a terrible smell of creosote hereabouts, has anybody been pasting his paintwork?'

'Not to my knowledge.'

Omally shrugged, 'Shall we play another round then?'

Pooley scrutinized his Piaget wristwatch. 'I feel a little unsettled,' he said. 'Perhaps we should adjourn now to the Swan for a cooling pint of Large to ease our fractured nerves.'

'That,' said Omally, smacking his hands together, 'is not a bad idea by any reckoning.'

5

Bitow . . . Bitow . . . Bitow . . . Bitow . . . Whap . . .
'What?' The ungodly sounds echoed across the library-silent saloon-bar of the Flying Swan, rattling the optics and jarring the patrons from their contemplation of the racing dailies. Neville the part-time barman clapped his hands about his ears and swore from between freshly clenched teeth.

Nicholas Roger Raffles Rathbone, currently serving his time as local paperlad, stood before the Captain Laser Alien Attack Machine, his feet at three of the clock and his shoulders painfully hunched in his bid to defend planet Earth from its never-ending stream of cosmic cousins ever bent upon conquest, doom, and destruction.

Bitow . . . Bitow . . . Bitow . . . Bitow . . . His right forefinger rattled away at the neutron bomb release button and a bead of perspiration formed upon his ample brow. 'Go on my son, go on.' Little streamers of coloured light, like some residue from a third-rate firework box, flew up the bluely-tinted video screen to where the horde of approaching spacecraft, appearing for all the world like so many stuffed olives, dipped and weaved.

Bitow . . . Whap . . . 'What?' Young Nick levelled his cherry-red boot at the machine, damaging several of his favourite toes.

Neville watched the performance with a face of despair. He too had made that gesture of defiance with an equal lack of success.

The boy Nick dug deeply into his denim pockets for

more small change, but found only a pound note, whose serial number corresponded exactly with one which had lain not long before in Norman's secret cashbox beneath his counter. He turned his back momentarily upon his humming adversary and bounced over to the bar counter. 'Give us change of a quid then, Nev.'

Neville viewed the diminutive figure with the lime-green coiffure. 'I cannot give out change,' he said maliciously. 'You will have to buy a drink.'

'OK then, a half of shandy and plenty of two-bobs in the change, the Captain awaits.'

Neville drew off a mere trickle of ale into the glass and topped it up from the drips tray. 'We've no lemonade,' he sneered.

'No sweat,' said Nick.

Neville noticed, as he passed the flat half-pint across the gleaming bar top, that the boy's right forefinger drummed out a continual tattoo upon an imaginary neutron bomb release button. Accepting the pound note, he rang up 'No Sale' and scooped out a fistful of pennies and halfpennies and a ten-bob piece. 'Sorry I can't let you have more than a couple of florins,' he told the bouncing boy, 'we are a little down on silver this morning.'

The boy shrugged. 'No sweat.' He was well acquainted with the old adage about a prophet being without honour in his own land, and he made a mental note that he would always in future take his perks in silver before settling in for a lunchtime's cosmic warfare. Without further ado he pocketed his ten-bob piece, swept up his pennies, pushed his half-pint pointedly aside and jogged back to the humming machine.

Pooley and Omally entered the Flying Swan. 'God save all here,' said the Irishman, as more bitowing rent the air, 'and a pox upon the Nipponese and all their hellish works.'

31

Raffles Rathbone heard not a word of this; he was hunched low, aiding the Captain in his bid to defeat Earth's attackers. His face was contorted into the kind of expression which made Joseph Carey Merrick such a big attraction in the Victorian side-shows. His right forefinger twitched in a localized St Vitus' Dance and his body quivered as if charged with static electricity.

Neville ground his teeth, loosening yet another expensive filling, and tore his eyes away from the loathsome spectacle and towards his approaching patrons. 'What is your pleasure, gentlemen?' he asked.

Pooley hoisted himself on to his favourite stool. 'Two pints of your very best, barlord,' he said. 'My companion is in the chair.'

Making much of his practised wrist action, Neville drew off two pints of the very very best. He eyed Omally with only the merest suspicion as the Irishman paid up without a fuss, guessing accurately that it was some debt of honour. His eyebrows were raised somewhat, however, to the shabby and mudbespattered appearance of the two drinkers. He thought to detect something slightly amiss. 'I think to detect something slightly amiss,' he observed.

John drew deeply upon his pint. 'You find me a puzzled man,' said he with some sincerity.

Pooley nodded, 'I also am puzzled,' he said tapping his chest.

The part-time barman stood silently a moment, hoping for a little elaboration, but when it became apparent that none was to be forthcoming he picked up a pint glass and began to polish it.

'You have had no luck yet with the disablement of that horror?' said Omally, gesturing over his shoulder towards the video machine.

Neville accelerated his polishing. 'None whatever,' he snarled. 'I have tried the hot soup through the vent, the

32

bent washer in the slot, assault with a deadly weapon. I have tried simply to cut the lead but the thing is welded into the wall.'

'Why not pull the fuse at the mains box?' Pooley asked.

Neville laughed hollowly. 'My first thought. Our friends from the brewery have thought of that. I have pulled every fuse in the place, but it still runs. It works off some separate power supply which doesn't even register on the electric meter. It cannot be switched off. Night and day it runs. I can hear it in my room, humming and humming. I swear that if something is not done soon I will tender my resignation, if only to save my sanity.'

'Steady on,' said Jim.

'Look at it!' Neville commanded. 'It is an obscenity, an abomination, an insult!' He placed one hand over his heart and the other palm downward upon the bar-top. 'Once,' said he, 'once, if you will recall, one could sit in this pub enjoying the converse of good friends well met. Once, in a corner booth, meditate upon such matters as took your fancy. Little, you will remember, and correct me if I am wrong or sinking into melancholy, little broke the harmony of the place but for the whisper of the feathered flight. Once . . . '

'Enough, enough,' said Jim. 'Hold hard now, you are bringing a lump to my throat which is causing some interference to my drinking.'

'I am not a man to panic,' said Neville, which all knew to be a blatant lie. 'But this thing is wearing down my resistance. I cannot take much more, I can tell you.'

Omally noted well the desperation upon the barman's face and felt sure that there was the definite possibility of financial advancement in it. 'You need to play a shrewd game with those mechanical lads,' he said, when he thought the time was right. 'A firm hand is all they understand.'

Neville's eyes strayed towards the jukebox, which had not uttered a sound these ten years, since Omally had applied a firm hand to its workings. It seemed a thing of little menace now compared with the video machine, but Neville could vividly recall the agonies he had gone through at the time. 'You feel that you might meet with such a challenge?' he asked in an even voice.

'Child's play,' said Omally, which made Pooley choke upon his ale.

'Good show.' Neville smiled bravely and pulled two more pints. 'These are on the house,' he said.

Old Pete, whose hearing was as acute as his right arm sound, overheard the last remark. 'Good morning, John, Jim,' he said, rising upon his stick. 'A fine day is it not?'

'It started poorly,' said Omally, 'but it is beginning to perk up. Cheers.'

'Been to the allotment then?' the ancient enquired, placing his empty glass upon the counter and indicating the mud-bespattered condition of the two secret golfers.

'Weeding,' said John, making motions with an ethereal shovel. 'Spring up overnight, those lads.'

Old Pete nodded sagely. 'It is strange,' said he, 'what things spring up upon an allotment patch overnight. Take my humble plot for instance. You'll never guess what I found on it the other day.'

Pooley, who had a kind of intuition regarding these things, kept silent.

'Golf tee,' said Old Pete in a harsh stage whisper.

'Large rum over here,' said Omally, rattling Pete's glass upon the bar.

'How unexpected,' said the wily old bastard. 'Bless you boys, bless you.'

Omally drank a moment in silence. 'Now tell me, Pete,' said he, when the ancient had taken several sips upon his free-man's, 'how spins the world for you at the present hour?'

Old Pete grunted non-committally. 'It is a case of mustn't grumble, I suppose.'

'No news then? Nothing out of the ordinary or untoward on the go?'

'Not that I can think of, did you have anything in mind?'

'No, nothing.' Omally made a breezy gesture. 'It is just, well, to be frank, Pete, it is well known that little, if anything, going on in the Borough ever slips by you, as your present drink will bear testimony to. I just thought that you might have some little snippet of interest up your four-buttoned sleeve.'

'You couldn't be a little more specific?' said Pete, draining his glass. 'So much happens hereabouts, as you know, to keep one's finger upon the pulse is a thirsty business.'

Omally looked towards Pooley, who shrugged. 'Same again please, Neville,' said John to the part-time barman, who had been hovering near at hand, ears waggling.

'All the way round?'

'All the way.'

The honours were done and to Neville's disgust Old Pete drew his benefactors away to the side-table, beneath which his dog Chips lay feigning slumber. The three men seated themselves. 'Would I be right in assuming that you have something on your mind, Omally?' the ancient asked.

'It is but a trivial matter,' Omally lied, 'hardly worth wasting your valuable time with, but I must confess that it causes me some perplexity.'

'Ask on then, John, you are two drinks to credit and I am by no means a hard man to deal with.'

'Then I shall get straight to the point. Have you seen a suspicious-looking character skulking around, on, or near the sacred soil of our allotments?'

Old Pete nodded. 'Of course I have,' he answered, 'both there and elsewhere.'

35

'Wearing a grey coverall suit, sallow complexion, high cheek-bones?'

'Looks like a young Jack Palance?'

'The very same.'

'I have seen several.'

'Oh dear,' said Pooley, 'more than one?'

'At least four. Take my warning, they have the mark of officialdom upon them. I saw one last week down by the cut, one yesterday on the corner of the Ealing Road, and there is one drinking this very minute in the far corner over by the gents' bog.'

'What?' Omally's head spun in the direction of the gents'. There in the darkened corner stood a sinister figure in a grey uniform. His features were blurry in the dim light, but it was almost certainly the same individual that he and Pooley had spied out on the allotment not half an hour earlier. As Omally watched, the figure turned his back upon them and strode through the door into the gents'.

'All right, Pete,' said Omally, turning to the ancient. 'Who is he?'

Old Pete shrugged. 'There you have me, I'm afraid. When first I saw them I took them for Council workers. They had some kind of instruments mounted on a tripod and appeared to be marking the ground. But I never got close enough to question them. They slipped away into side roads or off down alleyways upon my approach. This is the nearest that I have so far come to one of them.'

'But you are sure that there are more than one?' Pooley asked.

'I have seen as many as three of them together at one time. As like as the proverbial peas in a pod. Suspicious, I call it.'

'I shall go and question him.' Omally rose from his chair.

'Best wait till he comes out,' Jim suggested. 'It is hardly sporting to corner a man in the bog.'

'Do it now while you have him cornered,' said Old Pete. 'They are a sly crowd. I never saw that fellow enter the Swan and I was the first man in.'

'That settles it,' said John, drawing up his cuffs. 'I shall have it out with him.' Without further word he crossed the bar and pushed open the door to the gents'.

It closed gently behind him and a long minute passed. Pooley looked up at the Guinness clock and watched the second hand sweeping the dial. 'Do you think he's all right?' he whispered.

Old Pete nodded. 'Omally knows how to handle himself, it is well known that he is a Grand Master in the deadly fighting arts of Dimac.'

'It is much spoken of, certainly,' said Jim with some deliberation. As the second hand passed the twelve for the third time Pooley gripped the table and pulled himself to his feet. 'Something is wrong,' he said.

'He said he was going to have it out with the fellow, don't be so hasty, give him another minute.'

'I don't know, you say you never saw him come in, maybe he has several of his chums in there. I don't like the feel of this.'

Old Pete's dog Chips, who had not liked the feel of this from the word go, retreated silently between the legs of his ancient master. Jim was across the carpet and through the bog doorway in a matter of seconds. Once inside he froze in his tracks, his breath hung in his lungs, uncertain of which way it had been travelling, and his eyes bulged unpleasantly in their sockets. Before him stood John Omally, perspiration running freely down his face in grimy streaks. His tie hung over his shoulder college scarf fashion, and he swayed to and fro upon his heels.

Omally stared at Pooley and Pooley stared at Omally. 'Did he come out?' Omally's voice was a hoarse whisper.

Pooley shook his head. 'Then he must still be here then.'
Pooley nodded. 'But he's not.'

Pooley was uncertain whether to shake or nod over this.
'There's a terrible smell of creosote in here,' he said.
Omally pushed past him and lurched back into the bar
leaving Pooley staring about the tiled walls. Above him was
an air vent a mere six inches across. The one window was
heavily bolted from the inside and the two cubicle doors
stood open, exposing twin confessionals, each as empty
as the proverbial vessel, but making no noise whatever.
There was no conceivable mode of escape, but by the
single door which led directly into the bar. Pooley gave
his head a final shake, turned slowly upon his heel and
numbly followed Omally back into the saloon.

6

As the Memorial Library clock struck one in the distance, Norman finished topping up the battered Woodbine machine outside his corner shop. He locked the crumbling dispenser of coffin nails and pocketed Pooley's two washers, which had made their usual weekly appearance in the cash tray amongst the legitimate coin of the realm.

Norman re-entered his shop and bolted the door behind him, turning the OPEN sign to CLOSED. As he crossed the mottled linoleum he whistled softly to himself; sadly, as he had not yet retrieved his wayward teeth, the air sounded a little obscure. For some reason Norman had never quite got the hang of humming, so he contented himself with a bit of unmelodic finger-popping and what he described as 'a touch of the old Fred and Gingers' as he vanished away through the door behind the counter, and left his shop to gather dust for another Wednesday afternoon.

Norman's kitchenette served him as the traditional shop-keeper's lair, equipped with its obligatory bar-fire and gas-ring. But there, apart from these necessary appliances, all similarities ended. There was much of the alchemist's den about Norman's kitchenette. It was workroom, laboratory, research establishment, testing station and storage place for his somewhat excessive surplus stock of Danish glossies.

At present, the hellishly crowded retreat was base camp and ground control for Norman's latest and most ambitious project to date. Even had some NASA boffin cast his knowledgeable eye over the curious array of electronic hocus-pocus which now filled the tiny room, it was unlikely that he would have fathomed any purpose behind it all. The walls were lined with computer banks bristling with ancient radio valves and constructed from Sun Ray wireless sets and commandeered seedboxes. The floor was a veritable snakehouse of cables. The overall effect was one to set Heath Robinson spinning gaily in his grave.

Norman spat dangerously on his palms and rubbed them together. He picked his way carefully across the floor until he reached a great switchboard, of a type once favoured by Baron von Frankenstein. As Norman squared up before it, however, he had no intention of mouthing the now legendary words, 'We belong dead', but instead lisped a quick 'Here she goes' before doing the business.

With a violent flash and a sparkler fizz, the grotesque apparatus sprang, or, more accurately, lurched, into life. Lights twinkled upon the consoles and valves glowed dimly orange. Little pops and crackles, suggestive of constant electrical malfunction, broke out here and there, accompanied by a thin blue mist and an acrid smell which was music to Norman's nostrils.

The shopkeeper lowered himself on to an odd-legged kitchen chair before his master console and began to unwrap his tiny brown paper parcel. Peeling back the cotton-wool wadding, he exposed an exquisite little piece of circuitry, which he lifted carefully with a pair of philatelist's tweezers and examined through an oversized magnifying glass. It was beautiful, perfect in every degree, the product of craftsmanship and skill well beyond the perception of most folk. Norman whistled through his gums.

'Superbs,' he said. 'Superbs.'

He slotted the tiny thing into a polished housing upon the console and it slipped in with a pleasurable click. The last tiny piece in a large and very complicated jigsaw.

Norman clapped his hands together and rocked back and forwards upon his chair. It was all complete, all ready and waiting for a trial run. He had but to select two suitable areas of land and then, if all his calculations were correct . . . Norman's hand hovered over the console and it trembled not a little. His calculations surely were correct, weren't they?

Norman took down a clipboard and began to make ticks against a long and intricate list, which had been built up over many months, scribbled in variously coloured inks. As his Biro travelled down the paper Norman's memory travelled with it through those long, long months of speculation, theory, planning and plotting, of begging, borrowing, and building. The sleepless nights, the trepidation and the doubts. Most of all the doubts. What if it all came to nothing, what if it didn't work? He had damn near bankrupted himself over this one. What if the entire concept was a nonsense?

Norman sucked upon the end of his Biro. No, it couldn't be wrong; old Albert E had discontinued his researches on it back in Nineteen hundred and twenty-seven but the essential elements were still sound, it had to be correct. Just because Einstein had bottled out at the last moment didn't mean it couldn't be done.

Norman ticked off the final item on the list. It was all there, all present and correct, all shipshape and Bristol fashion, all just waiting for the off. He had but to choose two areas of land suitable for the test.

His hand did a little more hovering; he, like certain sportsmen in the vicinity, had no wish to draw attention to his project before its completion. Caution was the byword. The two tracts of land, one local and one in the area of the object he sought, would have to be unoccupied at the present time.

The latter was no problem. Norman boldly punched in the coordinates he knew so well, thirty degrees longitude, thirty degrees latitude and the minutiae of minutes. But as to a local site, this presented some difficulties. It was his aim to conduct the final experiment during the hours of darkness, when there would be few folk about to interfere. But for now, a little test run?

Norman snapped his fingers. 'Eurekas,' he whistled, taking up a Brentford street directory and thumbing through the dog-eared pages. The ideal spot. The St Mary's Allotment. The day being hot, all those dedicated tillers of God's good earth would by now be resting their leathern elbows upon the Swan's bar counter and lying about the dimensions of their marrows.

Norman punched in the appropriate coordinates and leant back in his chair, waiting for the power to build up sufficiently for transference to occur. He crossed his fingers, lisped what words he knew of the Latin litany and pressed a blood-red button which had until recently been the property of the local fire brigade.

A low purring rose from the electronic throat of the machinery, accompanied by a pulse-like beating. The lights upon the console sprang into redoubled illumination and the radio valves began to pulsate, expanding and contracting like some vertical crop of transparent onions. The little bulbs blinked in enigmatic sequences, passing back and forwards through the spectrum. Norman clapped his hands together and bobbed up and down in his chair. A thick blue smoke began to fill the room as the humming of the machinery rose several octaves into an ear-splitting whine. A strange pressure made itself felt in the kitchenette as if the gravitational field was being slowly increased.

Norman suddenly realized that he was unable to raise his hands from the console or his feet from the floor, and someone or something was apparently lowering two-hundredweight sacks of cement on to his shoulders. His ears popping sickeningly, he gritted his gums and made a desperate attempt to keep his eyelids up.

The ghastly whining and the terrible pressure increased. The lights grew brighter and brighter and the pulse beat ever faster. The apparatus was beginning to vibrate, window panes tumbled from their dried-putty housings and a crack swept across the ceiling. Beneath closed lids, Norman's eyes were thoroughly crossed. Without grace he left his chair and travelled downwards at great speed towards the linoleum.

All over Brentford electric appliances were beginning to fail: kettles ceased their whistlings, television pictures suddenly shrank to the size of matchboxes, the automated beer pumps at the New Inn trickled to a halt in mid-flow, and at the Swan the lights went out, leaving the rear section of the saloon-bar in darkness and the patrons blindly searching for their pints.

Omally groaned. 'It is the end of mankind as we know it,' he said. 'I should never have got up so early today.'

Pooley, who had had carrots the night before, topped up his pint from the Irishman's glass. 'Steady on, John,' he said in a soothing voice. 'It is a power cut, nothing more. We have been getting them more or less every Wednesday afternoon for months now.'

'But not like this.'

Old Pete's dog Chips set up a dismal howl which was unexpectedly taken up by Neville the part-time barman. 'Look at it! Look at it!' he wailed, pointing invisibly in the darkness. 'Look at the bloody thing!'

Bitow Bitow Bitow Bitow went the Captain Laser Alien Attack Machine, scornfully indifferent to the whims of the Southern Electricity Board, or anyone else for that matter.

43

In the tiny kitchenette to the rear of the corner shop there was a sharp and deafening twang, and a great bolt of lightning burst forth, charring the walls and upturning the banks of pulsating equipment. There followed a moment or two of very extreme silence. Smoke hung heavily in the air, cables swung to and fro like smouldering leander vines and the general atmosphere of the place had more than the hint of the charnel house about it.

At length, from beneath the fallen wreckage, something stirred. Slowly, and with much coughing, gasping and sighing, a blackened toothless figure rose painfully to his feet. He now lacked not only his upper set but also his eyebrows and sported a fetching, if somewhat bizarre, charcoal forelock. He kicked away the debris and fumbled about amidst the heaps of burned-out valves and twisted gubbins. 'Ahs,' he said, suddenly wielding a smoke-veiled gauge into view, 'success I thinks.'

Something had come through, and by the measurement upon that gauge it was a relatively substantial, goodly few hundredweight of something.

Norman wiped away a few loose eyelashes with a grimy knuckle, satisfied himself that there was no immediate danger of fire and sought his overcoat.

Small Dave had finished his midday deliveries and was taking his usual short cut back from the Butts Estate towards the Flying Swan for a well deserved pint of Large. As he shuffled across the allotment, his size four feet kicking up little dusty explosions, he whistled a plaintive lament, the title of which he had long forgotten. He had not travelled twenty yards down the path, however, when he caught sight of something which made him halt in mid-pace and doubt that sanity which so many had previously doubted in him.

Small Dave took off his cap and wiped it across his eyes. Was this a mirage, he wondered, or was he seeing things? Something overlarge and definitely out of place was grazing amongst his cabbages. It was a foul and scruffy-looking something of bulky proportion and it was emitting dismal grumbling sounds between great munches upon his prizewinning *Pringlea antiscorbutica*.

Dave screwed up his eyes. Could this be the Sasquatch perhaps? Or the Surrey Puma? Possibly it was the giant feral tom, which, legend held, stalked the allotments by night. The postman drew cautiously nearer, keeping even lower to the ground than cruel fate had naturally decreed. Ahead of him the creature's outline became more clearly defined and Small Dave knew that at least he was staring upon a beast of a known genus. Although this gave him little in the way of consolation.

The thing was of the genus *Camelus bactrianus*. It was a camel!

Small Dave's thoughts all became a little confused at this moment. He was never very good when it came to a confrontation with the unexpected. Arriving with a six-inch letter to discover a five-inch letter-box was enough to set him foaming at the mouth. Now, a camel on the allotment, a camel that was eating his precious cabbages, that was a something quite in a class by itself.

Dave's first thought, naturally enough, was that the thing should be driven off without delay. His second was that it was a very large camel and that as a species camels are notoriously malevolent creatures, who do not take kindly to interference during meal times. His third was that they are also valuable and there would no doubt be a handsome reward for anyone who should return a stray.

His fourth, fifth, sixth and seventh thoughts were loosely concerned with circuses, Romany showmen who were apt to snatch dwarves away for side-shows, an old Tod Browning movie he had once seen, and the rising cost of cabbages.

Small Dave's lower lip began to tremble and a look of complete imbecility spread over his gnomish countenance. He dithered a moment or two not knowing what to do, flapped his hands up and down as if in an attempt to gain flight, gave a great cry of despair, took to his heels and finally ran screaming from the allotment.

He had not been gone but a moment or two when a soot-besmirched head arose from behind a nearby water-butt. Apart from its lack of teeth and eyebrows, it bore a striking resemblance to Sir Lawrence Olivier in his famous portrayal of Othello.

A broad and slightly lunatic smile cleft the blackened face in two and a wicked chuckle rose in the throat of the watcher.

'Success indeeds,' whistled Norman, rubbing his hands together and dancing out from his hiding place. With a quick glance about to assure himself that he was now alone, he skipped over to the cabbage-chewing camel and snatched up its trailing halter line. 'Huts, huts,' he said. 'Imshees yallahs.' With hardly the slightest degree of persuasion and little or no force at all, Norman led the surprisingly docile brute away.

From behind Soap Distant's padlocked shed, yet another figure now emerged. This one wore a grey coverall suit, was of average height, with a slightly tanned complexion and high cheek-bones. He looked for all the world like a young Jack Palance. Through oval amber eyes he watched the shopkeeper and his anomalous charge depart. Drawing from a concealed pocket an instrument somewhat resembling a brass divining rod, he traced a runic symbol into the dusty soil of the allotment and then also departed upon light and silent feet.

7

When the lights returned once more to the Flying Swan, a moment or two after the holocaust in Norman's kitchenette, they exposed a frozen tableau of deceit and duplicity, which was a sad indictment upon the state of our society.

Neville stood poised behind the counter, knobkerry at the ready, to defend his optics against any straining hands.

Pooley held Omally's glass above his own, a stupefied expression upon his guilty face. Two professional domino players each had their hands in the spares box. Old Pete's dog was standing, leg raised, to the piano, and a veritable rogues' gallery of similar deeds was exposed the entire length of the bar.

Neville shook his head in disgust. 'You miserable bunch,' was all that he could say.

The only patron who had not shifted his position during the unscheduled blackout was a green-haired youth, who had been so engrossed in his war against the aliens that he had been totally oblivious to the entire event. *Bitow Bitow Bitow Bitow* crackled the machine. *Bitow, Bitow* . . . 'Bugger!' The lad restrained a petulant foot and slouched over to the bar counter. 'Where's me drink gone, Nev?' he asked.

The part-time barman shrugged. 'Ask this mutinous crew,' he suggested. Raffles Rathbone turned towards the assembled multitude, but they had by now returned to their previous occupations. Conversations hummed, darts whispered and glasses rose and fell. All was as it had ever been.

'Same again then is it?'

'Why not? Got sixteen thousand, personal high score, got me initials up there three times.'

'Oh goody goody,' sneered Neville. 'Are you sure you only want the half of shandy, I shouldn't crack a bottle of Bollinger, should I?'

'The half will be fine, thank you.' Neville did the honours.

The Swan settled down once more to its lunchtime normality, and such it would no doubt have enjoyed, had it not been for certain distant screams, which were borne upon the light spring breeze to announce the approach of a certain small and disconsolate postman.

'Camels! Camels on the allotment!' The cry reached the Swan shortly before Small Dave.

Omally choked into his beer. 'No more!' he spluttered, crossing himself. Pooley shook his head; it was proving to be a most eventful day and it was early yet. Neville reached once more for his knobkerry and Raffles Rathbone stood before the video machine, oblivious to the world about him.

Small Dave burst into the Swan, looking very much the worse for wear. He lurched up to the counter and ordered a large scotch. Neville looked down at the distraught postman, and it must be said that the makings of a fine smirk began to form at the edges of his mouth. Turning away he drew off a single for which he accepted double price. Small Dave tossed it back in one gulp as Neville had calculated and ordered another. 'C-C-Camels,' he continued.

Neville drew off a large one this time as a crowd was beginning to gather. 'So, Posty,' he said, pushing the glass across the counter towards the postman's straining hand, 'how goes the day for you then?'

48

Small Dave made pointing motions towards the general direction of the allotments. His lower lip quivered and he danced about in a state of obvious and acute agitation.

'No more postcards then?' Neville asked.

'C-C-Camels!' howled the midget.

Neville turned to Omally, who had dragged himself up to the bar counter. 'Do you think our postman is trying to tell us something, John?' he asked.

'He is saying camels,' said Jim Pooley helpfully.

'Ah, that is what it is, camels, eh?'

'C-C-Camels!'

'Yes, it is camels for certain,' said Omally.

'He has a lovely way with words,' said Neville, suddenly feeling quite cheerful, 'and a good eye for a picture postcard.'

'For God's sake! Camels, don't you understand?' Small Dave was growing increasingly purple and his voice was reaching a dangerous, champagne-glass-splitting kind of a pitch.

'Is he buying or selling, do you think?'

'I hadn't thought to enquire.' Neville squinted down at the postman, who was now down on all fours beating at the carpet. 'He is impersonating, I think.'

Old Pete hobbled up. He had experienced some luck recently over impersonating and wasn't going to miss out on a good thing. 'That's not the way of a camel,' he said authoritatively. 'That's more like a gerbil.'

Small Dave fainted, arms and legs spread flat out on the floor.

'That's a polar bear skin,' said Old Pete, 'and a very good one too!'

Small Dave was unceremoniously hauled up into a waiting chair. A small green bottle was grudgingly taken down from its haunt amongst the Spanish souvenirs behind the bar, uncorked and waggled beneath the midget's upturned nose.

'C-C-Camels!' went Small Dave, coming once more to what there were left of his senses.

'I find that his conversation has become a trifle dull of late,' said Neville.

'I think it might pay to hear him out.' Pooley thrust his way through the throng with a glass of water. The postman spied out his approach. 'What's that for?' he snapped. 'Going to give me a blanket bath, are you?'

Jim coughed politely. 'You are feeling a little better then? I thought perhaps you might like to discuss whatever is troubling you.'

'I should enjoy another scotch to steady myself.'

The crowd departed as one man; they had seen all this kind of stuff many many times before. The ruses and stratagems employed in the cause of the free drink were as numerous as they were varied. The cry of 'Camels', although unique in itself, did not seem particularly meritorious.

'But I saw them, I did, I did,' wailed Small Dave, as he watched the patrons' hurried departure. 'I swear.' He crossed himself above the heart. 'See this wet, see this dry. Come back fellas, come back.'

No-one had noticed John Omally quietly slipping away. He had become a man sorely tried of late, what with vanishing Council men and everything. The idea of camels upon the allotment was not one which appealed to him in the slightest. He could almost hear the clicking of tourists' Box Brownies and the flip-flopping of their beach-sandalled feet as they trampled over the golf course. It didn't bear thinking about. If there were rogue camels wandering around the allotment, Omally determined that they should be removed as quickly as possible.

John jogged down Moby Dick Terrace and up towards the allotment gates. Here he halted. All seemed quiet enough. A soft wind gently wrinkled the long grass at the boundary fence. A starling or two pecked away at somebody's recently sown seed and a small grey cat stretched luxuriously upon the roof of Pooley's hut. Nothing unusual here, all peace and tranquillity.

Omally took a few tentative steps forward. He passed the first concealed tee-box and noted with satisfaction that all was as it should be. He crept stealthily in and out between the shanty town of corrugated huts, sometimes springing up and squinting around, eyes shaded like some Indian tracker.

Then a most obvious thought struck him: there were only two entrances to the allotment and any camel would logically have to pass either in or out of these. Therefore any camel would be bound to leave some kind of spoor which could surely be followed.

Omally dropped to his knees upon the path and sought camel prints. He then rose slowly to his feet and patted at the knees of his trousers. What on earth am I doing? he asked himself. Seeking camel tracks upon a Brentford allotment, he answered. Have I become bereft of my senses? He thought it better not to answer that one. And even if I saw a camel track, how would I recognize it as one?

This took a bit of thinking out, but it was eventually reasoned that a camel track would look like no other track Omally had yet seen upon the allotment, and thus be recognized.

Omally shrugged and thrust his hands into his trouser pockets. He wandered slowly about, criss-crossing the pathway and keeping alert for anything untoward. He came very shortly upon the decimation of Small Dave's pride and joy. Half-munched cabbages lay strewn in every direction. Something had certainly been having its fill of the tasty veg. Omally stooped to examine a leaf and found to his wonder large and irregular toothmarks upon it.

'So,' said he, 'old Posty was not talking through his regulation headgear, something *has* been going on here.'

He scanned the ground but could make out nothing besides very human-looking footprints covering the well-trodden pathway. Some of these led off towards the Butts Estate entrance, but Omally felt disinclined to follow them. His eyes had just alighted upon something rather more interesting. Slightly in front of Soap Distant's padlocked shed, an image glowed faintly in the dirt. Omally strode over to it and peered down. He was certain the thing had not been there earlier.

The Irishman dropped once more to his hands and knees. It had an almost metallic quality to it, as if it had been wrought into the dirt in copper. But as to exactly what it was, that was another matter. Omally drew a tentative finger across its surface but the thing resisted his touch. He rose and raked his heel across it but the image remained inviolate.

John peered up into the sky. It wasn't being projected from above, was it? No, that was nonsense. But surely it had to come off, you couldn't print indelibly on dust. He scuffed at the ground with renewed vigour, raising a fine cloud of dust which slowly cleared to reveal the image glowing up once more, pristine and unscathed.

Omally stooped again and pressed his eye near to the thing. What was it? Obviously a symbol of some sort, or an insignia. There was a vaguely familiar look to it, as if it was something he had half glimpsed upon some occasion but never fully taken in. It had much of the rune about it also.

'So,' said a voice suddenly, 'you are a secret Mohammedan, are you, Omally?' The Irishman rose to confront a grinning Jim Pooley. 'Surely Mecca would be in the other direction?'

Omally dusted down his strides and gestured towards the gleaming symbol. 'Now what would you make of that, lad?' he asked.

Pooley gave the copper coloured image a quick perusal. 'Something buried in the ground?' he suggested.

Omally shook his head, although the thought had never crossed his mind.

'Is it a bench mark then? I've always wondered what those lads look like.'

'Not a bench mark, Jim.'

'It is then perhaps some protective amulet carelessly discarded by some wandering magician?' Although it seemed almost a possibility Omally gave that suggestion the old thumbs down. 'All right, I give up, what is it?'

'There you have me, but I will show you an interesting thing.' Omally picked up Pooley's spade, which was standing close at hand, raised it high above his head and drove it edgeways on towards the copper symbol with a murderous force. There was a sharp metallic clang as the spade's head glanced against the image, cleared Pooley's terrified face by the merest of inches and whistled off to land safely several plots away.

'Sorry,' said John, examining the stump of spade handle, 'but you no doubt get my drift.'

'You mean you cannot dig it out?' Omally shook his head. 'Right then.' Pooley spat on his palms and rubbed them briskly together.

'Before you start,' said Omally, 'be advised by me that it cannot be either erased, defaced or removed.'

Pooley, who had by now removed his jacket and was rolling up his sleeves, paused a moment and cocked his head on one side. 'It has a familiar look to it,' he said.

John nodded. 'I thought that myself, the thing strikes a chord somewhere along the line.'

Pooley, who needed only a small excuse to avoid physical labour, slipped his jacket back on. He took out a biro and *The Now Official Handbook of Allotment Golf*.

'Best mark it out of bounds,' said Omally.

Pooley shook his head and handed him the book. 'You're good with your hands, John,' he said, 'make a sketch of it on the back. If such a symbol has ever existed, or even does so now, there is one man in Brentford who is bound to know what it is.'

'Ah yes.' Omally smiled broadly and took both book and Biro. 'And that good man is, if I recall, never to be found without a decanter of five-year-old scotch very far from his elbow.'

'Quite so,' said Jim Pooley. 'And as we walk we will speak of many things, of sporting debts and broken spades.'

'And cabbages and camels,' said John Omally.

8

Professor Slocombe sat at his study desk, surrounded by the ever-present clutter of dusty tomes. Behind him twin shafts of sunlight entered the tall French windows and glittered upon his mane of pure white hair, casting a gaunt shadow across the mountain of books on to the exquisite Persian carpet which pelted the floor with clusters of golden roses.

The Professor peered through his ivory-rimmed pince-nez and painstakingly annotated the crackling yellow pages of an ancient book, the Count of St Germaine's treatise upon the transmutation of base metals and the improvement of diamonds. The similarities between his marginal jottings and the hand-inscribed text of the now legendary Count were such as would raise the eyebrows of many a seasoned graphologist.

Had it not been for the fact that the Count of St Germaine had cast his exaggerated shadow in the fashionable places of some three hundred years past, one would have been tempted to assume that both inscriptions were the product of a single hand, the Count's text appearing only the work of a younger and more sprightly individual. But even to suggest such a thing would be to trespass dangerously upon the shores of unreason, although it must be said that Old Pete, one of the Borough's most notable octogenarians, was wont to recall that when he was naught but a tousle-haired sprog, with ringworm and rickets, the Professor was already a gentleman of great age.

Around and about the study, the musty showcases were crowded with a profusion of extraordinary objects, the tall bookshelves bulged with rare volumes and the carved tables stood heavily burdened with brass oraries and silver astrolabes. All these wonders hovered in the half-light, exhibits of a private museum born to the Professor's esoteric taste. Golden, dusty motes hung in the sunlight shafts, and the room held a silence which was all its own. Beyond the French windows, the wonderful garden bloomed throughout every season with a luxuriant display of exotic flora. But beyond the walls existed a changing world for which the Professor had very little time. He trod the boundaries of the Borough each day at sunrise, attended certain local functions, principally the yearly darts tournament at the Flying Swan, and accepted his role as oracle and ornamental hermit to the folk of Brentford.

Omally's hobnails clattered across the cobbled stones of the Butts Estate, Pooley's blakeys offering a light accompaniment, as the two marched purposefully forward.

'No sign of the wandering camel trains then?' asked Jim.

Omally shrugged. 'Something had been giving Dave's cabbage patch quite a seeing to,' he said, 'but I saw no footprints.'

'Neville put the wee lad out, shortly after you'd gone.'

'Good thing too, last thing we need is a camel hunt on the allotment.'

The two men rounded a corner and reached the Professor's garden door. Here they paused a moment before pressing through. Neither man knew exactly why he did this; it was an unconscious action, as natural as blinking, or raising a pint glass to the lips. Omally pushed open the ever-unbolted door and he and Pooley entered the magical garden. The blooms swayed drowsily and enormous bees moved amongst them humming tunes which no man knew the words to.

The Professor turned not his head from his writing, but before his two visitors had come but a step or two towards the open French windows he called out gaily, 'Good afternoon, John, Jim. You are some distance from your watering hole with yet half an hour's drinking time left upon the Guinness clock.'

Pooley scrutinized his Piaget wristwatch, which had stopped. 'We come upon business of the utmost import,' he said, knowing well the Professor's contempt for the mundane, 'and seek your counsel.'

'Enter then. You know where the decanter is.'

After a rather undignified rush and the equally tasteless spectacle of two grown men squeezing together through the open French windows Pooley and Omally availed themselves of the Professor's hospitality. 'You are looking well, sir,' said Jim, now grinning up from a brimming shot-crystal tumbler. 'Are you engaged upon anything interesting in the way of research at present?'

The old man closed his book and smiled up at Pooley. 'The search for the philosopher's stone,' he said simply. 'But what of you fellows? How goes the golfing?'

Omally brought his winning smile into prominence. 'We pursue our sport as best we can, but the Council's henchmen have little love for our technique.'

Professor Slocombe chuckled. 'I have heard tell of your technique,' he said, 'and I suspect that your chances of membership to Gleneagles are pretty slight. I myself recently followed up some reports of UFO sightings above the allotments at night and my investigation disclosed a cache of luminously painted golf balls. Although your techniques are somewhat unorthodox, your enterprise is commendable.' The old man rose from his desk and decanted himself a gold watch. 'So,' he said at length, 'to what do I owe this unexpected pleasure?'

Pooley made free with a little polite coughing and drew

out *The Now Official Handbook of Allotment Golf* which he handed to the Professor. The snow-capped ancient raised his bristling eyebrows into a Gothic arch. 'If you seek an impartial judgement over some technicality of the game I will need time to study this document.'

'No, no,' said Jim, 'on the back.'

Professor Slocombe turned over the dog-eared exercise book and his dazzling facial archway elevated itself by another half inch. 'So,' he said, 'you think to test me out, do you, Jim?'

Pooley shook his head vigorously. 'No, sir,' said he, to the accompaniment of much heart crossing. 'No ruse here, I assure you. The thing has us rightly perplexed and that is a fact.'

'As such it would,' said Professor Slocombe. Crossing to one of the massive bookcases, the old man ran a slender finger, which terminated in a tiny girlish nail, along the leathern spines of a row of dusty-looking volumes. Selecting one, bound in a curious yellow hide and bearing a heraldic device and a Latin inscription, he bore it towards his cluttered desk. 'Clear those Lemurian maps aside please, John,' he said, 'and Jim, if you could put that pickled homunculus over on the side table we shall have room to work.'

Pooley laboured without success to shift a small black book roughly the size of a cigarette packet, but clearly of somewhat greater weight. Nudging him aside, the Professor lifted it as if it were a feather and tossed it into one of the leather-backed armchairs. 'Never try to move the books,' he told Jim. 'They are, you might say, protected.'

Jim shrugged hopelessly. He had known the Professor too long to doubt that he possessed certain talents which were somewhat above the everyday run of the mill.

'Now,' said the elder, spreading his book upon the partially cleared desk, 'let us see what we shall see. You have brought me something of a poser this time, but I think I shall be able to satisfy your curiosity. This tome,' he explained, fluttering his hands over the yellow volume, 'is the sole remaining copy of a work by one of the great masters of, shall we say, hidden lore.'

'We shall say it,' said John, 'and leave it at that.'

'The author's name was Cagliostro, and he dedicated his life, amongst other things, to the study of alchemic symbolism and in particular the runic ideogram.'

'Aha,' said Omally, 'so it is a rune then, such I thought it to be.'

'The first I've heard of it,' sniffed Pooley.

'It has the outward appearance of a rune,' the Professor continued, 'but it is a little more complex than that. Your true rune is simply a letter of the runic alphabet. Once one has mastered the system it is fairly easy to decipher the meaning. This, however, is an ideogram or ideograph, which is literally the graphic representation of an idea or ideas through the medium of symbolic characterization.'

'As clear as mud,' said Jim Pooley. 'I should have expected little else.'

'If you will bear with me for a while, I shall endeavour to make it clear to you.' The Professor straightened his ivory-framed spectacles and settled himself down before his book. Pooley turned his empty glass between his fingers. 'Feel at liberty to replenish it whenever you like, Jim,' said the old man without looking up. The pendulum upon the great ormolu mantelclock swung slowly, dividing the day up, and the afternoon began to pass. The Professor sat at his desk, the great book spread before him, his pale, slim hand lightly tracing over the printed text.

Pooley wandered aimlessly about the study, marvelling at how it could be that the more closely he scrutinized the many books the more blurry and indecipherable their titles became. They were indeed, as the Professor put it, 'protected'. At length he rubbed his eyes, shook his head in defeat, and sought other pursuits.

Omally, for his part, finished the decanter of five-year-old scotch and fell into what can accurately be described as a drunken stupor.

At very great length the mantelclock struck five. With opening time at the Swan drawing so perilously close, Pooley ventured to enquire as to whether the Professor was near to a solution.

'Oh, sorry, Jim,' said the old man, looking up, 'I had quite forgotten you were here.'

Pooley curled his lip. It was obvious that the Professor was never to be denied his bit of gamesmanship. 'You have deciphered the symbol then?'

'Why yes, of course. Perhaps you would care to awaken your companion.'

Pooley poked a bespittled finger into the sleeper's ear and Omally awoke with a start.

'Now then,' said Professor Slocombe, closing his book and leaning back in his chair. 'Your symbol is not without interest. It combines two runic characters and an enclosing alchemic symbol. I can tell you what it says, but as to what it means, I confess that at present I am able to offer little in the way of exactitude.'

'We will settle for what it says, then,' said Jim.

'All right.' Professor Slocombe held up Omally's sketch, and traced the lines of the symbol as he spoke. 'We have here the number ten, here the number five and here enclosing all the alchemic C.'

'A five, a ten and a letter C,' said Jim. 'I do not get it.'

'Of course you don't, it is an ideogram: the expression of an idea, if I might be allowed to interpret loosely?' The two men nodded. 'It says, I am "C" the fifth of the ten.'

The two men shook their heads. 'So what does that mean?' asked Omally.

'Search me,' said Professor Slocombe. 'Was there anything else?' Pooley and Omally stared at each other in bewilderment. This was quite unlike the Professor Slocombe they knew. No questions about where the symbol was found, no long and inexplicable monologues upon its history or purpose, in fact the big goodbye.

'There was one other thing,' said the rattled Omally, drawing a crumpled cabbage leaf from his pocket.

'If it is not too much trouble, I wonder if you would be kind enough to settle a small dispute. Would you enlighten us as to what species of voracious quadruped could have wrought this destruction upon Small Dave's cabbage patch?'

'His *Pringlea antiscorbutica*?'

'Exactly.' Omally handed the Professor the ruined leaf.

Professor Slocombe swivelled in his chair and held the leaf up to the light, examining it through the lens of a horn-handled magnifying glass. 'Flattened canines, prominent incisors, indicative of the herbivore, by the size and shape I should say that it was obvious.' Swinging back suddenly to Omally he flung him the leaf. 'I have no idea whatever as to how you accomplished that one,' he said. 'I would have said that you acquired a couple of jawbones from Gunnersbury Park Museum but for the saliva stains and the distinctive cross-hatching marks of mastication.'

'So you know what it was then?'

'Of course, it is *Camelus bactrianus*, the common Egyptian Camel.'

There was something very very odd about *Camelus bactrianus*, the common Egyptian Camel. Norman squatted on his haunches in his rented garage upon the Butts Estate and stared up at the brute. There was definitely something very very odd about it. Certainly it was a camel far from home and had been called into its present existence by means which were totally inexplicable, even to the best educated camel this side of the Sahara, but this did not explain its overwhelming oddness. Norman dug a finger into his nose and ruminated upon exactly what that very very oddness might be.

Very shortly it struck him with all the severity of a well-aimed half-brick. When he had been leading the thing away to his secret hideout, it had occurred to him at the time just how easy it had been to move. And he recalled that although he, an eight-stone weakling of the pre-Atlas-course persuasion, had left distinctive tracks, the camel, a beasty of eminently greater bulk, had left not a mark.

And now, there could be little doubt about it, the camel's feet no longer reached the ground. In fact, the creature was floating in open defiance of all the accepted laws of gravity, some eighteen inches above the deck.

'Now that's what I would call odd,' said Norman, startling the hovering ship of the desert and causing it to break wind loudly – a thing which, in itself, might be tolerable in the sandblown reaches of the Sahara, but which was no laughing matter in an eight-by-twelve lock-up garage. 'Ye gods,' mumbled Norman, covering his nose with a soot-stained pullover sleeve.

It was now that he noticed yet another untoward feature about the animal, which, had it been the property of the now legendary P.T. Barnum, would no doubt have earned that great showman a fortune rivalling that of Croesus himself: the camel had the appearance of being not quite in focus. Although Norman screwed up his eyes and viewed it from a variety of angles, the zero gravity quadruped remained a mite indistinct and somewhat fuzzy about the edges.

Norman took out an unpaid milk bill and scrawled a couple of dubious equations upon its rear. Weight being the all-important factor of his experiment, it was obvious that his calculations regarding molecular transfer were slightly at fault. He rose from his uncomfortable posture and, the air having cleared a little, picked up a clump of wisely commandeered cabbage leaves and offered them to the camel, now firmly lodged in the rafters. The thing, however, declined this savoury morsel and set up a plaintive crying which sent chills up the back of the scientific shopkeeper.

'Ssh . . . ssh, be quiets, damn yous,' whistled Norman, flapping his arms and searching desperately about for the wherewithal to silence the moaning creature. Something drastic would have to be done, of that there was no doubt. This camel, although living proof of his experiment's success, was also damning evidence against him, and its disclosure to the public at such a time, when he stood poised on the very threshold of a major breakthrough, could only spell doom to his plans in dirty big red letters.

Norman groaned plurally. That must not be allowed to happen. He had had run-ins with the popular press before, and he knew full well the dire consequences. Some way or other he would have to dispose of his hovering charge. Perhaps he could merely await nightfall then drag it outside and allow it to float away upon the wind. Norman shuddered, with his luck the camel would most likely rise to a point just beyond reach and hang there for all the world to see. Or far worse than that, it might sweep upwards into an aircraft's flight-path and cause a major disaster. These thoughts brought no consolation to the worried man.

The camel was still bewailing its lot in excessively loquacious terms and Norman, a man who was rapidly learning the true meaning of the word desperation, tore off his pullover and, having dragged the moaning beastie momentarily to ground level, stuffed the patchworked woolly over its head. A blessed silence descended upon the lock-up, and Norman breathed a twin sigh of relief. Perhaps, he mused, with its obviously unstable molecular structure the camel might simply deteriorate to such a point that a slight draught would waft it away into nothingness.

This seemed a little cruel, as the camel was something of an unwilling victim of circumstance, and Norman was not by nature a cruel or callous man. But considering the eventual good which his great quest would bring to the people of Brentford, the shopkeeper considered the sacrifice to be a small and necessary one.

It will thank me for it in the end, he told himself. To die in so noble a cause. I shall see to it that a memorial is built, the tomb of the unknown camel. We might even organize some kind of yearly festival in its honour. Camel Day, perhaps? Hold it on Plough Monday, incorporate a few morris dancers in Egyptian garb and a maypole or two, make a day of it. Yes, the camel had played its part and it would not go unrewarded.

Anyway, thought Norman, if it doesn't simply evaporate I can always speed the process up with a decent-sized weedkiller bomb.

9

Pooley and Omally sat at a secluded corner-table in the Flying Swan.

'I can't understand the Professor,' said Jim. 'Didn't seem to be himself at all.'

Omally shook his head, 'I don't know,' he replied. 'Appeared to me a clear case of keep-the-golfers-guessing. I suspect that he knows a good deal more than he was letting on to.'

'Not much ever gets by him. He certainly made short work of the cabbage leaf.'

Omally leant back in his seat and cast his arms wide. 'But where are we?' he asked. 'Nowhere at all! We have council men doing the impossible at their every opportunity, we have runic ideograms appearing magically upon the ground and camels working their way through the season's produce. I don't like any of it, it smacks to me of some great conspiracy to confound honest golfers and put them off their game.'

'I suspect that it goes a little deeper than that,' said Jim, 'but I agree that it does nothing to enhance the play. Perhaps we should quit the allotment now. Move on to pastures new. There are several large bombsites down near the docks surrounded by high walls. I know of a secret entrance or two.'

'Never,' said Omally boldly. 'I have had enough of running. If we do not make our stand now, the bastards will eventually drive us into the sea and I care little for the prospect of underwater golf.'

'Cork balls,' said Pooley.

'I beg your pardon?'

Bitow Bitow Bitow Bitow Bitow Whap . . . 'What?' Nicholas Roger Raffles Rathbone turned a full circle upon his heel and drove his reddening fists down on to the console of the Captain Laser Alien Attack Machine. 'You bastard!' he said earnestly. 'You bloody sneaked an extra saucer in there.' He turned towards the bar where Neville stood, his ears protected by cotton-wool balls and his hands feverishly at work with the polishing cloth. 'Have you altered this machine?' he cried.

'Get stuffed,' said Neville.

'I know the sequences,' Nick continued unabashed, 'thirty shots, then a big saucer, thirty-eight, then a mother ship. Somebody has tampered with this machine.'

Neville laid down his polishing cloth, plucked the ineffective cotton plugs from his ears and glowered across the bar. 'No-one has touched it,' he said, his words forming between two rows of teeth which were showing some signs of wear. 'No-one has touched, tampered or tinkered with it. No official brewery representative has ever called to service it. No engineers came to polish its paintwork, change its bulbs or fondle its inner workings, nor even to empty it of the king's ransom it must by now contain. It seemingly never breaks down, nor needs any maintenance, it runs from its own power supply and is a law unto itself. If you have any complaints I suggest that you address them directly to the machine. With any luck it will take exception to your manner and electrocute you!'

'Someone's been tampering,' said Nick, delving into his pockets for more two-bob bits, 'I know the sequences.'

The part-time barman turned away in disgust. 'Jim,' he

said, beckoning across the counter towards Pooley, 'might I have a word or two in your ear?'

Pooley hastened from his chair, favouring the possibility of a free drink. 'Your servant, bar lord,' said he.

'Jim,' said Neville, gesturing towards the hunched back of the green-haired youth, 'Jim, has Omally come up with anything yet regarding this abomination? I am at my wits' end. My letter of resignation is folded into the envelope and the stamp is on.'

Jim chewed upon his lip. It was obvious that Neville was speaking with great sincerity. It would be a tragedy indeed if Brentford lost the best part-time barman it ever had. Especially over so trivial a thing as a gambling machine.

'In truth,' lied Jim with great conviction, 'Omally and I have spent the entirety of the afternoon discussing this very matter. We were doing so even when you called me across. We are, I think, nearing a solution.'

'Ah,' said Neville, brightening, 'it is good to know that there are still friends in the camp. Have this one on the house.'

Pooley sank it at a single draught and strolled back to his seated companion.

'I saw that,' said Omally. 'What have you just talked me into?'

'Nothing much,' said Jim nonchalantly. 'It is just that Neville would prefer it if you would break the space machine now rather than later.'

Omally controlled himself quite remarkably. 'But I was of the impression that the thing is indestructable. Do you not feel that this small point might put me at a slight disadvantage?'

Pooley nudged his companion jovially in the rib area. 'Come now,' he said, 'this should provide a little light relief. Take your mind off your worries. What is it that you lads from the old country say? Do it for the crack, that's it, isn't it. The crack, eh?'

'The crack?' Omally shook his head in wonder. As if things weren't bad enough. He scratched at the stubble of his chin, which through the day had grown into what the Navy refer to as a full set, and cast a thoughtful eye towards the video machine. 'I have an idea,' he said, rising from his seat. 'Perhaps a success here might turn the tide of our fortunes. Give me a florin.' Pooley began to pat his pockets. 'Give me the florin,' Omally reiterated. Pooley paid up.

'Now, come Jim,' said the Irishman, 'and we will test the substance of this rogue apparatus.'

Neville the part-time barman watched the silver coin change hands and offered up a silent prayer to the dark and pagan deity of his personal preference.

Nicholas Roger Raffles Rathbone had a pile of not dissimilar coins of the realm stacked upon the chromium roof of the games machine. He was set in for the night.

'Stand aside, laddy,' said Omally in an authoritative tone. 'My friend here wishes to match wits with these extra-terrestrial laddos.'

'No way,' said Nick, turning not a verdant hair, 'I'm halfway through a game here.'

Omally leant down towards the youth and spoke a few words into a pointed, tattooed ear. The scourge of the cosmic commandos stepped aside. 'Be my guest,' he said politely. 'I will explain how it works.'

'That will not be necessary, thank you, off you go then, Jim.'

Pooley shook his head vigorously. 'Not me,' he said, 'these things give out dangerous X-rays. I'm not having my hair fall out and my fingernails drop off. No thank you.'

Omally patted his companion on the shoulder. 'Jim,' said he, 'who was it who set fire to my pop-up toaster?'

Pooley could not see the connection, but he nodded guiltily. 'It was me,' he said.

'And who overwound my alarm clock?'

'Also me.'

'And who fiddled with the tuner on the wireless set which had given me good and trouble-free listening for twenty years?'

Pooley looked away. 'Also me,' he said in a whisper.

'And who borrowed my electric razor and . . . '

'I didn't know you weren't supposed to use soap when shaving electric,' Pooley complained.

'Who was it?'

'Also me.'

'Then you will understand my reasoning that if there is one man capable of ruining, whether through chance, method or design, any piece of electrical apparatus with only the minimum of tampering then that person is you, James Pooley.'

Jim pushed in the florin and the video screen burst into colour. 'Lift off,' he said.

'You have to use the thrust booster to get optimum lift,' said Raffles Rathbone, prancing on his toes and pointing variously at the throbbing machine. 'Gauge the inclination of the saucers, if you count to three and fire just in front of them you can bring them down. Every third one is worth an extra hundred points, keep to the right and they can't . . . ' His voice trailed off as Omally dealt him a severe blow to the skull.

'Silence,' he said, 'Jim knows what he's doing.'

'I don't,' wailed Jim, wildly pressing buttons and joggling the joy stick.

'You're not here to win, Jim, only to break it.'

'Break it?' Raffles Rathbone renewed his frenzied dance. 'Break the machine? Oh, barman, barman, there is sabotage going on here, do something, do something.'

Neville smiled benevolently at the dancing youth. 'There is nothing I can do,' he said. 'All the patrons have a right to play the machine. Don't be so selfish.'

'Selfish? This is a conspiracy, I shall phone the brewery.'

John Omally, a man to whom the word tolerance meant about as much as the rules of backgammon, snatched up the squirming malcontent by his badge-covered lapels and held him high at arms' length. 'We don't want to go threatening the management now do we?' he asked.

'Ooh, I got one,' said Pooley suddenly. 'Blew him right out of the sky. And there goes another, *Bitow*. There's a knack to it you see.'

Omally let the dangling lad fall from his grasp. 'Any sign of damage yet?' he asked.

'I'm damaging their invasion fleet, look that's a hundred points, got the mother ship, you score double for that.'

Omally looked on in wonder. 'Come now, Jim,' he implored, 'try harder, apply a little more force.'

'I am, I am, there, took one straight out, you duck away to the side then, they can't get you there.'

'That's it,' said the fallen Raffles Rathbone. 'Count five from the last saucer across and the scout ship comes straight, down, you can get five hundred for him.'

A look of dire perplexity appeared upon Omally's ruddy face. 'Jim,' he said earnestly, 'what is happening here, Jim?'

'Nice one,' said Raffles Rathbone, 'when you get up to one thousand points you get an extra man. There, you got it.'

'No sweat,' said Jim Pooley.

Omally turned away from the machine and stalked over to the bar. Neville met his approach with a face like thunder. 'What is all this?' the part-time barman demanded. 'Treachery, is it?'

Omally shook his head ferociously, his honour was at stake here. 'Psychology,' he informed Neville.

'Oh, psychology is it, well silly old me, I could have sworn that he was enjoying himself.'

Omally smiled a sickly smile and tapped his nose. 'Leave it to Jim,' he counselled. 'He knows what he's doing. Wins over the machine's confidence, probes its defences, finds the weak spot and *Bitow!*'

'*Bitow*,' said Neville giving the Irishman what is universally known as the old fisheye. '*Bitow* it had better be.'

Omally grinned unconvincingly and ordered another pint.

Bitow Bitow Bitow Bitow Whap . . . 'What?'

'Aha,' yelled Raffles Rathbone, 'forgot to tell you about their strike ships. They got you that time. Care for a game of doubles?'

'Certainly,' said Jim, 'last to ten thousand gets the beer in.'

'You're on,' said the lad.

Omally hid his head in his hands and groaned.

At ten-thirty Neville called time, just to see what might happen. As ever the response was minimal. A few lingering tourists, up to enjoy the tours around the derelict gasworks, upped and had it away in search of their coaches, which had left an hour before. But by the local colour the cry was unheeded as ever. John Omally, whose face was now contorted into an expression which would have put the wind up Rondo Hatton, sat upon his barstool sipping at the fourth pint of Large he had been forced into buying himself during the course of the evening. Jim Pooley had spent the last four solid hours locked in mortal combat with the ever-alert invaders from the outer limits of the cosmic infinite.

For his part, young Nick had never been happier. He had borne the old slings and arrows of outrageous fortune regarding his involvement with the videotic projection of

71

the alien strike force for a goodly while. To be teamed up now with Jim Pooley, a man he had for long admired, gave him a definite feeling of invincibility. Together they would score maximum high points and get the mystery bonus. 'Get that man,' he yelled, dancing like a demented dervish. 'Give that lad some stick . . . nice one.'

Pooley paused at long last to take breath. His neutron bomb release finger had the cramp and he was beginning to suffer withdrawal symptoms from his self-imposed spell of drinklessness.

'I must rest now,' he told Rathbone. 'I heard our good barman calling for the towels up and the habits of a lifetime cannot be set aside in a single evening. I am called to the bar.'

'You are a mean player,' said the boy admiringly. 'It has been a pleasure to do battle with you.'

'You have the edge by virtue of practice,' replied Jim, 'but I'll give you a run for your money tomorrow lunchtime.'

'You're on,' said Raffles Rathbone.

When Jim found his way to the bar counter he was somewhat astonished by the full extent of Omally's hostility.

'What in the name of all the saints, including even those who have recently been given the big "E" by the present papacy, do you think you are up to?' the Irishman asked.

Pooley was unrepentant. 'Psychology?' he suggested.

'Psychology?'

'Yes, you know, win over the machine's confidence, probe its defences, find the weak spot then *Bitow*! Whose round is it?'

'Yours,' said Omally, 'Irrefutably yours.'

'I got fifteen thousand two hundred and one,' said Jim proudly, 'personal high score, take a bit of beating that.'

'Your head likewise.'

'It's in the wrist action,' Pooley continued informatively,

'and you have to know the sequences, once you know the sequences you can go for the high-scoring ships and simply dodge the lower ones. It's simple enough once you've sussed it out.'

'You're mad,' said Omally. 'You were right about the X-rays, they've burned out your brain.'

'Wrist action,' said Pooley, drumming his killing finger on to the bar. 'One, two, three, *Bitow,* move to the left, *Bitow, Bitow, Bitow.*'

'I will kill you.'

'Tell you what,' said Jim, 'I'll give you a game of doubles tomorrow. Nick will be here and he can give you a few pointers, you'll soon pick it up. Last one to two thousand points gets the drinks in, what do you say?'

Omally buried his face in his hands and began to sob plaintively. Pooley finished the Irishman's pint for him. 'You couldn't spare a couple of two-bobs, could you, John?' he asked. 'I just thought I'd get in another game before we go.'

10

Small Dave peeled open a packet of frozen *filet mignon amoureuse* and oozed it into the cankerous baking tray which had served his family for several generations. Turning the enamel oven up to regulo six, he popped the gourmet's nightmare on to a vacant shelf and slammed shut the door. This having been done to his satisfaction, the dwarfish postman slouched over to his sawn-down armchair and flung himself into it. He was not a happy man.

It is a sad fact that those unfortunates amongst us who are born lacking certain vital parts, or possess others to over-abundance, have good cause to bear grievance regarding their lots in life. Those blessed with the lucky humpty back, those who perpetually bump their heads upon the undersides of road bridges, or are capable of walking beneath bar stools without stooping, tend to feel that the gods have dealt with them rather shabbily.

Small Dave was one of this unhappy crew and he played the thing up for all it was worth. He took kindness for pity, the friendly word for the cutting jibe, and spent his days making life miserable for a community which would gladly have taken him as one of its own had he given it half a chance. When it came to having the old chip on the shoulder the little postman was in a class by himself. The arguments that many a famous man had been well below average height and that it wasn't a man's height that mattered, it was what he had in his heart, fell upon very deaf ears. Small Dave had resolved that if it stood taller than four feet and walked about, he hated it.

He was not exactly Mr Popular in Brentford. In fact, in a parish which tolerated almost every kind of eccentricity, he managed to achieve some notoriety.

This pleased his contemporaries, for, after all, they had wasted a lot of breath trying to convince him that you didn't have to be tall to be famous. Now they felt a lot less conscience-stricken about hating the vindictive, grudge-bearing wee bastard.

Small Dave dug his pointed nails into the chair's ragged arms and looked up at the clock. Nearly midnight, nearly time to get this camel business sorted out good and proper. He had been made to look very foolish this day, but he would have his revenge. Rising from his chair and setting flame to his acorn pipe, he paced the threadbare carpet, emitting plumes of sulphurous herbal smoke. At intervals he raised his fists towards heaven and at others he took to bouts of violent hand flapping.

At length the china Alsatian mantelclock struck the witching hour and Small Dave ceased his manic pacing. Striking one diminutive fist into the palm of its opposite number, he lurched from the room as if suddenly dragged forward by the ethereal cord which binds body and soul together. Up the staircase he went at a goodly pace, across a lino-covered landing, and up to the doorway of what estate agents laughingly refer to as the Master Bedroom.

Here he halted, breathing heavily, further hasty progress rendered impossible by the nature of the room's contents. It was literally filled with books. How the floor of the room was capable of supporting such a load was a matter for debate, but that the room contained what surely would have been sufficient to overstock an average public library was beyond doubt. The books cramming the open doorway formed a seemingly impenetrable barrier.

Small Dave looked furtively around, then withdrew a long key which he wore on a leather thong about his neck. Stooping, he found the hidden keyhole and swung open a tiny concealed door, formed from dummy bookbacks. With a curious vole-like snuffling, he dropped to all fours and scampered into the opening. The door of books swung silently shut behind him, leaving no trace of its presence.

Inside the room of books, Small Dave penetrated a tortuous labyrinth of tiny tunnels which were of his own creating. Deeper and deeper into the books he went, to the room's very core, where he finally emerged into a central chamber. It was a chamber wrought with exact precision into the interior of a perfect pyramid, aligned to the four cardinal points and fashioned from the choicest leather-bound volumes of the entire collection.

Within this extraordinary bower, illuminated by the room's original naked fly-specked bulb, were ranged an array of anomalous objects. A low dais surmounted by a single velvet cushion, a crystal, a milk bottle containing joss sticks, a framed picture of Edgar Allan Poe and a lone sprout under a glass dome.

Small Dave scrambled on to the velvet cushion and closed his eyes. The spines of the books stared down upon him, a multi-coloured leathern brickwork. He knew that he could never remove a single volume, for fear of premature burial, but as he had read every book in the room several times over and had memorized all by heart he had little need ever to consult them. His knowledge of the books transcended mere perusal and absorption of their printed words. He sought the deeper truths, and to do so it was necessary for him to consort with their very author. For if it was strange that such a chamber should exist and that such a collection of books should exist, then it was stranger still that each was the work of one single author: Edgar Allan Poe.

It was certain that if any of the Swan's patrons, who knew only Dave the postman while remaining totally unaware of Dave the mystic, had viewed this outré sanctum, they would have been forced to re-evaluate their views regarding his character. If they had witnessed the man who even now sat upon the dais, hands locked into the lamaic posture of meditation and legs bent painfully into a one-quarter lotus, they would have overwhelmingly agreed that the term vindictive, grudge-bearing wee bastard hardly applied here. Here it was more the case of vindictive, grudge-bearing wee lunatic bastard being a bit nearer the mark.

Small Dave began to whistle a wordless mantra of his own invention. His eyes were tightly closed and he swayed gently back and forth upon his cushion.

He had come to a decision regarding this camel business. He would ask help from the master himself, from the one man who had all the answers, old EAP. After all, had he not invented Dupin, the original consulting detective, and hadn't that original consulting detective been a dwarf like himself? Certainly Poe, who Dave had always noted with satisfaction was a man of less than average height, hadn't actually put it down in black and white, but all the implications were there. Dupin could never have noticed that body stuffed up the chimney in *Murders of the Rue Morgue*, if he hadn't been a little short-changed in the leg department.

Small Dave screwed up his eyes and thought 'Sprout'. It was no easy matter. Ever since he had first become a practising member of the Sacred Order of the Golden Sprout he had experienced quite a problem in coming to terms with the full potential power of that wily veg. His guru, one Reg Fulcanelli, a greengrocer from Chiswick, had spent a great deal of valuable time instructing Dave in the way of the sprout, but the wee lad simply did not seem to be grasping it. 'Know the sprout and know thyself,' Reg had told him, selecting a prime specimen from his window display and holding it up to the light. 'The sprout is all things to all men. And a law unto itself. Blessings be upon it.'

Small Dave had peered around the crowded green-grocery, wondering at the mountain of sprout sacks, the caseloads and boxfuls cramming every corner. 'You have an awful lot here,' he observed.

'You can't have too much of a good thing,' the perfect master had snapped. 'Do you want two pound of self-enlightenment or do you not?'

Small Dave hadn't actually reached the point of self-enlightenment as yet, but Reg had assured him that these things take a good deal of time and a great many sprouts.

Dave contorted his face and rocked ever harder. Ahead of him in the blackness beneath his eyelids the mental image of the sprout became clearer, growing and growing until it appeared the size of the room. Reg had explained that to ascend to the astral, one had to enter the sprout and become at one with it. When one had reached this state of cosmic consciousness all things were possible.

A bead of perspiration rolled down to the end of Dave's upturned nose. He could almost smell the sprout, it was so real, but he did not seem to be getting anywhere with the astral travelling side of it. He took a deep breath and prepared himself for one really hard try.

Downstairs in Small Dave's ancient enamel oven the now unfrozen *filet mignon amoureuse* was beginning to blacken about the edges. Soon the plastic packets of sauce which he had carelessly neglected to remove from the foil container would ignite causing an explosion, not loud, but of sufficient force to spring the worn lock upon the oven's door and spill the burning contents on to the carpet. The flames would take hold upon a pile of *Psychic News* and spread to the length of net curtain which Small Dave had been meaning to put up properly for some weeks.

Small Dave, however, would remain unconscious of this until the conflagration had reached the point which sets schoolboys dancing and causes neighbours from a safe distance to bring out chairs and cheerfully await the arrival of the appliances.

It is interesting to note that, although these things had not as yet actually come to pass, it could be stated with absolute accuracy that they would most certainly occur. That such could be so accurately predicted might in a way, it is to be supposed, argue greatly in favour of such things as precognition and astral projection.

Small Dave would argue in favour of the latter, because by some strange freak of chance, while his physical self sat in a state of complete ignorance regarding its imminent cremation, his astral body now stood upon a mysterious cloudy plane confronting the slightly transparent figure of a man in a Victorian garb with an oversized head and narrow bow tie.

'Mr Poe?' the foggy postman enquired. 'Mr Edgar Allan Poe?'

'Small Dave?' said that famous author. 'You took your time getting here.' He indicated something the ethereal dwarf clutched in his right hand. 'Why the sprout?' he asked.

II

Norman had returned to his kitchenette, leaving his camel snoring peacefully in the eaves of his lock-up garage, its head in a Fair Isle snood. He surveyed the wreckage of his precious equipment and wondered what was to be done. He was going to need a goodly few replacement parts if he ever hoped to restore it. It was going to be another quid or two's worth of postcard ads in all the local newsagents: 'Enthusiast requires old wireless sets/parts, etc., for charity work. Will collect, distance no object.' That had served him pretty well so far. And if the worst came to the worst then he would have to put in a bit more midnight alleyway skulking about the rear of Murray's Electrical in the High Street.

Norman picked his way amongst the tangled wreckage and pondered his lot; it didn't seem to be much of a lot at the present time. It was bound to cost him big bucks no matter how it went, but at least he had the satisfaction of knowing that his theory was at least partially correct. The evil-smelling ship of the desert lodged in his garage testified amply to that. But there was certainly something amiss about his calculations. They would need a bit of rechecking; it was all a matter of weight, all very much a matter of weight.

Norman unearthed his chair and slumped into it. It had been an exhausting day all in all. As he sat, his chin cupped in his hand, his mind wandered slowly back to the moment which had been the source of inspiration for this great and wonderful project. Strange to recount, it had all begun one lunchtime in the saloon-bar of the Flying Swan.

Norman had been listening with little interest to a discussion between Jim Pooley and John Omally, regarding a book Jim had but recently borrowed from the Memorial Library upon the Great Mysteries of the Ancient Past. The conversation had wandered variously about, with Pooley stating that in his opinion Stonehenge was nothing more than scaffolding and that the builders, some megalithic forerunners to Geo. Wimpey and Co., had never actually got around to erecting the building. Doubtless a pub, he considered.

Omally, nodding sagely, added that this was the case with many ancient structures, that their original purposes were sorely misinterpreted by the uninspired scholars of today. The Colosseum, he said, had very much the look of a multi-storey carpark to him, and the Parthenon a cinema. 'Look at the Odeon in Northfields Avenue,' he said, 'the façade is damn near identical.'

Norman was about to make a very obvious remark when Pooley suddenly said, 'It definitely wasn't built as a tomb.'

'What, the Odeon Northfields? No, I don't think so.'

'Not the Odeon, the Great Pyramid at Giza.'

'Oh, that body.' Omally nodded his head. 'Surely I have read somewhere that it was the work of them extra-terrestrial lads who used to carry a lot of weight back in those times.'

Pooley shook his head. 'That I doubt.'

'What then?' Omally asked, draining his glass and replacing it noisily upon the bar counter.

Pooley, who could recognize a captive audience when he saw one queuing up for a one-pint ticket, ordered two more of whatever it was they were drinking at the time and continued. 'It was the ticking of the old Guinness clock up there which solved the thing for me.'

'Oh, you consider the Great Pyramid to have been a pub also?'

'Hardly that.'

'Then might I make so bold as to inquire how such a humble thing as the Guinness clock leads you to solve a riddle which has baffled students of Egyptology for several thousands of years?'

'It is simplicity itself,' said Jim, but of course it was nothing of the sort. 'The ticking of the Guinness clock put me in mind, naturally enough, of Big Ben.'

'Naturally enough.'

'Now as you may have noticed, Big Ben is a very large clock with a pendulum so great that it would easily reach from here, right down the passage and into the gents.'

Omally whistled. 'As big as that, eh?'

'As big, and this huge clock is kept accurately ticking away by the piles of pennies placed upon that pendulum by the builders of the thing. Am I right?'

'You are,' said Omally agreeably, 'you are indeed.'

'Well then!' said Pooley triumphantly.

'Well then what?'

Pooley sighed; he was clearly speaking to an idiot. 'The Great Pyramid is to the planet Earth what the penny piles are to Big Ben's pendulum. Shall I explain fully?'

'Perhaps you should, Jim, but make it a quick one, eh?'

'Well then, as we are all aware, these ancient Egyptians were a pretty canny bunch. Greatly skilled at plotting the heavens and working things out on the old slide rule. Well, it is my belief that sometime back then some sort of catastrophe, no doubt of a cosmic nature, occurred and pushed the Earth a little off its axis. There is a great deal of evidence to support this, the sudden extinction of the mammoths, the shifting of the Polar caps, all this kind of thing.'

Omally yawned. 'Sorry,' he said.

'Now these Egyptian lads were not to be caught napping and when they realized that impending doom was heading their way they did the only logical thing and took corrective measures.'

'Corrective measures?' The bottom of Omally's glass was already in sight and he could feel the dartboard calling.

'Corrective measures they took,' said Jim, 'by building a kind of counterbalance upon the Earth's surface to keep the thing running on trim. They selected the exact spot which bisects exactly the continents and oceans. They aligned their construction to the four cardinal points and then whammo, or not whammo, as the case may be. There you are, you see, case proven, we have a great deal to thank those ancient sunburned builders for.'

Omally seemed strangely doubtful. 'There has been a lot of building work done about the world since that time,' he said, 'some of which I can personally vouch for. With all that weight being unevenly distributed about the place, I have the feeling that your old pyramid would become somewhat overwhelmed.'

Pooley shook his head. 'The pyramid is a unique structure, it has an exact weight, mass, and density ratio to the planet itself. It is the one construction which will fill the bill exactly. The stones quarried for it were cut to carefully calculated sizes and shapes, each is an integral part interlocking like a Chinese puzzle. The inner chambers are aligned in such a way as to channel certain earth currents to maximum effect. It is much more than simply a big lump of rock. No matter how many other buildings go up all over the world, the pyramid will still maintain its function. To alter the Earth's motion one would have to actually move the Great Pyramid.'

'I'll chalk up then,' said Omally, but the remark was apparently not directed to Jim Pooley.

Norman, however, was entranced. Could there possibly be any conceivable truth behind Pooley's ramblings? It all seemed impossibly far-fetched. But what if it were so? The implications were staggering! If one could actually alter the course of the Earth by moving the Great Pyramid about, then one could wield quite a lot of weight, in more than one sense only. A bit of a tilt northwards and Brentford would enjoy tropical summers, a mite more later in the year and there would be tropical winters too. It was all in the wrist action.

It would be quite a task, though, the Great Pyramid was estimated to weigh upwards of five million, nine hundred and twenty-three thousand, four hundred tons. It would take more than a builder's lorry and a bunch of willing lads on double bubble. Possibly he could bribe coachloads of tourists into each bringing back a bit with them. That would be a lengthy business though.

Norman's gigantic intellect went into overdrive. He had been experimenting for years with a concept based upon Einstein's unified field theory, which was concerned primarily with the invisibilizing and teleportation of solid objects. It was rumoured that the US Navy had made a successful experiment during the war, creating some kind of magnetic camouflage which to all intents and purposes made an entire battle cruiser vanish momentarily. Einstein himself, it was said, had forbidden any further experimentation, due to the disastrous effects visited upon the crew.

Norman had recalled thinking on more than one occasion that Einstein, although an individual given to the rare flash of inspiration, had for the most part been a little too windy by half. Now if the Great Pyramid could be teleported from one site to another it might be very instructive to observe the results . . .

Norman scuffed his feet amongst the wreckage. It had all been so long ago, a lot of peanuts had lodged under the old bridge since then. But he had proved that at least some of it was possible. In fact, the more he thought about it the more he realized that to teleport a live camel from the Nile Delta to the St Mary's allotment, in a matter of seconds, wasn't a bad day's work after all. He was definitely well on his way.

Norman smiled contentedly, picked his way over to the corner sink and, drawing back the undercurtain, took out a bottle of Small Dave's home-made cabbage beer, a crate of which he had taken in payment for an unpaid yearly subscription to *Psychic News*. It was a little on the earthy side and had more than a hint of the wily sprout about it, but it did creep up on you and was always of use if your lighter had run low.

'The ultimate quest,' said Norman, raising the bottle towards the charred ceiling of the war-torn kitchenette.

It had long been a habit of his, one born it is to be believed at a Cowboy Night he had attended some years previously, for Norman to wrench the hard-edged cap from the bottle's neck with his teeth before draining deeply from its glassy throat.

In his enthusiasm he quite forgot the matter of his wayward dentures.

The ensuing scream rattled chimney pots several streets away and caused many of the 'sleeping just' to stir in their slumber and cross themselves fitfully.

12

Elsewhere other early recumbents were stirring to the sound of fire-engine bells and the cheers of an assembled throng of spectators. There was a fair amount of noise and chaos, smoke and flame, when the front bedroom floor at twenty-seven Silver Birch Terrace collapsed, bringing with it a hundred-thousand volumes of Poe and an apparently comatose postman of below average height.

When the firemen, who had been amusing themselves by flooding neighbouring front rooms and washing out carefully-laid gardens, finally finished their work upon Small Dave's house, the ambulance men, who had been grudgingly aroused from their dominoes, moved in to claim the corpse in the interests of medical science. They were more than surprised to find the postman sitting virtually uncharred in the ruins of his living room, legs crossed and bearing a baked sprout in his right hand. He wore a smiling and benign expression upon his elfin face and seemed to be humming something. Shrugging helplessly, they wrapped him up in a red blanket and bundled him into the ambulance.

When the sound of its departing bells had faded, along with those of the appliance, away into the night, the observers of the holocaust drifted away to brew cocoa and prepare for their beds. Eventually just two members of the jolly band remained, one a fellow of Irish extraction and the other a man with a twitching right forefinger.

'What now?' asked John Omally.

'A nocturnal tournament?' Pooley suggested. 'One for the road before we turn in, how does double or quits suit you?'

'Very well, I think you owe me something for the evening of embarrassment you have given me. Care to put an extra wager upon the course record?'

Pooley, who considered his sobriety to give him the natural edge, nodded enthusiastically and the two men wandered off towards the allotment. Omally affected the occasional drunken side-step in the hope of adding weight to Pooley's conviction and causing him to bet a little more recklessly.

It was a clear night. A hunter's moon swam above in the heavens, edging the corrugated sheds with a priceless silver. The course was illuminated to such a degree that there was no need for the employment of the miner's helmets Pooley had improvised for late matches.

The allotment gates were barred and bolted. An officious Council lackey had also seen to it that they were now surmounted by a row of murderous looking barbs and a tangle of barbed wire. Exactly why, nobody could guess. Pooley and Omally were obliged to use their own private entrance.

'A nine-holer or the full eighteen, Jim?'

'The night is yet young and I feel more than equal to the task, remembering that you are already deeply in my debt.' Pooley quietly unlocked his shed and withdrew the two sets of hidden clubs.

Omally tossed a coin. 'Heads,' he said, as the copper coin spun into the night sky.

Had the falling coin actually struck terra firma, as one might naturally have assumed that it would, it is possible that the events which followed might never have occurred. It is possible, but it is unlikely. The coin tumbled towards the allotment dust, until it reached a point about three inches above it, and then an extraordinary thing occurred. The coin suddenly arrested its downward journey and hovered in the air as if now reluctant to return to the planet of its origin.

The two golfers stared at it in dumb disbelief. 'Now that is what I would call a trick,' said Jim, when he eventually found his voice. 'You really must teach it to me on some occasion. Wires is it, or magnetism?'

Omally shook his head. 'None of my doing,' he said, crossing his heart solemnly, 'but it has come up heads so I suggest that you tee off first.'

'Not so fast,' Pooley replied. 'The coin has not yet reached the deck, it might have a couple of turns left in it.'

'It has clearly stopped falling,' said John, 'and that is good enough for me. Kindly tee off.'

'I think not,' said Jim, shaking his head slowly and firmly. 'I am not a man to call cheat, but the coin's behaviour leads me to believe that something a little phony is going on here. Kindly toss it again.'

'You want the best out of three then?'

'No, the best out of one. I should like the coin, as the biblical seed itself, to fall upon the stony ground!'

Omally shrugged. 'I confess my own astonishment at the coin's anarchistic behaviour, but I feel deeply insulted that you should even hint at duplicity upon my part. Trust being the bond which cements our long friendship, I suggest that we simply let the matter drop, or in this case hover.'

'Toss the coin again,' said Jim Pooley.

'As you will,' said Omally, who had now determined that he would cheat the second toss come what may. He stooped down and reached out a hand towards the hovering coin. He was rewarded almost instantaneously by a crackle of blue flame which scorched his fingertips and sent him reeling backwards into the shadows as if suddenly hit by a speeding locomotive. 'Ooh, ouch, damn and blast,' came a voice from the darkness.

Pooley sniggered. 'Must be a hotter night than I thought, John,' he said, 'Get a touch of static did you?'

Omally gave out with a brief burst of obscenities.

'Tut tut.' Pooley stretched out a tentative boot to nudge the copper coin aside. This, in the light of Omally's experience, was an ill-considered move upon his part. For his folly he received a similar charge of energy which caught his steel toecap, arched up the back of his leg and hit him squarely in the groin. 'Erg,' he said, which was in technical terms basically accurate. Clutching at his privy parts, he sank to his knees, eyes crossed.

Omally crawled over to his gasping companion's doubled form. 'I take the oath that this is none of my doing,' he said, blowing upon his charred finger-ends.

Pooley said, 'Erg,' once more, which was at least an encouraging sign that life still remained in him.

'Oh no!' said Omally suddenly. 'Not again.' The dust beneath the hovering coin had cleared to reveal the grinning metallic face of yet another runic ideogram. As the two men watched, a faint glow seemed to engulf it; growing steadily, as if somehow charged from beneath, it bathed the symbol in a sharp white light.

But it was no light of Earth. Although the symbol glowed with a dazzling brilliance, the light seemed self-contained and threw no illumination on to the awe-struck faces of the two golfers. Then, with an audible crackle, the light rose in a green column, a clear laser-like shaft, directly into the night sky.

'Erg, erg,' went Jim, gesticulating wildly in many directions. All over the allotments identical columns of light were rising. They soared into the black void of space, and although they dwindled to whitened hairs, there seemed no end to their journeyings.

'Say this isn't happening,' Omally implored.

Pooley could only offer another 'Erg', which was of no comfort whatever. In fact, as a means of communication the word 'Erg' was proving something of a dead loss.

Just then the lights went out. One by one they snapped off, leaving the night as it were untouched, although Pooley and Omally knew very much to the contrary. Pooley at last found a tiny croaking voice which had been hiding at the back of his throat. 'What were they, John?'

Omally shook his head. 'I think that it is possibly God's way of telling us to give up golf.'

Pooley found this explanation doubtful to say the least. 'God, I think, is generally a little more direct about these things. A great man for a thunderbolt is God. But whatever it was, it was the final straw, the allotment has lost its charm for me.'

'I can sympathize.' Omally struggled to his feet and took to dusting down his tweeds with his one good hand. 'With wandering camels, vanishing council spies, symbols and searchlights, there does seem to be an unwonted amount of activity hereabouts of late.'

'I'm for telling the Professor,' said Jim, getting a perfect mental image of a whisky decanter.

Omally had taken to soaking his scorched fingers in a nearby water-butt. 'I think,' said he, 'that the Professor has pressing business of his own. But, as you see, the coin has now reached the ground.' He pointed towards where the rogue penny now lay upon the exposed symbol. 'And even though it is still "heads", in the face of the unfortunate accident which befell you I am willing to concede the toss.'

'Thank you.' Pooley stroked his trouser region gingerly, the old three-piece suite was smarting like a good 'un. 'I have quite gone off golf now, I should prefer a glass or two of nerve tonic rather better.'

'Aha!' Omally tapped his nose. 'I think there might be a bottle or two of such stuff maturing even now in my hut, would you care to step across?'

'I would indeed, but slowly now, I am not feeling at my best.'

The two men wended their way over the allotment, treading warily and taking great lengths to avoid those areas where the strange symbols lay glowing faintly in the moonlight.

Omally's plot was always a matter for discussion and debate amongst his fellow allotment-holders. John tended to steer clear of the general run-of-the-mill, socially acceptable forms of crop and specialize rather in things with unpronounceable Latin names and heady fragrances. Sniffing moggies often emerged from his plot vacant-eyed and staggering.

Pooley stepped carefully across Omally's bed of flowering mandrake and gestured towards a row of towering belladonna. 'You have an unsavoury looking crop on at present,' he said, by way of making conversation.

'Export orders mostly,' John told him. The shed itself had a good deal of the gingerbread cottage about it, with its trelliswork of climbing wolfsbane and its poppy-filled window boxes. Omally unpadlocked the door and picked up a couple of picture postcards from the welcome mat. One of these carried upon its face a rooftop view of Brentford. Omally read this one aloud: 'Encountering difficulties dismantling Ark due to petrified condition, may be forced to bring it down in one piece. Regards to all, Archroy.'

'Do you actually believe any of the stuff he writes?' Pooley asked.

Omally shrugged his broad and padded shoulders. 'Who is to say? He sends these cards to Neville and one or two other prominent Brentonians. I suspect there will shortly be a request for financial assistance with the Ark's transportation. No doubt he will wish to have the money orders forwarded to some post-office box in West Ealing.'

'You are a hard man, John.'

'I am a realist,' said the realist.

Omally's bottles were unearthed and drinks were poured. The two lazed variously upon potato sacks, sharing a Woodbine and musing upon this and that. As the contents of the bottles dwindled, likewise did the musing upon this and that. More and more did this musing spiral inwards, its vagueness and generalities crystallizing with each inward sweep to become definites and absolutes. And thus did these definites and absolutes eventually centre upon the woes and anguishes of interrupted golf tournaments and, in particular, their own.

'It is becoming intolerable,' said Pooley, draining his enamel mug and refilling it immediately.

'Unbearable,' said Omally, doing likewise.

'Something must be done.'

'Absolutely.'

'Something drastic.'

'Quite so.'

'My bottle is empty,' said Jim.

Omally tossed him another.

'Good health to you, John.'

'And to yourself.'

Three hours and as many bottles later the matter was coming very near to being resolved. A vote was being taken and by a show of hands it was carried unanimously. It was agreed that with the aid of two long-handled shovels, each fitted with rubber handgrips as a precautionary measure, the mysterious symbols would be dug from the ground. They would be transported by wheelbarrow, similarly insulated about the handle regions, to the river and therein unceremoniously dumped. With these obstacles to play satisfactorily removed, attention would be turned towards the matter of the council spies. It had not been fully resolved as to the exact course of action to be taken over this, but it was generally agreed that the employment of stout sticks would play a part in it.

The moon had by now run a fair distance along its nightly course, and when the men emerged from Omally's hut the allotment had about it the quality of a haunted place. There was a harsh, collars-up chill in the air and the low moon now cast long and sinister shadows across a deathly-tinted ground. The prospect of digging up a potential minefield held little if any appeal whatsoever.

'Best make a fresh start in the morning,' said Pooley, rubbing his hands briskly together. 'I'm for my cosy nest, bed ways is best ways and all that.'

Omally grasped the retreating Jim firmly by his thread-bare collar. 'Not so fast, Pooley,' said he, 'you are not going to bottle out on this now.' Jim thought to detect a lack of conviction in the Irishman's tone. 'I suggest a compromise.'

Pooley hovered on his toes. 'You mean do it in shifts, you dig tonight, I tomorrow, I applaud that.'

'Hardly.' Omally tightened his grip. 'I mean rather that we go round and set markers beside the symbols so we will be able to locate them. Then we both dig tomorrow.'

Pooley thought this not only sound but also far less strenuous. 'That is using the old grey matter,' he told John. 'Now, if you will release your grip, which is causing no little interference to my general welfare about the throat regions, I shall do my best to assist you.'

Now began the inevitable discussion upon the best method of accomplishing the task in hand. Pooley suggested the hardy sprout as a piece of vegetable matter suitable for the job. In the interests of good taste Omally put up the spud as the ideal substitute. The war then waged between bean poles loaded with tinfoil, shredded newspaper laid out in the form of pentagrams and a whole host of objects ranging from the noble and worthy to the positively obscene. Finally, after Pooley had made a suggestion so ludicrous as to bring the naturally short-tempered Irishman within a hairbreadth of killing him there and then, Omally put his foot down once and for all.

'Enough, enough,' he shouted. 'We will not mark them at all, we shall merely pace around the allotment and make notes as to each location as we come upon it. That is that.'

If Pooley had worn a hat he would have taken it off to his companion and cast it into the air. 'Brilliant,' he said, shaking his head in admiration. 'How do you do it, John?'

'It's a gift, I believe.'

Pooley pulled out the *Now Official Handbook of Allotment Golf* and handed it to Omally. 'Let us go,' he said. 'The field is yours.'

Now, it is to be remembered that both men had imbibed considerable quantities of potato gin, a drink not noted for its sobering qualities, and that the light was extremely poor. Had it not been for these two facts it is just possible that the job might have been accomplished with some degree of success. As it was, in no time at all, the two men found themselves crossing and recrossing their tracks and scrawling illegible diagrams and unreadable locative descriptions all over the exercise book.

'We have done this one already,' said Pooley, lurching to one side of a glowing symbol. 'I'm sure we've done this one.'

Omally shook his head, 'No, no,' he said, 'it is as clear as clear, look, you can see the way we came.' He tapped at the notebook and as he did so the moon crept away behind a large cloud, leaving them in total darkness. 'Bugger,' said John, 'I cannot seem to find my way.'

'Best call it off then,' said Pooley, 'bad light stops play, nothing more to be done, bed is calling.'

'My hearing is acute,' Omally warned. 'One move and I strike you down.'

'But, John.'

'But nothing.'

The two men stood a moment awaiting the return of the moon. 'What is that?' Omally asked, quite without warning.

'What is what?' Pooley replied sulkily.

Omally gestured invisibly to a point not far distant, where something definitely untoward was occurring. 'That there.'

Pooley peered about in the uncertain light and it did not take him long to see it. 'Right,' said Jim, 'that is definitely me finished. The Pooleys know when their time is up.'

'Keep your gaping gob shut,' whispered Omally hoarsely, as he leapt forward and dragged the quitter to the dust.

Coming from the direction of Soap Distant's abandoned hut a soft red light was growing. The door of the heavily bolted shed was slowly opening, showing a ghostly red glow.

'Would you look at that?' gasped Dublin's finest.

'I should prefer not,' said Pooley, climbing to his feet and preparing for the off.

Omally clutched at his companion, catching him by a ragged trouser cuff. 'Look,' said he, 'now that is a thing.'

From all points of the allotment shadowy forms were moving, figures indistinct and fuzzy about the edges, striding like automata, ever in the direction of the weird red light. 'Ye gods,' whispered Jim as one passed near enough to expose his angular profile, 'the council spies, dozens of them.'

Omally dragged Pooley once more towards terra. 'I would counsel silence,' he whispered, 'and the keeping of the now legendary low profile.'

'I feel sick,' moaned Jim.

The gaunt figures strode ever onwards. Silently they moved amongst the many scattered obstructions upon the allotment soil. Never a one turned his head from his goal and each walked with a mechanical precision.

Pooley and Omally watched their progress with wide eyes and slack jaws. 'We should follow them,' said John, 'see what they're up to.'

'With the corner up we should.'

'Poltroon. Come on man, let's sort the thing out.'

Pooley sloped his drunken shoulders. 'John,' said he, 'are you honestly suggesting that any good whatsoever will come from following this gang of weirdos? I feel rather that we would be walking straight into a trap. This is only my opinion of course, and it is greatly influenced by the state of blind panic I find myself in at present. There is something altogether wrong about every bit of this. Let us leave the allotment now, depart for ever, never to return. What do you say?'

Omally weighed up the situation. Things did seem a little iffy. They were greatly outnumbered and there was definitely something unnatural about the striding men. Perhaps it would be wiser to run now and ask questions later. But there were a lot of questions that needed asking and now might be the best time to ask them, emboldened as they both were, or he at least, by the surfeit of alcohol pumping about the old arteries. 'Come on, Jim,' he said, encouragingly. 'One quick look at what they're up to, what harm can it do? After the day we've had nothing else can happen to us, can it?'

Pooley thought that it possibly could, and as it turned out Pooley was absolutely correct.

13

Ahead the red light glowed evilly and the spectral figures moved into its aura to become cardboard silhouettes. Pooley and Omally lurched along to the rear of the strange brigade as silently as their inebriate blunderings would allow. None of the queer horde turned a head, although the sounds of their pursuers, as they stumbled amongst corrugated plot dividers and galvanized watering cans, rang loudly across the silent allotments. As the stark figures neared the light they fell into line and strode through the doorway of Soap Distant's hut like so many clockwork soldiers.

When the last of them had entered, the light grew to a blinding intensity then dimmed away to nothingness. 'There,' said Pooley, faltering in his footsteps, 'a trick of the light, nothing more, probably landing lights on a Jumbo or some such. Off to our beds now then, eh?'

Omally prodded him in the loins with the rake he had wisely appropriated in the interests of self-preservation. 'Onward, Pooley,' he ordered. 'We will get to the bottom of this.'

His words, as it happened, could not have been more poorly chosen, but Omally, of course, was not to know that at this time. The two men neared Soap's hut and peered through the open doorway. There was nothing to be seen but sheer, unutterable, unfathomable darkness.

'Lighter,' Omally commanded. Pooley brought out his aged Zippo and sucked at the wick. Omally snatched at the well-worn smoker's friend and as the flame bravely illuminated the hut's interior the two men gave forth with twin whistles of dismay.

The shed was empty: four corrugated walls, a ceiling of slatted asbestos and a concrete floor.

John Omally groaned. Pooley shook his head in wonder. 'These council lads certainly leave the great Houdini with egg on his chin,' he said respectfully. 'How do you suppose they do it?'

'I utterly refuse to believe this,' said Omally, holding the lighter aloft and stepping boldly through the doorway. 'There is no conceivable way they could all have . . . '

He never actually finished the sentence. Pooley's lighter was suddenly extinguished and Omally's words were swallowed up as if sucked into some great and terrible vacuum.

'John?' Pooley found himself alone in the darkness. 'John, this is not funny.' His voice echoed hollowly in the sinister hut.

'Oh dear me,' said Jim Pooley.

The moon slowly withdrew itself from its cloudy lair and shone a broad beam of light through the open doorway. The tiny hut was empty. John Omally had simply ceased to exist. Jim snatched up Omally's discarded rake, prodding ahead of him as he gingerly moved forward. The moon was still shining brightly and now, along the nearby rooftops, the thin red line of dawn was spreading.

'Oh!' The tip of Pooley's protruding rake had of a sudden become strangely fuzzy and ill-defined. Another step forward and Pooley noted to his utter stupefaction that it had vanished altogether into empty air. He withdrew it hastily and ran his finger along its length; it was intact. Jim looked at the rake and then at the empty shed before him, he scratched at his head and then at his chin, he weighed the thing up and tried to make some sense of it.

The shed was obviously not what it at first appeared. An

ingenious camouflage indeed. But to camouflage what, and, most importantly, where was John? Obviously somewhere behind the simulated reality of the empty shed lurked another something, and obviously it was a thoroughly unwholesome something which boded ill for unwary golfers.

Pooley approached the doorway once more, and thrust the rake in up to the hilt. He waggled it about and swished it to and fro; it met with no apparent resistance. Jim pulled out the rake and stood a moment rescratching his head. It really was a very clever thing indeed. Possibly that was how these council lads had eluded them before. Probably the one in the Swan's bog had simply switched on some sort of 3-D projector, whipped up an image of an empty cubicle and sat down on the seat for a good sneer whilst Omally got foamy about the jaws. They were probably standing there in the shed even now doing the same.

Pooley took a step backwards. He'd show the buggers! Wielding the rake in as menacing a manner as he could, he took a deep if drunken breath and rushed at the image. 'Ooooooooooh,' went Jim Pooley as the concrete floor of the shed dissolved beneath his feet, plunging him down into the perpetual darkness of the now legendary bottomless pit.

How far Jim fell, and how long his plummet into the nether regions of the great beneath actually took, must remain for ever a matter for conjecture. That his life had plenty of time to flash before his eyes was of little consolation, although it did give an occasion for him to recall that during it he had consumed a very great deal of alcohol. Also, that should he survive this, he had every intention of consuming a great deal more.

Finally, however, after what had been up until then a relatively uneventful if windy fall to oblivion, Pooley's descending form made a painful and quite unexpected contact with a body of ice-cold and seemingly unfathomable water.

'Ow . . . *ooh!*' wailed that unhappiest of men. '*Ow . . . ooh* and *glug.*' Pooley surfaced after several desperate and drowning moments, mouthed several very timely and well-expressed obscenities and sank once more into the subterranean depths.

'I forgive all,' he vowed as his head bobbed aloft for a second time. Possibly Jim would have survived for a goodly while bobbing up and down in this fashion. It is more likely, however, that he would have breathed his last as he went down for that famous old third time, had help not arrived from a most unexpected quarter.

'Climb aboard, Jim,' said a voice which struck a strange chord in Pooley's rapidly numbing brain. Jim squinted up from his watery grave to realize for the first time that he was no longer in darkness. Above him he could see the cowled head and shoulders of a man, leaning from what appeared to be a coracle of skin and bark, extending a rugged-looking oar. Without hesitation Pooley clutched at the thing and was unceremoniously hauled aboard. Huddled low in one end of the curious craft lay John Omally, swathed in blankets.

'Nice of you to drop in,' said the Irishman with the rattling teeth. Pooley made some attempts to wring out his tweed lapels, but soon gave up and resigned himself to death by pneumonia.

'Where are we?' he asked, peering about him.

A wan light emanating from some luminescent substance within the very rocks, which swept dome-like and dizzying high above them, illuminated a monstrous cavern. The black waters of the subterranean lake spread away in every direction, losing themselves into a great vastness of absolutely nothing.

It all looked a little worrying.

Jim shuddered, and not from the icy cold which now knotted his every muscle. It was the sheer mind-stunning hugeness of the place, and the fact that it actually existed somewhere deep beneath the roads where he daily set his feet. And those waters, what might lurk in them? It didn't bear thinking about. Jim turned to his saviour.

'You have my thanks, sir,' said he, 'but tell me . . .' His words trailed off as the dark figure turned from the oar he had been carefully slotting into its rowlock and confronted the dripping Brentonian. 'Soap?' said Jim. 'Soap, is that you?'

The boatman slipped back the cowl which covered his head and grinned wolfishly, 'Have I changed so much then, Pooley?' he asked.

Jim surveyed the darkly-clad figure, whose black robes threw the deathlike pallor of his face into ghastly contrast. His hair was peroxide blond and his eyebrows and lashes naught but snowy bristles. Soap was as white as the proverbial sheet. Pooley recalled the ruddy-faced Hollow Earth theorist with the sparkling green eyes who had regaled them with talk of Rigdenjyepo and the denizens of the world beneath. He also recalled only too well that terrible night when Soap had invited him and Omally down into a fantastic tunnel system beneath his house to witness the opening of what Soap believed to be the Portal to Inner Earth.

Pooley and Omally had made a rapid exit from the workings, but Soap had gone through with the thing and opened what turned out to be the stopcocks of the old flood sluices of Brentford Docks. An entire stretch of Grand Union Canal had drained forthwith into Soap's diggings and that had been the last Brentford had seen of the Hollow Earther.

Pooley stared at Soap in disbelief. 'You do appear slightly altered in your appearance,' he said carefully, as he gazed into the latter's eyes, now pink as an albino's, and slightly luminous.

'Five years below can alter any man,' said Soap, re-adjusting his cowl. 'I have seen things down here that would stagger the senses of the strongest man. I have seen sights which would drive the sanity from your head quicker than shit off a shovel.'

Pooley now also recalled that he and Omally had always been of the opinion that Soap was a dangerous lunatic.

'Yes,' said Jim, 'indeed, ah well then, again my thanks for the old life-saving and now if you would kindly show us the way out of here. I feel that it must be nearing my breakfast time.'

Omally piped up with, 'I have pork in the press if you'd care to come topside with us, Soap me old mate.'

The hooded figure said no more, but sat carefully down and applied himself to the oars. The curious little craft, with its extraordinary crew, slowly edged its way across the pitch-black waters. How Soap could have any idea of which way he was travelling seemed totally beyond conjecture. Hours may have passed, or merely minutes; time did not seem to apply here. Pooley's Piaget wristwatch had now ceased its ticking for good and all and maintained a sullen rusting silence. The high dome of rocks seemed unchanging and Omally wondered on occasions whether they were actually moving at all. Presently, however, a thin line of white appeared upon the horizon.

'Land ho,' said Soap, grinning at his marrow-chilled passengers.

'Would there be any chance of light at the end of the long dark tunnel?' Pooley asked. 'Such as nutrition, or possibly the warming quaff of ale or lick of spirits?'

Soap tapped at his nose in a manner which the two remembered only too well. 'You will be well cared for, you have been long expected.' Upon that doubtful note he withdrew once more into silence and rowed on towards land.

The island, for such it now showed itself to be, was a

strange enough place by any reckoning. As Soap beached the craft and ushered the two ashore, Pooley viewed the place with the gravest misgivings. There was a dreadful prehistoric gloom about it; if the black waters were bad enough, this was somehow worse.

The island was a long, rough crescent, covered for the most part with enormous stalagmites. These gave it the appearance of the half-submerged jawbone of some long-dead behemoth. Pooley felt instinctively that to set foot on such a thing was direly wrong and his thoughts were shared by Omally. Yet both were wet, cold, hungry, and demoralized, and with little complaint they numbly followed Soap along the bone-white beach to a craggy outcropping which seemed the highest point of the bleak landfall.

'Would you kindly turn your backs a moment?' Soap asked politely. Pooley eyed his colleague and the blue-faced Irishman shrugged in his blanket shawl. Soap was but a moment in performing whatever action he had in mind, and when the two turned back, a great doorway yawned in the faceless rock revealing a comfortable-looking room of extraordinary size.

'Step inside quickly now, please. I have no wish to expose the entrance any longer than need be. There are eyes everywhere, even here.'

Pooley shook his head in redoubled wonder and the two men scuttled inside, followed by their amiable if enigmatic host. The door swung shut, predictably leaving no trace whatsoever of its existence.

'Now,' said Soap, 'cup of tea, is it?'

A thin smile flickered momentarily upon Omally's arctic boat-race, 'Only Soap Distant could offer a cup of tea at the Earth's core.'

'There have been others,' said Soap, indicating the letters A.S. which were scratched into the stonework of one of the walls. 'But that is another story entirely.'

Pooley cast his eyes about the room. It had all the makings of the average Brentford front sitter: the moquette three-piece, the nylon carpet, the occasional table whose occasion was yet to come, the fitted bookshelves and the television set. But for the hewn rock walls and the obvious lack of windows one might have been fooled into believing that all was suburban mundanity.

'Surely reception hereabouts must be a little ropey?' said Jim, indicating the television.

'Kept purely through nostalgia for my former existence,' said Soap. 'Now, my suggestion of a nice hot cuppa is eliciting very little in the way of positive response. I have some fine Riesling in my cellar, or perhaps some Bordeaux rosé? Shall I open a case or two?'

'That would be the thing,' said Pooley, with some enthusiasm, 'events have sorely taxed us of late.'

Soap Distant vanished from the room, away down a flight of hewn rock steps which had not been previously mentioned.

Pooley and Omally sat a moment in silence before the great man of Eire gave voice. 'If I might say so, Jim,' John ventured, 'your suggestion of having it away to our cosy beds and starting afresh on the morrow was one which I really should have picked up on before it went out of fashion.'

'I blame nobody,' said the noble Jim, 'but would sincerely ask what in the name of all the holies we are doing in this godforsaken place and how we might facilitate our escape?'

Soap appeared from the cellar, cradling several bottles of wine in his arms. 'The day is yet saved,' he said, beaming hideously. 'The cellar brims with vintage vino of all varieties. I have brought up a selection.'

Omally, who was certain that the day was very far from being saved, rubbed his hands thoughtfully together. 'Why are we here, Soap?' he asked.

'Well now, that is a question and no mistake,' the other replied. 'Some incline towards the theory of a divine creator with reasons of his own for doing things. Others favour the theory of natural selection or hint that we are nothing more than an accident of DNA. I myself have a rather more radical theory.'

'No doubt,' said John sourly, 'but you know perfectly well that is not what I meant. Why are we, that is Pooley and myself, here, that is, sitting upon this ghastly settee, slowly but surely freezing to death?'

Soap popped the corks from two of the bottles and handed them one apiece to his guests. 'In words of one syllable,' said Soap, 'you are in big schtuck. I think that you might do well to take a sup or two before I fill you in on the details.'

The two sub-zero golfers did not need telling twice, and in a matter of seconds two bottles of vintage Rhine wine had vanished away into the nether regions of two stomachs. 'The floor would seem to be yours,' said Jim wiping his chin. 'Is there any more of this?'

Soap handed over two more bottles and positioned himself in a dignified pose against the stucco fireplace.

'As you will remember,' he said, 'I have spoken to you many times in the past about the family Distant's conviction that an entire world exists here, beneath the Earth's surface, and that it is peopled by superbeings, benign and benevolent, who would bestow the great wealth of their knowledge upon the man from above who came in peace to speak with them.' John and Jim nodded thoughtfully. 'Well, I was wrong.'

'Tough luck,' said Omally. 'Say la vee as the French say.'

'Are you certain?' Pooley asked. Soap had always spoken with such conviction that even though Jim considered him to be three-halfpence short of a shilling, he had half romantically wondered whether his tales might be true.

'I am indeed certain,' said Soap. 'It is the exact opposite. There are dwellers beneath, but far from being benign and benevolent they are foul and evil and intent upon one thing only: to leave this world of darkness and conquer the sun-soaked realm above.' Soap's pink eyes travelled upwards and John and Jim's followed them.

'Now, now,' said Omally. 'I cannot believe all this. Surely if it were so, these fellows would have emerged years ago. They could surely have dug their way out. How did they come to be here in the first place?'

'Ah,' said Soap, giving his nose an annoyingly significant tap. 'That is a tale indeed, and if you have time I will tell it.'

'It would seem,' said John, 'that unless you feel so inclined as to lead us skywards, then we have all the time in the world.'

'Certainly you are a captive audience, but I must impress upon you that this is a very important business, and that your help is sorely needed. I have no wish to return to the surface, my world is here. But neither do I have the wish to see mankind destroyed by these beings, or worse still, driven here to plague me.'

John took off one of his boots and emptied the contents into a nearby aspidistra pot. 'Go on then,' he said, 'let's hear it.'

Soap withdrew a shining disc from an inner pocket and held it towards his guests. 'You recognize this, no doubt?'

Pooley peered at it and nodded. 'The symbol is the same as those on the allotment. You wouldn't happen to know what it means, by any chance?'

'I would, and so would Professor Slocombe.'

'Well, he certainly didn't feel fit to confide in us. "C" the fifth of the ten was all we got for it.'

'I was in the room when he told you,' said Soap. 'The Professor and I have known about the symbols and the plans of the Cereans for some time. We agreed that we should enlist help to assist with their destruction. Men of enterprise, we agreed, men of sterling stuff, good men and true, hearts of oak, valorous men with big . . . '

'Yes, yes,' said Omally, 'naturally you thought of us.'

'Actually no,' said Soap, 'we had hoped that Small Dave might be passing, but as you turned up . . . '

'Thanks a lot,' said Omally.

'I nearly drowned,' said Jim.

'Just my little joke,' said Soap, smiling sweetly. 'The Professor said that you two were his first choice.'

Pooley groaned pathetically, 'It would seem, John,' said he, 'that we have been press-ganged.'

Omally nodded bleakly. 'As running is obviously out of the question, I suggest that we waste no more time. Tell your tale, Soap.'

'Thank you, John, I expected at least a blow or two to the head. I am glad you are taking it so well. What I am about to tell you might seem a little hard to believe, but I can assure you it is all true.'

'No doubt,' said Omally.

'The symbol upon this disc' – Soap held the glittering item aloft – 'means literally what the Professor told you. "I am 'C' the fifth of the ten." It is the insignia of the planet Ceres which was once the tenth planet in our solar system, fifth from the sun. Ceres was the home world to a most advanced race of beings who commuted between the planets much in the way that you or I might take a sixty-five up to Ealing Broadway. Their world was small and their population large. They needed another planet similar to theirs for colonization. Naturally enough their eyes turned towards Earth, a world at that time only sporting a primitive society which offered little opposition to such an advanced race. They sent out scout parties, who were pleased to discover that the simple Earthers hailed them as gods. No doubt the Cereans would be running the place even now had not their warlike natures got the best of them. A great war developed upon Ceres and whilst a considerable number of the lads were here arranging matters to their satisfaction their entire planet was totally destroyed, leaving them marooned.

'The cataclysm was, if you will pardon the expression, somewhat earth-shattering, and the shocks were felt here. A travelling asteroid, the Moon as we now know it, was blown into orbit around the Earth causing absolute devastation. Half of the world was flooded. Those Cereans who survived the holocaust did so by withdrawing here and sealing themselves in. Little remained to ever prove their existence but for legend.

'The Cerean survivors never lost hope, although they were few in number and the centuries which passed saw mankind's development slowly approaching that of their own. Still they remained, waiting and plotting. For they had one thing to wait and plot for.

'Shortly before the planet's destruction the men of Ceres had sent a great strike force out of this solar system to seek other stars and other worlds. The Cereans knew that they would some day return and, finding no Ceres, would put two and two together and revisit the Earth. Thus they have remained, waiting and waiting, preparing for this return. They are doing so still and their time has almost come. Even as I speak the Cerean strike force is streaking across the Cosmos bound for Earth. And they have only one thing upon their minds.'

Soap ceased his fantastic monologue, and Pooley and Omally stared at him dumb and slack-jawed. 'If you don't mind me saying so,' said John at length, 'and please do not construe this as any criticism of yourself or your character, that is the most absurd piece of nonsense I have ever had the misfortune of listening to.'

'I have seen the film of it,' said Pooley, 'dubbed from the original Japanese it was.'

'And the lights upon the allotment,' said Soap, 'what would you take those to be?'

'The work of the council,' said Omally firmly, 'another plot to confound honest golfers.'

Soap burst into a paroxysm of laughter. Tears rolled down his pale cheeks and he clutched at his stomach.

'Come now,' said Pooley, 'it is no laughing matter, those lads have it in for us.'

'Have it in for you?' gasped Soap between convulsions. 'You witness a test run of laser-operated gravitational landing beams, the product of a technology beyond comprehension, and you put it down to the work of Brentford Council?'

'If you will pardon me,' said Pooley, somewhat offended, 'if it is the product of a technology beyond comprehension I hardly feel that we can be blamed for finding it so.'

'Quite,' said Omally.

'And your journey here through the solid concrete floor of an empty allotment shed?'

'I have been meaning to ask somebody about that,' said John.

'It was a hologram,' said Pooley, matter-of-factly.

'Oh, of course, one of those lads.'

'I must apologize for your rapid descent,' Soap explained. 'I had a great deal of trouble in keeping the door open long enough for you both to enter. I was unable, however, to stop the Cereans bringing down the lift.'

'Come now,' said Pooley, who had always been fond of the phrase, 'be fair Soap, all this is a little hard to swallow.'

'Nevertheless, it is true. As true as the fact that you are

sitting here, a mile and a half beneath Penge, drinking one-hundred-and-fifty-year-old Rhine wine.'

'Penge?' Pooley shook his head once more. 'Where the hell is Penge?'

'I've never been quite certain myself, but I'm told that it's a very nice place.'

John and Jim finished their second bottles and sat in silence wondering what in the world they were to do next. Omally sat glowering into the carpet. Pooley took off his jacket, which was starting to steam at the shoulders. 'All right,' he said at last, 'say that we do believe you.'

'I don't,' Omally interrupted.

'Yes, well, say that we did. What do you suppose we can do about it? How can we – ' he indicated himself and his bedraggled companion ' – how can we battle it out with an intergalactic strike force? I myself possess a barlow knife which is good for whittling and Omally has an air pistol. Could you perhaps chip in with a few Sam missiles and the odd thermonuclear device?'

'Sadly no,' said Soap. 'But I am open to any suggestions at this time.'

'I have one to make,' said John Omally bitterly. Pooley covered his ears.

14

Small Dave lay in his hospital bed for some days before the doctors released him. He seemed sound enough physically, a little scorched about the extremities, but nothing more. It was his mental state which put the wind up the hospital staff. The constant talking to himself. Still, there was no law as yet against that sort of thing, and he wasn't a private patient, was he? The doctors consequently turned the dwarf postman out on to the street and left him to fend for himself.

At length he returned to the boarded-up shell which had been his family seat for countless generations. As he stood peering up at the blackened brickwork there was little emotion to be found upon his elfin face. With a mere shrug, a brief display of hand-flapping, and a word or two to an invisible companion, he turned upon his heel and shambled away towards the Ealing Road.

Neville watched him pass from the Swan's doorway. 'Vindictive, grudge-bearing wee bastard,' was all the part-time barman had to say.

As the dwarf receded into the distance, Neville noted to his dismay that a bouncing, striding figure, sporting a lime-green coiffure and a natty line in bondage trousers, was rapidly approaching, his denim pockets bulging with coin of the realm and his trigger finger already a-twitch. It was, in fact, twitching at a rate exactly equivalent to that of the nervous tic the part-time barman had recently developed in his good eye.

'Damn,' said Neville, as Raffles Rathbone offered him a cheery wave. The bouncing boy squeezed past him into the saloon-bar and jogged up to the Captain Laser Alien Attack Machine. 'Good morning to you,' he said, addressing the thing directly. 'Ready for the off?'

With a single movement he tore aside the 'Out of Order' sign Neville had Sellotaped over the video screen and cast it across the floor.

'Broken,' said the part-time barman, without turning from his position in the doorway. 'Coin jammed in the mechanism, won't work.'

Nick eyed the barman's rear quarters with suspicion. 'I'll give it a try, to make sure,' he said slowly.

'Brewery say to leave it, might blow up if anyone tampers with it.'

'Can't see any coin,' said the lad, squinting into the slot.

'I have my orders. Have to wait for the engineer.'

'Really?' Nick's ill-matched eyes flickered between the barman's back and the humming machine. A florin hovered in his hand and a look of indecision wrinkled his brow.

Neville turned suddenly. 'Best leave it, eh?'

The coin was an inch from the slot and the youth's hand was beginning to tremble. A certain electricity entered the air, and with it the distinctive wail of a harmonica, as next door in the rear yard of the Star of Bombay Curry Garden, Archie Karachi performed an apt rendition of 'Do Not Forsake Me Oh My Darling'. It was not that he had any knowledge of the drama enacting itself within the saloon-bar of the Swan, but rather that his son's bar-mitzvah was coming up and he wanted to put on a decent show.

Neville's nervous tic accelerated slightly, but he fixed the boy with a piercing gaze of the type favoured by cobras whilst surveying their four-footed lunch. Nick for his part was not really equal to such a battle of wills. He did his best to look determined, but a bead of perspiration appeared upon his lofty hairline and, taking with it a quantity of green dye, descended towards the bridge of his nose, leaving an unpleasant slug trail behind it.

'Leave it, eh?' said Neville.

'I . . . er.' The boy blew the green bead from the tip of his nose. A minute passed, a long long minute. Nothing moved in the Swan but for a twitching eyelid, and a synchronized right forefinger. Nick's face was now striped, giving him the appearance of a sniper peering through long grass.

Neville's good eye was starting to water. Somebody had to crack.

'I'll have a half of shandy please,' said the boy, breathing a great sigh of relief. Neville smiled broadly and turned towards the pumps.

There was a sudden metallic click, a clunk and then . . . *Bitow Bitow Bitow Bitow* went the Captain Laser Alien Attack Machine.

'It's all right,' said Nick sweetly, 'it's mended. You can phone up the brewery and tell them to cancel the engineer.'

Neville ground his teeth sickeningly and clutched at the counter top. He had been so close. So very, very close.

Old Pete entered the Flying Swan, Chips close upon his well-worn heels. 'Good day to you, Neville,' said the ancient. 'A large dark rum if you please.'

Neville did the business, the exact coinage changed hands, and the part-time barman rang up 'No Sale'.

Old Pete eyed the player at the games machine with contempt and unplugged his hearing aid. 'Pardon me whilst I withdraw into a world of silence,' he told Neville.

'Have you seen anything of Pooley and Omally?' the part-time barman asked.

'Pardon?' said Old Pete.

'Pooley and Omally!' shouted Neville. 'Plug the thing in, you old fool!'

Pete refitted his jack plug. 'Haven't seen them,' he said, sipping at his drink.

'It has been more than a week now,' said Neville, with a hint of bitterness in his voice. 'They are supposed to be doing a little bit of work for me. I fear that they have had it away on their toes.'

Old Pete shook his snowy head. 'Perhaps the Four Horsemen has dropped its prices or the Red Lion has got a stripper in.'

Bitow Bitow Bitow Bitow Bitow went the Captain Laser Alien Attack Machine.

Bitow Bitow – Whap – 'What?' Raffles Rathbone turned upon Neville. 'You've been at this again,' he said, curling his lip. 'The sequences have changed again, it's not fair.'

'Get stuffed,' Neville told him.

'But it doesn't give you a fair chance,' whined the young sportsman. 'That's the second time the sequences have changed.' He stalked over to the bar counter. 'Give me a light ale,' he said bravely.

Neville whistled through his ruined teeth. 'A whole half, eh, and no lemonade?'

'Straight,' said the lad.

Old Pete eyed the youth with distaste. Young Chips licked his lips and considered the boy's ankles. Neville poured a half of light and Raffles Rathbone flung a handful of silver across the counter. Neville obligingly short-changed him.

'Anything new with you?' Old Pete asked the barman when the shock-headed hooligan had returned once more to the humming machine.

'Very little,' said Neville. 'I had another postcard from Archroy. Delivered, I hasten to add, by a relief postman of charm and good character, who chooses to deliver a fellow's mail unread.'

Old Pete chuckled. 'Wee Dave still shacked up in the loony ward at the Cottage Hospital then?'

'No, he's out, but happily he has not returned to the round.'

'Vindictive, grudge-bearing wee bastard,' said Old Pete. 'So what of Archroy, how fares the lad upon his travels?'

'He claims to have discovered Noah's Ark upon the peak of Ararat,' said Neville rather proudly. 'His last card said that he has employed a gang of Kurds to work upon chipping the lower portion of the great vessel from the glacial floor. It is tough going by all accounts.'

'It would be.' Old Pete stifled a snigger.

Neville shrugged. 'It is a queer business. I confess that I do not know exactly what to make of it. It would be a rare one if it were true. I can't help feeling that there is a catch in it somewhere and that it will cost me dearly.'

'Well,' said Old Pete, in a tone of great seriousness, 'do not get me wrong, for I am no churchman, but I will tell you a strange thing. During the Hitlerian War I was serving as warden in a refugee centre in South London. One night I got chatting with a young Russian, and he showed me four photographs which he claimed to be of the Ark of Noah.' Neville's good eye widened. 'They were old grainy sepia prints, much travelled and much stained, but he treated them as if they were holy relics. He'd been torpedoed off a troop ship and he claimed that the photos had saved his life. It seems that the folk who live around Ararat have always known of the Ark's existence. Apparently it is visible for only a few short months, once or twice a century, and during this time their holy men make a pilgrimage up the mountainside to scrape off pitch from the hull. This they make into amulets as a protection against drowning.'

Neville was fascinated. 'But how did this fellow come by the photographs?'

Old Pete rattled his empty glass on the counter and feigned deafness. Neville snatched it up from his fist and refilled it. Old Pete continued with his story. 'Told me that his father got them from one of a party of Russians who rediscovered the thing during the time of the Czar.'

'And did you think them genuine?'

'Who can say? They were definitely photographs of some very old and very large vessel half submerged in a glacier. I confess that I never took a lot of notice of them at the time. There was an air raid going on.'

'But what happened to the young Russian?'

'Got blown up!' said Old Pete maliciously. 'Seems that the photographs offered no protection against that kind of thing.'

'You made it all up,' sneered Neville, reaching for a glass and his polishing cloth.

Old Pete took out his shabby-looking wallet and laid it reverently upon the bar. 'And what if I told you that he gave me one of the photographs and that I have been carrying it with me for more than thirty years? What would you say to that, oh doubting Thomas?'

Neville's twitch, which had taken a temporary leave of absence, returned reinvigorated. 'He didn't? You haven't . . . ?'

Old Pete swept up his wallet and thrust it back into his pocket. 'Course I bloody haven't!' he said triumphantly. 'You'll believe any damn thing at times, won't you, Neville?'

The part-time barman bit upon a filling. That was twice he had been done down in a single lunchtime and he would have no more of it. Silently he swore a great and terrible oath to his pagan deity, that he would unremittingly bar for life the next person, no matter whom it might be, who tried to get one over on him. To make it more binding he pricked his finger and drew the blood the length of his knobkerry. There was no getting out of a vow like that.

'Give me the same again please, Neville,' said the chuckling ancient.

Norman entered the Flying Swan looking somewhat ashen. Neville hadn't seen him for some time and he marvelled at the shopkeeper's lack of eyebrows and apparently hand-carved wooden teeth. Some new frippery of fashion amongst the shop-keeping fraternity, he supposed.

'Give me one of those,' said Norman, gesturing towards the scotch.

'Closed for stock-taking?' Neville asked. 'Or have the health people been sampling your toffees again?'

'Just pour the drink.' Neville did so.

Norman suddenly stiffened. 'Has Small Dave been in here?' he asked, squinting about the bar.

'No,' said Neville, 'but I think I am about ready for him now.'

'You're not,' moaned Norman, 'take my word for it.' As he had already thrown the scotch down his throat, Neville refilled his glass. 'He was in my place and there is something not altogether right about him.'

'There never was.'

'This is different.' Norman peered over his shoulder to assure himself that he had not been followed in. 'He knows things.'

'Course he knows things, he's always reading your damned mail and squinting through people's letter-boxes. Vindictive, grudge-bearing wee . . .'

'Yes, I know all that, but listen!' Norman composed himself. Neville took the opportunity to collect payment for the drinks. 'He comes into my shop,' said Norman, 'wants his copy of *Psychic News*. Isn't in, says I. He mutters away to himself for a moment and then, it's third from the bottom of the pile, says he. With the bloody corner up, says I.'

'Well of course you did,' said Neville.

'May I continue?' Neville nodded and Norman drew him closer and spoke in hushed and confidential tones. Old Pete turned up his hearing aid and placed it upon the counter.

'I root through the pile of papers and there it is, plain as plain, third up from the bottom, just like he'd said. Here you go then, says I. Five Woodbine also, says himself. I hand him a packet, he has another mutter then tells me they're stale. Without even opening them! I get in a lather then, but I open up the packet just to be polite, and damn if the things aren't as dry as dust.' Neville looked at Old Pete, who merely shrugged. Young Chips, however, was taking it all in. 'Anyway,' Norman continued, 'he then points to another packet on the shelf and says that he understands that they are all right and so he'll take them. If this wasn't bad enough, as he's leaving the shop, he tells me that my false teeth are going mouldy under the counter.'

'And were they?' asked Old Pete.

Norman drew a furry-looking set of National Healthers from his pocket and tossed them on to the bar top. 'Lost them a week or more back. He couldn't possibly have guessed they were there.'

'Curious,' said Neville, scratching at his greying temples.

'But that's not the worst of it.'

'You mean there's more?'

'Oh yes.' Norman's voice had a disarmingly tremulous pitch to it. 'He said *we* must be off now. *We*, that's what he said. But *we* will be back. With that the shop door opens by itself, he walks out and the thing closes behind him of its own accord.'

'Norman,' said Neville in a calm and even voice, 'Norman, you are barred for life. Kindly get out of my pub and never, ever, ever return.'

15

Professor Slocombe was at his desk, busily at work amongst his books, when two bedraggled and heavily bearded travellers appeared at his French windows. 'Come in, lads,' he said cheerily, 'I am sure I do not need to inform you where I keep the decanter.'

'Do you know how far it is to Penge?' asked John Omally.

'I've never troubled to find out, although they tell me that it's very nice.'

'Oh, very pleasant,' said Pooley, 'but a fair hitch from Brentford.'

'My apologies,' said the old man, when the two men were both seated and clutching at their brimming glasses. 'But you see, I had no wish to force your hands over this matter. I was not altogether certain that if I simply confronted you with the truth you would believe it. Rather, I considered that if matters were simply allowed to run their course, your inquisitiveness would get the better of you and you would involve yourselves. My surmise was accurate, I see.'

'As ever,' said Pooley.

'You quite suit the beards.'

'Soap Distant doesn't own a razor.'

'Apparently he hasn't grown a hair on his face in five years.'

'An interesting man,' said the Professor, 'if a trifle eccentric.'

Omally's attention had become drawn to an elaborate brass device which now stood upon a pedestal in the centre of the Professor's study. 'What is that body?' he asked.

'An orrery,' said the old gentleman. 'I thought it might interest you.'

'Pre-eminently,' said Omally. 'I find little in life more interesting than an orrery.'

Professor Slocombe raised an admonitory eyebrow, but after a moment of brief consideration regarding the deprivations suffered by his guests over the last few days he lowered it again.

'Let me show you,' he said, gesturing towards the instrument. The two men grudgingly rose from their comfy chairs, carefully bearing their glasses.

'It's a mechanical device of great age,' the Professor explained, 'demonstrating the movement of the planets about our Sun and their relative positions to one another during their endless journeys.' He drew their attention to a brazen sphere. 'Here is the Earth,' he said, 'and here the legendary planet Ceres. You can see that its path of orbit lay exactly between those of Mars and Jupiter. Fifth from the Sun. I have no wish to labour this point, but might I explain that although it was a comparatively small world its mass and density were such that its destruction caused a chain reaction in our system which had very serious consequences hereabouts.'

'So we heard.'

The Professor began to hand-crank the amazing piece of machinery and the brass globes pirouetted about the central sphere in a pleasing *danse ronde*.

'Here upon this small date counter you can follow the time-scale of each yearly revolution.'

Pooley and Omally watched the years tick by as the tiny planets spun on their courses.

'Now here,' said the old man, halting the mechanism,

'is where the catastrophe occurred. You will notice the alignment of the planets, almost a straight line from the Earth. With the destruction of Ceres the gravitational effects would have been shattering.'

Pooley noted the date upon the tiny brass counter. 'The time of the Biblical Flood,' said he.

'Exactly. I personally subscribe to the theory of Ceres' existence and of its destruction,' said Professor Slocombe. 'It ties up a good many historical loose ends, and I will go further. It is stated in the Bible that after the waters of the great Flood subsided, God set his bow in the heavens as a sign that no such event would occur again. I believe that the popular view that it was the rainbow is incorrect. Rainbows must surely have been observed before the time of the Flood. More likely, I think, that it is to our Moon that the Almighty alluded, the lunar disc's journey describing as it does a bow-like arc in the sky each night.'

'Has a certain ring to it,' Pooley agreed. 'But what puzzles me is to why these Cereans should choose Brentford of all places as a landing site. I take it that by what Soap said regarding gravitational landing beams this is, in fact, the case.'

'Indeed yes, Brentford has been singled out as the target. I thought originally that it was Soap's network of tunnels which had drawn them, but I find that the Cerean tunnel system extends beneath a greater part of the globe. My second thought was that some great centre existed here in the distant past, possibly a previous landing site, but I can find no evidence to support this.'

'What then?'

'I feel it to be the influence of the Brentford Triangle!'

'The Brentford what?' said both men in unison.

The Professor poured a scotch from the crystal decanter and seating himself in a fireside chair did his very best to explain. 'The borough which is Brentford proper,' he said, 'exists within the bounds of a great triangle. The sides of this figure are the Grand Union Canal, the Great West Road and the River Thames. These follow the courses of three major ley lines. As you may know, these are lines of subterranean force which, although never having been fully explained, nevertheless appear to exert an influence upon the surface of the planet. I walk the boundaries of the borough every day and I have dowsed these lines many times. They never move.

'The ancients knew of their existence and aligned their tumuli, barrows, standing stones and circles upon them. Apparently they believed that the power could be tapped. Sadly, down through the centuries man has built across the leys, interrupting their flow and nullifying their power.'

'So,' said Pooley, 'if the power of the leys is lost, why do you attach any significance to this Brentford Triangle business?'

The Professor tapped at his nose, and for the first time both Pooley and Omally realized where Soap Distant had got the habit from. 'Simply because man appears to have lost touch with the leys' power does not mean that other creatures also have. Certain are still susceptible, the most obvious being our feathered friends.'

'Darts?' queried Pooley. The Professor ignored him.

'I have written something of a monograph upon the subject. Migrating birds inevitably take identical routes each year, and these invariably run along the major ley lines of the countrywide system.'

'This all seems a bit iffy,' Omally remarked. 'Are you suggesting that Cereans, like birds, navigate by ley lines?'

'I am suggesting that an advanced civilization such as theirs must surely have discovered them. And here at a time when they were uninterrupted. As the lines appear never to move, they are surely ideal for navigation. The maps of Earth no doubt gather dust in the Cerean ships' computer banks even now. Ready when required.'

'I suppose it is feasible,' Omally conceded. 'But even so, why choose Brentford? Why not Avebury, Glastonbury, Stonehenge or somewhere?'

The Professor rose from his chair and crossed the room to where something rested upon an ornate Victorian easel covered by a green baize cloth. Drawing this aside, he exposed a large mounted map of the district. The lines of the great triangle had been inked in red and stood out clearly.

'Impressive,' said Omally.

'But, as you say, hardly sufficient. It would certainly seem more logical that the Cereans would choose one of the better-known ley centres of this country. No, there is something more here, some inner pattern which I am failing to observe. I am sure it is staring me right in the face, but I cannot find it. Something is shining out like a beacon into space guiding these beings upon their way.'

Pooley and Omally followed the old man over to the map and stood peering over his shoulders. They turned their heads from one side to the other, made as to speak, then reconsidered, traced the courses of the streets, and pointed variously at random. At length they looked at one another and shrugged.

'I cannot see anything,' said Jim, 'just roads and houses, shops and pubs.' With the mention of the latter two pairs of eyes turned simultaneously towards the great ormolu mantel-clock, which obligingly struck five o'clock.

'Nearly opening time,' said Omally. 'I have been a week without a pint of Large. Possibly, Professor, we might continue this discussion over a refreshing bevvy or two?'

The Professor smiled gently and withdrew from his desk a folded map of the neighbourhood. 'You certainly deserve a drink,' he said, 'and here' – he took out a crisp new five-pound note – 'have it on me.'

Pooley accepted both map and fiver. 'Thank you,' he said, 'this is most kind. Will you not join us for one?'

'I think not,' said the old man. 'Study the map though and employ your wits. I ask only one favour: please bring me a pound's worth of silver from the Swan's cash register. From there and nowhere else, do you understand?'

'The motive or the request?'

The old man smiled and tapped again at his nose.

'One question,' said Omally, as he and Jim were turning to leave. 'Suppose by the vaguest of chances we were to discover this pattern, what could we do?'

The Professor shrugged his ancient shoulders. 'No knowledge is ever wasted. You know my methods. I never make a move before acquainting myself with every last piece of relevant information.'

'Yes, but . . . ' Jim made a rustling sound with the five-pound note. 'We will be in touch,' said John Omally.

'Good luck,' said the Professor, returning to his desk. 'I shall look forward to hearing from you.'

John and Jim wandered off towards the Flying Swan. 'At least one good thing has come out of all this,' said Jim after a while.

'Then you will kindly enlighten me as to what it is, because it has certainly slipped by me in the heat of the moment.'

'Well,' said Pooley, 'at least now we know that the strangers upon the allotment are not from the council, so we can continue our game.'

'You are wise beyond your years, Jim,' said Omally, dealing his companion a weltering blow to the skull.

16

Neville sat alone at a side table in his favourite darkened corner of the empty saloon-bar. He heard the library clock faintly chiming the hour over towards the Butts Estate and sighed a deep and heartfelt sigh.

This was one of the part-time barman's favourite times, when, the optics replenished, the pumps checked, and the glasses polished, he could sit alone for the short half-hour before opening and reflect upon days gone by and days possibly yet to come.

This afternoon, however, the barman felt oddly ill at ease. Something was going on in the borough, something sinister, and he could smell it. Although whatever it was lurked just out of earshot and beyond his range of vision, Neville knew he could smell it. And what he could smell, he most definitely did not like. It was musty and tomb-like and had the sulphurous odour of the pit to it, and it made him feel awkward and uneasy.

The part-time barman's long thin hand snaked out from the darkness and drew away a tumbler of scotch from the table top. There came a sipping sound, a slight smacking of lips, and another great dismal sigh. Neville leant forward to replace the glass and his nose cleaved through the veil of shadow, a stark white triangle.

He shook his head vigorously in an attempt to free himself of the gloomy feeling which oppressed him. The feeling would not be so easily dislodged, however. Neville took a deep, deep breath, as a drunken man will do under the mistaken belief that it will clear his head. The effort was wasted of course, and the part-time barman slumped away into the darkness taking his scotch with him.

Something was very wrong in Brentford, he just knew it. Some dirty big sword of Damocles was hanging over the place, waiting to drop at any minute. His nose told him so and his nose was never wrong. Certainly the Swan's patrons scoffed and sneered at his extra-nasal perception, but he knew what was what when it came to a good sniff. It was a family gift, his mad Uncle Jimmy had told him when he was but a scrawny sprog. The entire clan possessed it in varying degrees, and had done so since some half-forgotten time, in the pagan past, at the very dawn of mankind. Down through the centuries it came, father to son, turning up again and again and again. A great and wonderful gift it was, a blessing from the elder gods, which should never be used for personal gain or profit. 'But what exactly is it?' the young Neville had asked his musty-looking relative. 'Search me,' said Uncle Jimmy. 'I'm on your mother's side.'

Neville had total recall when it came to his childhood. He could remember every dismal dreary moment of it, with soul-destroying clarity. He, the gangling lad, always head and shoulders above his classmates and always sniffing. Such children do not have any easy time of it. And with the coming of his teens it got no better. Although highly sexed and eager to make the acquaintance of nubile young ladies, Neville's gaunt, stooping figure, with its slightly effeminate affectations, had attracted the attention of quite the wrong sort of person. Big fat girls, some sporting cropped heads and tattoos, had sought to smother him with their unsavoury affections. Young fellow-me-lads of the limp-wristed persuasion were forever asking him around for coffee to listen to their Miles Davis records with the lights out. Neville shuddered, grim times.

He had given up all thoughts of being a young buck and a bit of a ladies' man at an early age, and had fallen naturally enough into the role of aesthete. He had dutifully nurtured a six-hair goatee and frayed the bottom of his jeans. He had done the whole bit: the Aldermaston marches, which he joined for the last half mile to arrive in Trafalgar Square amidst cheering crowds; the long nights in coffee bars discussing Jack Kerouac and René Magritte over cold cups of espresso; the dufflecoats and Jesus boots, the night-school fine arts courses. But he never got his end away.

He had met many a big-breasted girl in a floppy sweater, smelling of joss sticks, who spoke to him of love being free and every experience being sacred. But they always ended up at the art teacher's pad and he back at home with his mum.

He'd never been one of them, and he couldn't blame it all on his nose. He was simply an outsider. That he was an individualist and an original meant little to a lad with stirrings in the groin department.

Neville rose from his seat and padded across the threadbare carpet to the whisky optic. Surely things hadn't been all that bad, had they? Certainly his childhood and years of puberty had not exactly been the stuff of dreams, but there had been moments of joy, moments of pleasure, hadn't there?

Neville's total recall could not totally recall any. Still, things weren't all that bad now. He was the Swan's full-time part-time barman, and it was an office which made him as happy as any he could imagine.

If he had known when he was fifteen that this lay in store for him, he would never have suffered such agonies of self-doubt when he realized that he could not understand a single bit of Bob Dylan's 'Gates of Eden'.

But how had he come to get the job in the first place? It had been a strange enough business by any accounts.

Neville remembered the advert in the *Brentford Mercury*: 'Part-time barman required, hours and salary negotiable, apply in person. Flying Swan.'

Now in his late twenties and making a career out of unemployment, Neville had jettisoned the camphor bags and forced himself into his one suit, given his brothel creepers a coat of Kiwi, and wandered down to the Swan to present himself. The acting part-time barman, who shortly afterwards absconded with a month's takings and several cases of scotch, had given him the summary once-over. He asked if he thought he could pull a pint, then hired him on the spot.

As to who the actual tenant of the Flying Swan was, Neville had not the slightest idea. The paint had flaked off the licensee plate outside, and those who swore they knew the man like a brother gave conflicting accounts as to his appearance. Neville had been handed the keys, told to take his wages from the disabled cash register, and left to get on with it. It had been a rare challenge but he had risen to it. He had no knowledge of running a pub but he had learned fast, and the ever-alert locals had only ever caught him the once on any particular dodge. He had single-handedly turned the Swan from a down-at-heel spit and gob saloon to a down-at-heel success. He had organized the trophy-winning darts team, who had now held the local shield for a record five consecutive years. He had supervised the numerous raffles and alehouse events, acted as oracle and confessor to local drunks, and strangely and happily had evolved into an accepted part of the Brentford landscape.

He was at home and he was happy.

Neville's smile broadened slightly, but a grim thought took off its edges. The brewery. Although they had no objection whatsoever to his residency, him being basically honest and the pub now running at a handsome profit, the brewery gave him no rest. They were forever suggesting special

events, talking of modernization, and installing things . . .
His eyes strayed involuntarily towards the bulky contours
of the humming monster which he had now covered with a
dust sheet tightly secured with baling wire.

Neville tossed back his scotch and looked up at the
Guinness clock; nearly five-thirty, nearly opening time.
He squared up his scholar's stoop and took another deep
breath. He would just have to pull himself together.
Embark upon a course of positive activism. Be polite
to his patrons, tolerant of their foibles, and indulgent
towards their eccentricities. He would smile and think
good thoughts, peace on earth, good will towards men.
That kind of thing. He was certain that if he tried very
very hard the horrid odour would waft itself away, to be
replaced by the honeysuckle fragrance of spring.

From not far away the library clock struck the half-hour,
and Neville the part-time barman flicked on the lights,
took himself over to the door, and opened up. On the
doorstep stood two bearded men.

'Good evening, barlord,' said Jim Pooley.

'God save all here,' said John Omally.

Neville ushered them into the bar without a word. Now
was the present and what was to happen happened now
and hereafter and it surely couldn't be all bad, could it?
The two men, however, seemed to be accompanied by a
most extraordinary smell. Neville pinched at his nostrils
and managed a somewhat sickly grin. 'Your pleasure,
gentlemen?' he asked when he had installed himself behind
the jump, and his two patrons had resumed residency of the
two barstools which had known not the pleasure of their
backsides for more than a week. 'What will it be?'

Pooley carefully withdrew from his pocket the five-
pound note, which had not left his clammy grip since it had
been handed to him, and placed it upon the bar counter.

Neville's eyebrows soared into a Gothic arch. He had

hoped that if he thought positively things might turn out OK, but this? This transcended even his wildest expectations. Jim Pooley with a five-pound note?

And it got worse. 'Two pints of Large please, Neville,' said Pooley, smiling almost as hideously as the barman, 'and have one yourself!'

Neville could feel a prickling sensation rising at the back of his neck. Have one yourself? He had read in paperback novels of the phrase being used by patrons of saloon-bars, but he had never actually encountered it in real life. 'Pardon,' said the part-time barman, 'might I have that last bit again.'

'Have one yourself,' Pooley reiterated.

Neville felt at his pulse. Could this really be? Or had he perhaps died and gone to some kind of barman's Valhalla or happy drinking ground? The nervous tic went into overdrive.

Omally, who was growing somewhat thirsty, made the suggestion that if Neville wanted to take advantage of Jim's generosity it would be better if he dropped the amateur theatricals and did so at once. Neville hastened to oblige. 'Thank you Jim,' he said. 'I don't know what got into me then. Your kindness is well received, I thank you.'

Still mumbling the phrase 'Have one yourself' under his breath, Neville pulled two pints of the Swan's finest. As he did so he took the opportunity to study the two men, whose eyes were now fastened by invisible chains to the rising liquid. The beards were odd enough in themselves, but that Pooley's shirt appeared to have shrunk by at least two sizes and that the colour of Omally's regimental tie had run on to his neck were things of exceeding strangeness. Caught in a sudden downpour perhaps? Neville could not remember any rain. The ducking-stool then? Some lynch mob of cuckolded husbands exacting a medieval revenge? That seemed feasible.

The barman passed the two exquisitely drawn pints across the counter and took possession of the magical blue note, which he held to the light as a matter of course. Having waited respectfully whilst Pooley and Omally took the first step towards quenching their long thirst he said at length, 'Well now, gentlemen, we have not had the pleasure of your company for more than a week. You have not been taken with the sickness I hope, nor struck by tragic circumstances.'

Pooley shook his head. 'We have been in Penge,' he said.

'Penge,' said Omally, nodding vigorously.

'Ah,' said Neville thoughtfully. 'I haven't actually been there myself, but I understand that it's very nice.'

'Splendid,' said Pooley.

'Very nice indeed,' his colleague agreed. 'You'd love it.'

Neville shrugged and turned away to cash up the traditional 'No Sale' and extract for himself the price of a large scotch. As he did so Pooley remembered the Professor's request.

'Could I have a pound's worth of change while you're at it?' he asked politely.

Neville froze in his tracks. A pound's worth of change? So that was it, eh? The old 'have one yourself, barman' was nothing more than the Judas kiss. Pooley planned to play the video machine. 'You bastard!' screamed Neville, turning upon the drinker.

'Pardon me?' said Jim.

'Pound's worth of change is it? Pound's worth of change? You treacherous dog.'

'Come now,' said Jim, 'steady on.'

'Steady on? Steady on? Have one yourself barman and a pound's worth of change while you're at it! What do you take me for?'

'Seemed a reasonable request to me.' Pooley looked towards Omally, who was covering his drink. 'What is going on, John?' he asked.

Omally, who was certainly never one to be slow on the uptake, explained the situation. 'I think that our good barman here believes that you want the money to play the video machine.'

Pooley, whose mind had been focused upon matters quite removed from video games, suddenly clicked. 'Oh,' he said, 'good idea, make it thirty-bobs' worth, Neville.'

'AAAAAAGH!' went the part-time barman, reaching for his knobkerry.

Pooley saw the hand vanishing below counter level and knew it to be a very bad sign. 'Come now,' he implored, backing away from the bar, 'be reasonable. I haven't played it in a week, I was just getting the hang of it. Look, let's just say the quid's-worth and call it quits.'

Neville brought the cudgel into prominence. 'I've had enough,' he shouted, hefting it in a quivering fist. 'You traitor. Touch the thing and you are barred, barred for life. Already today have I barred one regular, another will do no harm.'

'Who is the unhappy fellow?' asked Omally who, feeling himself to have no part in the present altercation, had not shifted from his seat.

'Norman,' growled Neville. 'Out, barred for life, finished, gone!'

Omally did his best to remain calm. 'Norman?'

'Norman.'

'Norman Hartnell of the corner shop?'

'That Norman, yes.'

'Norman Hartnell, the finest darts player this side of the Thames? Norman the captain of the Swan's darts team? The five times trophy-winning darts team? The very darts team that plays at home for the championship on the twenty-ninth? That Norman you have barred for life?'

What colour had not already drained from Neville's naturally anaemic face took this opportunity to make an exit via his carpet-slipper soles.

'I . . . I . . . ' The barman rocked to and fro upon his heels; his good eye slowly ceased its ticking and became glazed, focused apparently upon some point far beyond the walls of the Swan. He had quite forgotten the darts tournament. The most important local sporting event of the entire calendar. Without Norman the team stood little hope of retaining the shield for a sixth year. What had he done? The locals would kill him. They would tar and feather him and ride him out of the town on a rail for this. Darts wasn't just a game in Brentford, it was a religion, and the Flying Swan its high temple. A bead of perspiration appeared in the very centre of Neville's forehead and clung to it in an appropriately religious fashion like some crystal caste mark. 'I . . . I . . . I . . .' he continued.

Old Pete entered the Swan, Chips as ever upon his heels. Being naturally alert, he spied out the barman's unnatural behaviour almost at once. 'Evening to you, Omally,' he said, nudging the Irishman's arm. 'Haven't missed anything, have I?'

'Sorry?' Omally, although a man rarely rattled, had been severely shaken by the barman's frightful disclosure.

'The mime,' said Old Pete. 'I'm very good at these. Spied out Norman's Quasimodo some days back and won an ounce of tobacco. This one looks quite easy, what's the prize?'

Omally scratched his whiskers. 'What are you talking about?'

The old loon put his head upon one side and stroked his chin. 'Is it a film or a television programme?' he asked. 'Do I get any clues?'

'It's a book,' said Pooley, taking the opportunity to

retrieve his pint before retreating to a safe distance.

'I . . . I . . . I . . .' went Neville.

'Must be the Bible then,' said Old Pete. 'Not that I've ever read it. Should say by the look of the stick and everything that it's either Moses parting the Red Sea or Samson slaying all those Philippinos with the jawbone of an ass.'

Young Chips, who was of a more metaphysical bent, suspected that it was more likely Lobsang Rampa's *The Third Eye*, with the caste mark and the glassy stare and what was quite obviously some kind of mantra based upon the concept of self-realization; the I.

Neville slowly replaced his knobkerry, and turned to the cash register where he drew out Pooley's change, including amongst it thirty shillings'-worth of florins. Preventing patrons from playing Captain Laser machines did not seem to be of much importance any more. 'Enjoy your game,' he said, handing the still flinching Jim the money.

Old Pete shook his head. 'Can't abide a poor sport,' he said. 'Guessed it in one, did I? Told you I was good. What about the prize then?' Neville, however, had wandered away to the end of the bar where he now stood polishing an imaginary glass with an invisible bar cloth. 'What about a drink then?' The ancient turned imploringly towards Pooley and Omally, but the two had taken themselves off to a side table where they now sat muttering over an outspread map. 'I won it fair and square,' said Old Pete to his dog. Chips shrugged, he had a bad feeling about all this and wished as usual to remain non-committal.

Jim Pooley ran his finger up and down the cartographical representation of Brentford and made a wash-handbasin out of his bottom lip. 'This really is all getting rather dire,' he said. 'Spacemen on the allotment, starships on the attack, and the Flying Swan without a darts captain. Are we dreaming all this or can it really be true?'

Omally fingered his beard and examined the tide marks

about his cuff. 'It's true enough,' said he, 'and I think we might do no better than to apply ourselves to the problem in the hope that a solution might be forthcoming.'

'We'll have to do something about Neville.' Pooley peered over his shoulder towards the dejected figure. 'I can't stand seeing him like that.'

'All in good time,' said Omally, giving his nose a tap. 'I am sure I shall be able to effect some compromise which will satisfy both parties and get us one or two freemans into the bargain. For now though the map must be the thing.'

Jim had his doubts but applied himself once more. 'What are we looking for?' he asked very shortly.

Omally took out his Asprey's fountain pen, which by virtue of its quality had withstood its ordeal by water with remarkable aplomb, or la plume, as the French would have it. 'If a pattern exists here I shall have it,' he said boldly. 'When it comes to solving a conundrum, the Omallys take over from where the fellow with the calabash and the deerstalker left off. Kindly turn the map in my direction.'

'Whilst you are solving the Enigmatic Case of the Cerean Cipher,' said Pooley sarcastically, 'I shall be off to the bar for another brace of Large. I am at least getting pleasure from my newly acquired wealth.'

The ordnance survey map had received more than a little attention on his return. 'Looks very nice,' he said. 'I didn't know that there was a streak of William Morris in you, John. Taken to designing wallpaper, is it?'

'Silence,' said Omally. 'If it is here, I will have it.'

Jim sucked at his pint. 'What are all those?' he asked, pointing to a network of squiggles.

'The drainage system of the borough.'

'Very good, and those?'

'All the houses that to my knowledge have recently fitted loft insulation.'

'You are nothing if not thorough. And the curlicues?'

'That is a personal matter, I have left nothing to chance.'

Pooley stifled a snigger. 'You surely don't believe that an alien strikeforce has plotted out the homes of your female conquests as a guideline to their invasion?'

'You can never tell with aliens.'

'Indeed.' Pooley watched the Irishman making crosses along a nearby side-road. 'Might I venture to ask what you are plotting now?'

'Morris Minors,' said Omally.

Jim stroked his beard reflectively. 'John,' he said, 'I think that you are going about this in the wrong way. The Professor suggested that we look for some kind of landmarks, surely?'

'All right then.' Omally handed Jim his cherished pen. 'You are obviously in tune with the Professor's reasoning, you find it.'

Pooley pushed out his lip once more but rose to the challenge. 'Right then,' he said, 'landmarks it is. What do we have?'

'The War Memorial.' Pooley marked a cross. 'The Public Library.' Pooley marked another.

Twenty minutes later the map had the appearance of a spot the ball contest form that had been filled in by a millionaire.

'I've run out,' said Omally.

'So has your pen,' said Jim, handing his friend the now ruined instrument. The two peered over the devastated map. 'One bloody big mess,' said Jim. 'I cannot make out a thing.'

'Certainly the crosses appear a little random.'

'I almost thought we had it with the subscribers to *Angling Times* though.'

'I could do with another drink.'

'We haven't done those yet.'

Omally pressed his hands to his temples. 'There is

not enough ink in the country to plot every drinker in Brentford.'

'Go and get them in then.' Pooley handed John one of the Professor's pound notes. 'I'll keep at it.'

Omally was a goodly time at the bar. Croughton the pot-bellied potman, finding himself under the sudden overwhelming strain of handling the bar single-handed while Neville sought divine guidance, had begun to crack and was panicking over the drinks. The Swan now swelled with customers and arguments were breaking out over cloudy beer and short change. Omally, seizing the kind of opportunity which comes only once in a lifetime, argued furiously that he had paid with a fiver; the flustered potman, being in no fit state to argue back, duly doled out the change without a whimper.

Omally pocketed the four well-won oncers, reasoning that the news of such an event might well unbalance the sensitive Pooley's mind and put him at a disadvantage over the map plotting. When he returned to the table bearing the drinks he was somewhat surprised to find that the expression Jim Pooley now wore upon his face mirrored exactly that of Neville the part-time barman. 'Jim?' asked John. 'Jim, are you all right?'

Pooley nodded gently. 'I've found it,' he said in a distant voice. Omally peered over the map. There being no ink left in the pen, Pooley had pierced the points of his speculation through with defunct matchsticks. A pattern stood out clearly and perfectly defined. It was immediately recognizable as the heavenly constellation of Ursa Major, better known to friend and foe alike as The Plough.

'What are they?' Omally asked, squinting at the crucified map.

'It's the pubs,' said Pooley in a quavering voice. 'Every house owned by this brewery.'

Omally marked them off. It was true. All seven of the

brewery pubs lay in the positions of the septentriones: the New Inn, the Princess Royal, The Four Horsemen, and the rest. And yes, sure as sure, there it was, there could be no mistake: at the point which marked Polaris, the North Star in Ursa Minor – the Flying Swan. 'God's teeth,' said John Omally.

'Let the buggers land then,' said Jim. 'I am not for destroying every decent drinking-house in Brentford.'

'I am behind you there, friend,' said John, 'but what can it mean? The Swan at the very hub, what can it mean?'

'I shudder to think.'

'Roll the map up,' said John, 'we must tell the Professor at once.'

Pooley, who still had upon his person the price of several more pints, was reticent and suggested that perhaps there was no immediate rush. The Professor could hardly have expected them to solve the thing so swiftly. Perhaps a celebration pint or two was called for.

'A sound idea,' said Omally heartily. 'In fact, as you have done so well, I suggest that we dispense with pints and go immediately on to shorts!'

'A fine idea,' said Jim, 'I will get a couple of gold ones in.' Thus saying he rose from his seat and made for the bar. Quite a crush had now developed, and even Pooley's practised elbows were hard put to it to gain him a favourable position. As he stood, waggling his pound note and trying to make himself heard, Jim suddenly felt a most unpleasant chill running up his spine. Pooley, taking this to be some after-effect of his discovery, shuddered briefly and tried to make himself heard. He found to his horror that his voice had suddenly deserted him. And it was then that he noticed for the first time that there was a strong smell of creosote in the air. Pooley clutched at his throat and gagged violently. As he did so a firm and unyielding hand caught his elbow, and held it in a vicelike grip.

Jim turned towards his tormentor and found himself staring into a face which only a mother could love. There was more than a touch of the Orient about it, slightly tanned, the cheekbones high and prominent, and the eyes slightly luminescent. It was a face in fact which bore an uncanny resemblance to a young Jack Palance. The figure was dressed in an immaculate black suit and had about him the feeling of impossible cleanliness.

These details Pooley's brain took in, but it was somewhat later before he was actually able to relate them verbally. For the present the awful clone of the legendary Hollywood star was steering the muted Jim through the crowd and towards the Swan's door.

Pooley, realizing that the fate which lay in store for him, if not actually worse than death itself, was probably none other than the very same thing, began to struggle for all he was worth. He swung around upon his kidnapper and with deadly accuracy kneed him in the groin. Had he known anything whatever about Cerean anatomy, however, he would have gone immediately for the left armpit. As it was, his blow did little other than damage one of the Cerean's sinuses.

Pooley was nearing the end of the bar counter by now and the Swan's doorway was perilously close. His mouth opened and closed, paying silent tribute to Edvard Munch's most famous painting. The patrons of the Swan, it appeared, cared little for Pooley's plight and paid him not the slightest heed.

At the end of the bar stood Neville, staring into space. Pooley made one single-handed and desperate grab towards his bar apron. Even in a blind panic he knew better than to go for the tie. That being the first thing a drunk ever goes for, and Neville being the professional he was, the part-time barman always wore a clip-on. Pooley caught the apron and the outcome was not a pleasant thing to behold.

Neville's genitalia, which were correctly placed for a man of Earth, were suddenly drawn into violent and painful contact with the tap spout of one of the Swan's finest traditional hand-drawn ales.

'AAAAAAAAAGH!' went Neville the part-time barman, the searing agony suddenly reviving him from his vertical catalepsy.

The sound reverberated about the bar, silencing every conversation and turning every head. Omally, startled by the cry, leapt from his seat, and glimpsed Pooley's dire predicament.

The Cerean tugged once again upon Pooley's elbow, and Jim, who would not have released his grip for all the Lapsang Souchong south of the Yellow River, dragged the barman forward for a second time.

'AAAAAAAAAGH!' the part-time barman reiterated, as his cobblers smote the beer engine anew. All thoughts of darts teams and barred captains were suddenly driven from his head and he howled in pain and did his utmost to free himself of Pooley's maniacal hold.

The Swan's patrons, momentarily stunned by the first cry, were emboldened by the second. Tempers had been growing more and more frayed during the evening and this altercation offered a fine opportunity for giving vent to pent-up emotions. The crowd began to advance upon the threesome, and Omally was in the vanguard. With a Gaelic cry which would surely have put the wind up King Billy himself, Omally made a grab at the Cerean.

The darkly-clad figure shook him off as if he were but a speck of dandruff upon his finely-tailored shoulder. Omally tumbled to the deck, cursing and spitting. Several members of the Swan's drinking élite laid powerful hold upon Pooley, with the result that Neville, who was rapidly giving up all thoughts of potential parenthood, found his good eye crossing once more.

The ensuing *mêlée* was notable for many things, not least the extraordinary display of divided loyalties. One faction was definitely pro-Neville, being firmly of the belief that Pooley had attacked the barman, and that the man in black was attempting to restrain him. Another took it that Neville, whose behaviour that evening had not exactly been exemplary, had gone for Pooley, and that the man in black was one of the brewery's dark forces, assisting in that loyal patron's expulsion from the Swan. A third, which counted but one in its number, and this a son of Eire, was of an entirely different opinion altogether.

It must be stated that other factions existed also. These were formed either from fellows who felt that now was as good a time as any to end some personal vendetta, or from those who by their very natures necessarily misinterpret any given situation. Their participation was notable mainly for its enthusiastic and seemingly indiscriminate violence.

Young Chips, who could smell a nigger in a woodpile even with his nose bandaged, set immediately to work upon the Cerean's ankles.

Pooley had by now, under the welter of blows, lost hold upon Neville's apron, and, as the part-time barman lapsed from consciousness and sank gracefully behind the bar, found himself being borne once more towards the doorway. Towards the very doorway, in fact, where John Omally now stood, brandishing a beer bottle.

'Leave hold,' roared the Irishman. Pooley's mouth opened and closed and a lip reader would have covered his eyes at the obscenity.

The Cerean squared up to the obstacle in his path and raised his left hand to strike. Omally swung his bottle and, it must be reasoned, more from luck than judgement, struck the villain a devastating blow to the left armpit.

As he lost his grip upon Pooley, several of the pro-Neville brigade fell upon the barman's attacker with relish.

The Cerean staggered towards Omally, who, having the advantage of fighting upon home territory, stepped nimbly aside and tripped him through the Swan's open doorway and into the street.

Outside, parked close to the kerb, stood an automobile that was a collector's dream. It was ink-black and gleaming, a showroom piece. The handbook had it down as a nineteen-fifty-eight Cadillac Sedan, the deluxe model. In the driving seat sat a man of average height, wearing an immaculate black suit. He bore an uncanny resemblance to a young Jack Palance and favoured a creosote aftershave. It took him but a moment to leave the car and gain the pavement, but by then the chaos of flailing fists which now filled the Swan was spilling into the street.

The pro-Pooley faction, who knew a brewery henchman when they saw one, and who were currently occupied in assaulting the one who was rolling about clutching at his armpit, saw another quarry and wasted little time in taking the opportunity to vent their spleen.

Archie Karachi, who ran the Star of Bombay Curry Garden next door to the Swan, was a man who knew a race riot when he saw one. Thrusting a vindaloo-stained digit into his telephone dial, he rang out a rapid nine, nine, nine. Being also a man of few words, and most of those Hindi, his message was succinct and to the point. 'Bloody big riot in Swan,' he bawled above the ever increasing din, 'many men injured, many dead.'

The blue serge lads of the Brentford nick were not long in responding to this alarm call. With the station grossly over-manned, as befits a district with a low crime rate, what they craved was a bit of real police action. A bit of truncheon-wielding, collarbone-breaking, down to the cells for a bit of summary justice, real police action. Within minutes, several squad cars and a meat wagon were haring along the wrong side of Brentford High Street, through the red lights, and up the down lane of the one-way system, bound for the Flying Swan. Within the wheel-screeching vehicles constables were belting on flak jackets, tinkering with the fittings of their riot shields, and drumming CS gas canisters into their open left palms with increasing vigour.

What had started out as a localized punch-up, had now developed into wholesale slaughter. The numbers involved in the *mêlée* had been swelled significantly by the arrival of a gang of yobbos from the flatblocks opposite. Those crop-headed aficionados of the steely toecap had been met head on by the students of the Brentford Temple of Dimac Martial Arts Society, who had been limbering up for their evening's training schedule with a fifteen-mile run. Neither of these warrior bands having the slightest idea what all the fuss was about, or which was the favourable side to support, had contented themselves with exercising their respective martial skills upon one another. Although this did nothing to ease the situation, to the crowds of onlookers who now lined the opposite pavements and crammed into every available upstairs window, it added that little extra something which makes a really decent riot worthwhile.

With sirens blaring and amber lights flashing, the squad cars slewed to a halt at the rear of a war-torn Cadillac. This development was wildly applauded by the onlookers, many of whom had thought to bring out stools and kitchen chairs, that they might better enjoy the event. As hot-dog men and ice-cream sellers, who have an almost magical knack of appearing at such moments, moved amongst the spectators, the Brentford bobbies went about their business with a will, striking down friend and foe alike. With every concussion inflicted the crowd hoorahed anew and, like the season-ticket holders at the Circus Maximus in days gone by, turned their thumbs towards the pavement.

To the very rear of this scene of massacre, pressed close to the wall of the Flying Swan, two bearded golfing types watched the carnage with expressions of dire perplexity. 'Gather up the map,' said John Omally. 'I feel that we have pressing business elsewhere.'

Easing their way with as little fuss as possible through the Swan's doorway, they passed into the now deserted saloon-bar. Deserted that is, but for a certain part-time barman who now lay painlessly unconscious in the foetal position behind the jump, and an old gentleman and his dog, who were playing dominoes at a side-table.

'Goodnight to you Pooley and Omally,' said Old Pete. 'You will be taking your leave via the rear wall I have no doubt.'

Pooley scooped up the map and stuffed it into an inside pocket. 'Offer my condolences to Neville,' he said. 'I expect that it is too much to hope that he will awake with amnesia.'

'You never can tell,' said the ancient, returning to his game. 'Give my regards to Professor Slocombe.'

17

Professor Slocombe peered over the pen-besmirched, match-riddled map with profound interest. At length he leant back in his chair and stared a goodly while into space.

'Well?' asked John, who had been shifting from one foot to the other for what seemed like an age. 'Has Pooley found it?'

The Professor pulled himself from his chair and crossed the room to one of his bookcases. Easing out an overlarge tome, he returned with it to his desk. 'Undoubtedly,' he said, in a toneless voice. 'If you will pardon my professional pride, I might say I am a little miffed. I have sought the pattern for weeks and you find it in a couple of hours.'

'I think we had the natural edge,' said Omally.

Pooley, whose injured parts were now beginning to pain him like the very devil, lay slumped in an armchair, a hand clasping the neck of the whisky decanter. 'I only hope that it will help,' he said. 'Those lads are on to us, and I escaped death by a mere hairbreadth this night.'

'We have by no means reached a solution,' said the Professor, in a leaden tone. 'But we are on the way.'

Omally peered over the old man's shoulders as he leafed through his great book. 'What are you looking for now?'

'This book is the Brentford Land Register,' the Professor explained. 'The pubs you have plotted were all built during the last one hundred years. It will be instructive to learn what existed upon the sites prior to their construction.'

'Ah,' said John, 'I think I follow your line of thought.'

'I think my right elbow is fractured,' said Jim Pooley.

The Professor thumbed over several pages. 'Yes,' he said. 'Here we have it. The Four Horsemen, built upon the site of the cattle trough and village hand pump.' He turned several more pages. 'The New Inn, upon this site there has been a coaching house for several hundred years, it has always boasted an excellent cellar and a natural water supply. Built in 1898, the North Star, a significant name you will agree, founded upon Brentford's deepest fresh-water well.' The Professor slammed the book shut. 'I need not continue,' he said, 'I think the point is clearly made.'

'My collarbone is gone in at least three places,' said Jim.

'It can't be the water supply,' said Omally. 'That is ludicrous. Aliens do not steer themselves through space guided by the village waterworks. Anyway, every house in Brentford has water, every house in the country, surely?'

'You fail to grasp it,' said the Professor. 'What we have here is a carefully guided natural watercourse, with the accompanying electrical field which all underground water naturally carries, culminating in a series of node points. The node points channel the ley earth-forces through the system, terminating at the Flying Swan. If you will look upon the map you will see that the Swan is built exactly one third up from the Thames base line of the Brentford Triangle. Exactly the same position as the King's Chamber in the Great Pyramid. A very powerful position indeed.'

'It all appears to me a little over-circuitous,' said Omally. 'Why not simply stick up a row of landing lights? If these Cerean lads have all the wits that you attribute to them, surely they could tamper with the National Grid and form a dirty big cross of lighted areas across half of Britain?'

'Possibly,' the Professor replied, 'they might be able to do that for an hour, possibly for a day, but this pattern has been glowing into space for a hundred years, unnoticed by man and untouched. It is reinforced by the structures built above it, pubs, thriving pubs. This is Brentford; nobody ever knocks down a pub here.'

'True,' said Omally. 'We have little truck with iconoclasts hereabouts.'

'This beacon could go on radiating energy for a thousand years. After all, the Cereans had no idea how long they would have to wait to be rescued.'

'There is definitely evidence of a cracked rib here,' said Pooley, feeling at his chest.

'All is surely lost,' said Omally.

'I didn't say it was terminal,' Pooley replied. 'Just a job for a skilled surgeon or two.'

Professor Slocombe stroked his chin. 'At this very moment,' he said, 'somewhere on the outer rim of the galaxy, the Cerean Strike Force is heading towards its homeworld. Finding none, it will inevitably be turning here, guided by the descendants of its stranded forebears. Unless otherwise diverted or destroyed, they will home in upon their landing area, and I do not believe that we can expect any of that "We bring greetings from a distant star" benign cosmic super-race attitude to be very much in evidence upon their arrival. We must work at this thing; I do not believe that it is without solution.'

'My ankle's gone,' grizzled Pooley. 'I shall walk with a limp for the rest of my life.'

'Do put a sock in it, Pooley,' said the Professor.

'But I'm wounded,' said the wounded Pooley. 'Somebody might show a little compassion.'

'I don't think you realize the gravity of the situation.'

'On the contrary,' said Jim, waggling a right wrist which was quite obviously a job for the fracture clinic. 'I've never missed an episode of "The Outer Limits" – true, I've been in the bog during many a title sequence, or slept through the last five minutes, but I know what I'm talking about.

None of this smacks to me of sound science fiction. All this sort of stuff does not occur in the shadow of the gasworks. Alien invaders, who we all know to be green in colour and pictured accurately upon the front page of the *Eagle*, do not muck about with council water supplies or conveniently arrange for the location of public drinking-houses. I take this opportunity to voice my opinion and pooh pooh the whole idea. There is a poultice wanting upon these knees and more than one of my fillings has come adrift.'

'An uncle of mine has connections with the Provos,' said Omally. 'If you will sanction the exemption of the Swan, I might arrange for the levelling of every other relevant pub in Brentford.'

Professor Slocombe smiled ruefully. 'That, I think, might be a little too extreme,' he said. 'I am sure that a less drastic solution can be found.'

'Nobody ever listens to me,' said Jim, going into a sulk.

'As I see it,' said Professor Slocombe, 'the Flying Swan is the epicentre of the entire configuration. It has been so aligned as to act as the focal point. The harnessed Earth forces flow through the alignment and culminate therein. There must be something located either within the Swan or beneath it into which the energy flows. Something acting as locative centre or communicating beacon to these beings. As to what it is, I have not the slightest idea.'

'Maybe it's the darts team,' said Pooley. 'We've held the shield for five years. Perhaps your lads have infiltrated the team and are guiding their mates in through a series of pre-planned double tops.'

'You are not being obstructive are you, Jim?' the Professor asked.

'What, me? With the collapsed lung and the damaged cerebral cortex? Perish the thought.' Pooley took up his glass in a grazed fist and refilled it.

'Now we know where it is,' said the Professor, 'it surely cannot be that difficult to find it.'

'But what are we looking for?' asked Omally. 'You find a great triangle, we find the constellation of the Plough.'

'I find it,' said Pooley.

'Pooley finds it,' said Omally, 'one thing leads to another, but we just go around in circles. What are we looking for?'

'I think I can make a reasonable guess,' said Professor Slocombe. 'We are looking for something which is the product of a high technology. Something which utilizes the vast power fed into it and acts as the ultimate homing beacon. It must have been placed in the Swan during the last year or so, for it was only during this time that the Earthbound Cereans gained knowledge of their prodigals' return and wished to announce their own presence.'

Pooley shrugged. 'Product of a high technology, runs off its own power supply and recently installed in the Swan. Can't see anything filling that bill, it would have to be pretty well camouflag . . . ' Pooley ceased his discourse in mid-sentence. An image had suddenly appeared in his brain. It was so strong and crystal clear that it blotted out everything else. It was the image of a large bulky-looking object shrouded beneath a groundsheet and secured with baling wire, and it was humming and humming and humming.

'By the light of burning martyrs,' said John Omally. 'It has been staring us in the face for months and we never even twigged.'

'What is it?' the Professor demanded. 'You know, don't you?'

'Oh, yes,' said Jim Pooley. 'We know well enough, but believe me the thing will not be easily tampered with. It will take an electronics expert with the brain of an Einstein to dismantle it, and where are we going to get one of those in Brentford?'

Norman Hartnell was not a happy man. Apart from being barred from the Swan with darts night rapidly approaching, which was the kind of thing that could easily drive a sensitive soul such as himself to the point of suicide, he also was suffering a grave amount of concern over his camel. Still wedged firmly into the eaves of his lock-up garage, and gaining bulk from its hearty consumption of cabbage leaves, the beast still showed no inclination whatever to return to Earth. On top of these two insoluble problems, Small Dave's untimely return to Brentford and his disconcerting perceptions were causing the shopkeeper a good deal of grief. He really would have to get rid of the camel. It was damning evidence by any account, and he also had the definite feeling that Small Dave was on to him. The nasty vindictive grudge-bearing wee bastard seemed to be dogging his every move. If he was ever to transfer the Great Pyramid of Cheops from its present foundations in Egypt to its planned relocation upon the turf of Brentford football ground, he really couldn't have the dwarfish postman blundering in and spoiling everything before the project was completed.

Norman dropped into his kitchen chair and did a bit of heavy thinking. The mantelclock struck eleven, time once more to feed the camel. Norman glanced despairingly about; perhaps he should simply blow the garage up. The trouble was that he was really growing quite attached to the mouldy-looking quadruped.

He'd never been allowed to have a pet when he was a lad, and dogs didn't exactly take to him. But Simon, well, Simon was different; he didn't snap at your ankles or climb on your furniture. True, he didn't exactly do anything other than sleep in the rafters and roar for food when hungry, but there was something about the brute which touched Norman. Possibly it was his helplessness, relying upon him, as it did, for his every requirement. Perhaps it was that he had Simon exclusively to himself, nobody forever patting at him and offering him biscuits. Whatever it was, there was something. Simon was all right. He was cheap to feed, living as he did upon Small Dave's cabbages, and his droppings made excellent manure for the roses. Norman wondered for one bright moment whether a camel might be trained to eat dwarves; shouldn't be but a mouthful or two. Pity camels were exclusively vegetarian.

Norman rose from his chair, drew on his shabby overcoat and put out the kitchen light. Stepping silently through the darkened shop, he put his eye to the door's glass and peered out at the Ealing Road. All seemed quiet, but for the distant sound of police sirens. Small Dave was nowhere to be seen.

The shopkeeper drew the bolt upon the door and slipped out into the night. He scuttled away down Albany Road, keeping wherever possible in the shadows. Down the empty street he hurried, with many a furtive glance to assure himself that he was not being followed.

Young Chips, who was returning from some canine equivalent of a lodge meeting, had been watching the shopkeeper's progress for some moments. Now where is Norman off to, he asked himself, and who is the character in the Victorian garb hard upon his heels? If I wasn't half the dog I believe myself to be, I would be certain that that is none other than the famed American author, Edgar Allan Poe. Scratching distractedly at a verminous ear, the dog lifted his leg at a neighbour's Morris Minor, and had it away for home.

Norman reached the allotment gates and peered around. He had the uncanny feeling that he was being watched, but as there was no-one visible he put the thing down to nerves and applied his skeleton key to the lock. A wan moon shone down upon the allotments, and when Norman had had his evil way with Small Dave's already depleted cabbage crop, no living being watched him depart with his swag.

The row of lock-up garages slept in the darkness. As Norman raised the door upon its well-oiled hinges, nothing stirred in the Brentford night. 'Simon,' he said in a soothing tone, 'din dins.'

Having closed the door behind him, he switched on the light, illuminating the tiny lock-up. Simon looked down from his uncomfortable eyrie, and Norman sought some trace of compassion upon the brute's grotesque visage. 'Yum yums,' he said kindly. 'Chow time.'

If camels are capable of displaying emotions, other than the 'go for the groin if cornered' variety, Simon was strangely reticent about putting his about. As he hung in the air, the great ugly-looking beast did little other than to drool a bit and break wind. 'You cheeky boy,' said Norman. 'It's your favourite.'

Behind him, Edgar Allan Poe eased himself through the closed garage door and stood in the shadows watching Norman making a holy show of himself. Simon saw Edgar at once, and Simon did not like the look of Edgar one little bit.

'WAAAAAARK!' went Simon the zero-gravity camel.

'Come, come,' said Norman, flapping his hands, 'there is nothing to get upset about. It's really only cabbage, your favourite.'

'WAAAAAARK!' the disconsolate brute continued.

'Shhh!' said the shopkeeper. 'Calm yourself, please.'

'WAAAAAARK!' Simon set to wriggling vigorously amongst the eaves.

'Stop it, stop it!' Norman frantically waved the cabbage leaves about. 'You'll have the whole neighbourhood up.'

Edgar Allan Poe was fascinated. Times had certainly changed since he had shuffled off the old mortal coil. Small Dave had spent a goodly amount of time impressing upon him the importance of finding a camel. But to think that people actually kept them as pets now, and that they were no longer tethered to the planet of their birth by gravity. That was quite something. 'Stone me,' said Edgar Allan Poe.

John and Jim were taking the long route home. After the incident earlier that evening at the Swan they had no wish to cross the allotment after dark. It was a brisk, cloudless night, and as they slouched along, sharing a late-night Woodbine, they were ill-prepared for the ghastly wailing cries which suddenly reached their ears.

'What is it?' Pooley halted in mid-slouch.

Omally peered up and down the deserted street and over his shoulder to where the allotment fence flanked an area of sinister blackness.

'It is the plaintive cry of the banshee,' said he, crossing himself. 'Back in the old country no man would question that sound. Rather he would steal away to his own dear hovel and sleep with his head in the family Bible and his feet in the fireplace.'

'I have never fully understood the ways of the Irish,' said Jim, also crossing himself just to be on the safe side. 'But I believe them to be a people not without their fair share of common sense, best we have it away on our toes then.'

Another horrific cry rose into the night, raising the small hairs on two ill-washed necks, and causing Pooley's teeth to chatter noisily. This one, however, was followed almost at once by vile but oddly reassuring streams of invective, which could only have arisen from one local and very human throat.

'Could that be who I think it could?' Pooley asked.

'If you mean that very electronics expert with the brain of a veritable Einstein to whom you previously alluded, then I think that it might just be.'

The two men strained their ears for another sound, but

none was forthcoming. Slowly, they proceeded along the street, halting outside the row of lock-up garages. 'Would you look at that,' said Omally, pointing to where a line of orange light showed beneath one of the doors. 'Now what would you take that to be?'

'I would take it to be another trap,' said Jim. 'I have recently had a very bad experience through entering sheds without being asked.'

Omally shuddered. The thought of those icy-black subterranean waters was never far from his mind. 'Caution then?' he asked, creeping close to the door and pressing his ear to it.

It was at that exact moment that Edgar Allan Poe, who had been badly shaken by the floating, screaming camel, chose to make his exit from the garage. Passing discreetly through the solid wood of the garage door he slid right into the skulking Omally. For one ghastly moment the two forms, one solid and smelling strongly of drink, the other ectoplasmic and probably incapable of bearing any scent whatever, merged into one.

'Holy Mary, Mother of God!' screamed Omally, clutching at his head. 'The very devil himself has poked his clammy finger into my ear.'

'Who's out there?' Norman spun away from Simon, who was now silent beneath the falcon hood of a potato sack which had been rammed over his head.

'Night watchman,' said Pooley unconvincingly. 'Twelve o'clock and all's well. Goodnight to you, stranger.'

'Pooley, is that you?'

'Norman?'

The garage door rose a couple of feet and Norman's face appeared, peeping through the opening. 'Is Small Dave with you?' asked the persecuted shopkeeper.

'That vindictive grudge-bearing wee bastard? Certainly not.'

Norman crawled out under the door and drew it rapidly down behind him. 'Just servicing the old Morris Minor,' he said.

'Sounds a bit iffy,' said Omally.

'A bit of gear trouble, nothing more.'

'Let me have a look at it then.' Omally was all smiles. 'I know the old Morris engine like the back of my hand.' He extended this very appendage towards the garage doorhandle, but Norman barred his way.

'Nothing to concern yourself about,' he said, 'nothing I cannot handle.'

'Oh, no trouble, I assure you. Nothing I like better than getting to grips with a monkey wrench and a set of allan keys.'

'No, no,' said Norman, 'I think not, it is growing late now and I have to be up early in the morning.'

'No problem then, I have no a.m. appointments, to me the night is yet young. Leave me the garage key and I will post it through your letter-box as soon as I am done.'

'You are kindness personified,' said Norman, 'but I could not impose upon you in such a fashion. My conscience would not allow it. I will just lock up and then we shall stroll home together.' He stooped to refasten the padlock.

'You'd better switch the light off before you go,' said Jim Pooley.

Norman's hand hovered over the padlock. A look of terrible indecision crossed his face.

'Allow me,' said John Omally, thrusting the shopkeeper aside and taking the handle firmly in two hands. 'I should just like to have a look at this car of yours before we depart.'

'Please don't,' whined the shopkeeper, but it was too late. The door flew upwards and the light from the lock-up garage flooded the street, exposing Norman's secret to the world.

Pooley took a step backwards. 'My God,' was all that he had to say.

Omally, however, was made of sterner stuff. 'Now, there we have a thing,' he said, nudging the cowering shopkeeper. 'Now there we have a thing indeed.'

Norman's brain was reeling, but he did his best to affect an attitude of bland composure. 'There, then,' he said, 'satisfied? Now if you don't mind, it is growing late.'

Omally stepped forward into the garage and pointed upwards. 'Norman,' he said, 'there is a camel asleep in your rafters.'

'Camel?' said Norman. 'Camel? I don't see any camel.'

'It is definitely a camel,' said John. 'If it were a dromedary it would have but one hump.'

'You have been drinking, I believe,' said Norman. 'I can assure you that there is nothing here but a Morris Minor with a tetchy gearbox. I have read of folk suffering such hallucinations when they have imbibed too freely. Come, let us depart, we shall speak no more of these things.'

'It's definitely a camel,' said Jim.

'Dear me,' said Norman shaking his head, 'another victim of Bacchus, and so young.'

'Why is it in the rafters?' Pooley asked. 'I was always of the opinion that camels preferred to nest at ground level and in somewhat sunnier climes.'

'Perhaps it is a new strain?' said Omally. 'Perhaps Norman has created some new strain of camel which he is attempting to keep secret from the world? Such a camel would no doubt revolutionize desert travel.'

Norman chewed upon his lip. 'Please be careful where you stand, Omally,' he said. 'Some of the primer on the bonnet is still wet.'

Omally put his arm about the shopkeeper's shoulder. 'Why not just make this easy on yourself?' he asked.

'Although I accept that mentally you are a fearsome adversary, surely you must realize that the game is up? Cease this folly, I beg you.'

'Don't scuff the spare wheel with your hobnails,' said Norman.

Pooley raised his hand to speak. 'If I might make a suggestion,' he said, 'I think that the matter could be easily settled with a little practical demonstration.'

'Yes?' said Norman doubtfully.

'Well, you suggest that Omally and I are suffering some kind of mental aberration regarding this camel.'

'You are.'

'And we say that your Morris Minor is only notable for its complete and utter invisibility.'

'Huh!'

Pooley drew out his pocket lighter and struck fire. 'You rev up your Morris,' he said, 'and I shall toast the feet of my camel.'

'No, no!' Norman leapt into life. 'Not toast his feet, not toast the feet of my Simon.'

'The camel has it,' said Jim Pooley.

Norman sank to his knees and began to sob piteously. Omally suggested that Jim should lower the garage door and this he did.

'Come, come,' said Omally to the crumpled shopkeeper, 'there is no need for this undignified behaviour. Clearly we have intruded upon some private business. We have no wish to interfere, we are men of discretion, aren't we, Jim?'

'Noted for it.'

'Not men to take advantage of such a situation are we, Jim?'

'Certainly not.'

'Even though this manifestation is clearly of such singularity that any newspaper reporter worthy of his salt would pay handsomely for an exclusive.'

'Say no more,' moaned Norman between sobs. 'Name your price. I am a poor man but we can possibly come to some arrangement. A higher credit rating, perhaps.'

Omally held up his hand. 'Sir,' he said, 'are you suggesting that I would stoop to blackmail? That I would debase the quality of our long-standing friendship with vile extortion?'

'Such I believe to be the case,' said Norman dismally.

'Well then,' said Omally, rubbing his hands together, 'let us get down to business, I have a proposition to put to you.'

18

After leaving Norman's garage in the early hours of the morning, Pooley found little joy in the comforts of his cosy bed. He had listened with awe and not a little terror to the amazing revelations which Omally had skilfully wrung from the shopkeeper. Although Jim had plaintively reiterated that the Earth-balancing-pyramid theory which Norman had overheard, that lunchtime so long ago, was gleaned from the pages of an old comic book, as usual nobody had listened to him. What small, fitful periods of sleep he had managed were made frightful with dreams of great floating camels, materializing pyramids and invading spacemen.

At around six o'clock Pooley gave the whole thing up as a bad job, dragged on an overcoat, thrust a trilby hat on to his hirsute head, and trudged off round to the Professor's house.

The old man sat as ever at his desk, studying his books, and no doubt preparing himself for the worst. He waved Pooley to an armchair without looking up and said, 'I hope you are not going to tell me that during the few short hours that you have been gone you have solved the thing.'

'Partially,' said Jim without enthusiasm. 'But I think John should take full credit this time.'

The old man shook his head. 'Do you ever feel that we are not altogether the masters of our own destinies?' he asked.

'No,' said Jim. 'Never.'

'And so, what do you have to tell me?'

'You will not like it.'

'Do I ever?'

Pooley eyed the whisky decanter as a source of inspiration but his stomach made an unspeakable sound.

'Would you care to take breakfast with me, Jim?' the Professor asked. 'I generally have a little something at about this time.'

'I would indeed,' said Jim. 'Truly I am as ravenous as Ganesha's rat.'

The Professor tinkled a small Burmese brass bell, and within a few seconds there came a knocking at the study door which announced the arrival of Professor Slocombe's elderly retainer Gammon, bearing an overlarge butler's tray loaded to the gunwhales with breakfast for two.

It was Pooley's turn to shake his head. 'How could he possibly know that I was here?'

Professor Slocombe smiled. 'You ask me to give away my secrets?' he said, somewhat gaily. 'Where would I be if you deny me my mystique?'

'You have mystique enough for twenty,' said Jim.

'Then I will share this one with you, for it is simplicity itself.' He rang the small bell again and Gammon, looking up from the coffee he was pouring into the fine Dresden china cups, said, 'Certainly, sir, two lumps it is.'

'It is a code with the bell-ringing,' said the enlightened Jim.

The Professor nodded his old head. 'You have found me out,' said he. In reality, of course, Pooley had done nothing of the kind.

Gammon departed at a mental command, closing the door behind him. Pooley set about the demolition of the steaming trayload. Between great chewings and swallowings, he did his best to relate to the Professor all that he had seen and heard that night.

Professor Slocombe picked delicately at his morning repast and listened to it all with the greatest interest. When Pooley had finished his long, rambling, and not a little confused monologue, he rose from his chair and took out a Turkish cigarette from the polished humidor. Lighting this with an ember from the grate, he waggled the thing at Pooley, and spoke through a cloud of steely-blue smoke. 'You would not be having one over on me here, would you Pooley?' he asked.

'I swear not.'

'Norman has a camel in his lock-up garage which he teleported from the Nile delta and which openly defies the law of gravity?'

'Not openly. Norman is keeping the matter very much to himself.'

'And he plans to alter the Earth's axis by teleporting the Great Pyramid of Cheops into Brentford football ground?'

'That's about the size of it.'

Professor Slocombe fingered the lobe of his left ear. 'We live in interesting times,' he said.

Pooley shrugged and pushed a remaining portion of buttered toast into his mouth.

'The idea does have a certain charm, though,' said Professor Slocombe. 'I should really have to sit down and work it out with a slide rule. For the moment, however, I feel it would be better if he was dissuaded from going ahead with it. I think we should nip it in the bud.'

'I think John and I can fit that in between engagements,' said Pooley sarcastically. The Professor raised an eyebrow towards him, and he fell back to his toast chewing.

'How near to completion do you believe his project to be?'

Pooley shrugged again. 'Days away, by the manner in which he spoke. Omally, using his usual ingenuity, suggested that he might avail himself of any serviceable components from the Captain Laser machine, once he had successfully disabled it. That idea alone was enough to win him over to the cause. What with thinly-veiled threats of exposure and the assurance that his action would not only save mankind as we know it, but also secure him readmission to the Swan in time for the darts tournament, he was putty in Omally's grubby mitt.'

'It would certainly be nice to clear all this up before darts night,' said the Professor enthusiastically. 'I have booked a table at the Swan, I would not care to miss it for the world.'

'Let us pray that none of us do,' said Pooley. 'Would there be any chance of a little more toast?' Professor Slocombe reached for his small brass bell. 'I know perfectly well that it is not how you do it,' said Jim.

'The toast is on the way,' said Professor Slocombe, smiling broadly.

Neville limped painfully up the stairs to his room, bearing with him the special mid-week edition of the *Brentford Mercury*, which had flopped unexpectedly through the Swan's letter-box. Propping it against the marmalade pot, he lowered himself amid much tooth-grinding on to the gaily-coloured bathing ring, which rested somewhat incongruously upon his dining chair.

As he sipped at his coffee he perused the extraordinary news sheet. BRENTFORD HOLOCAUST! screamed the six-inch banner headline with typically restrained conservatism. *'Many arrests in Battle of Brentford, rival gangs clash in open street warfare.'*

Neville shook his head in wonder at it all. How had the trouble started? It was all a little hazy. That Pooley and Omally were involved, he was certain. He would bar them without further ado.

He groaned dismally and clutched at his tender parts.

He surely could not afford to bar any more clients; something desperate was going to have to be done to persuade Norman to return to the fold. And Old Pete; he was sure he had barred him, but he was equally certain that the old reprobate had been in the night before. Perhaps he hadn't. He would bar him again just to be on the safe side.

He perused the long columns of journalistic licence which covered the *Mercury*'s front page. It had been some kind of political rally, so it appeared, the Brownshirts or the League of St George. Apparently these extremists had been drawn into combat with the martial acolytes of the Brentford Temple of Dimac. The police had acted bravely and justly, although greatly outnumbered. There was some talk of decorations at the Palace.

Neville skimmed along the lines of print, seeking to find some reference to the original cause of the incident, but none was forthcoming. The Swan didn't even get a mention, nor did the names of any of the regulars appear amongst the list of arrested villains destined to go up before the beak this very morning. With the arrival of the boys in blue the Swan's stalwarts had either melted away into the night or retired to the tranquillity of the saloon-bar to engage in games of darts and dominoes.

He read the final paragraph. The gallant bobbies had, so it was stated, become involved in a hair-raising car chase through Brentford with a black nineteen-fifties Cadillac which had roared away from the scene of the crime during the height of the disturbances. They had pursued it through the maze of backstreets until unaccountably losing it in a cul-de-sac.

Neville folded the paper and flung it into the fireplace. He would get to the bottom of all this, just as soon as he could get it all clear in his mind. But for now only two things mattered: firstly, that Norman be reinstated as soon as possible in a manner in which neither party would lose face and one which would not anger his pagan deity; and, secondly, that the ice pack which he now wore strapped between his legs got another top-up from the fridge.

Small Dave sat in the sewage outlet pipe at the old dock, which he now called home. His face wore a manic expression into which it had been moulding itself, a little more permanently, with each passing day. He had given up such niceties as hygiene, and now lived for only one thing.

Dire and unremitting vengeance!

Some way further up the pipe, hovering in the darkness, was a misty figure, visible only to the small postman and to certain members of the animal élite.

Small Dave ground his teeth and spat into the daylight. So Norman had the camel penned up in his garage upon the Butts Estate, did he? He had always suspected the shopkeeper, and now Edgar had confirmed his suspicions.

'We have him,' sneered the dwarf, raising a tiny fist towards the sky. 'Right where we want him.' He grinned towards the spectre, exposing two rows of evil-looking yellow teeth. Edgar Allan Poe shifted uneasily in the darkness. He was not at all happy about any of this. He had made a big mistake in allowing himself to become involved with this diminutive lunatic, and sorely craved to return to the astral plane. Although a grey and foggy realm, which offered little in the way of pleasurable diversion, it was infinitely preferable to this madhouse any day of the week.

Sadly, by the very nature of the laws which govern such matters, he was unable to gain release, other than through the courtesy of the being who had called him into service. The mighty fire which had raged through Small Dave's house, eating up many thousands of copies of his books, had acted as some kind of sacrificial catalyst which now bound him to the material world.

Edgar Allan Poe was thoroughly Earthbound, and he was in a very, very bad mood.

At a little after eleven-thirty John Omally reached the Flying Swan. He would have reached it sooner but for the throng of reporters from the national dailies who had accosted him in the street. With his usual courtesy and willingness to be of assistance he had granted several exclusive interviews on the spot.

Yes, he had been there in the thick of it, braving the rubber bullets and the tear-gas. Yes, he had been the last man standing, by virtue of his mastery in the deadly fighting arts of Dimac. No, he had only saved the lives of three of his companions, not four, as was popularly believed. And no, he was sorry, he could not allow any photographs to be taken, modesty forbidding him to take more than his fair share of credit in saving the day.

Patting at his now heavily burdened pockets, Omally entered the Flying Swan. Neville was at the counter's end, supported upon the gaily-coloured rubber bathing ring which he had Sellotaped to the top of a bar stool. He was studying a picture postcard which boasted a rooftop view of Brentford, but upon Omally's approach he laid this aside and viewed the Irishman with distaste.

'You are not welcome here,' he said in no uncertain terms.

John smiled sweetly. 'Come now,' he said, 'let us not be at odds. You have no axe to grind with me. I come as the bearer of glad tidings. All your troubles are over.'

Neville's good eye widened. 'All my troubles are over?' he roared, but the exertion sent blood rushing to certain areas which were better for the time being left bloodless and kosher. 'I am a ruined man,' he whispered hoarsely, between clenched teeth.

'A regrettable business,' said John. 'If I ever see that

fellow in the black suit again, I shall do for him.'

Neville said, 'Hm,' and pulled the Irishman the pint of his preference.

'Have one yourself,' said John.

Although the deadly phrase burned like a branding iron upon Neville's soul, he was loath to refuse and so drew himself a large medicinal scotch.

'About this being my lucky day then?' he said, when he had carefully re-established himself upon his rubber ring. 'You will pardon my cynicism I hope, but as the bearer of glad tidings you must surely rival the angel of death announcing the first innings score at the battle of Armageddon.'

'Nevertheless,' said Omally, 'if you will hear me out then you will find what I have to say greatly to your advantage.'

Neville sighed deeply and felt at his groin. 'I believe that I am getting old,' he told Omally. 'Do you know that I no longer look forward to Christmas?'

John shook his head. He didn't know that, although he wondered how it might be relevant.

'I haven't had a birthday card in ten years.'

'Sad,' said John.

'At times I wonder whether it is all worthwhile. Whether life is really worth all the pain, disappointment, and misery.' He looked towards Omally with a sad good eye. 'People take advantage of my good nature,' he said.

'No?' said John. 'Do they?'

'They do. I bend over backwards to help people and what do I get?' Omally shook his head. 'Stabs in the back is all I get.' Neville made motions to where his braces, had he worn any, would have crossed. 'Stabs in the back.'

'I really, genuinely, can help you out,' said Omally with conviction. 'I swear it.'

'If only it were so,' moaned Neville. 'If only I could

see some ray of hope. Some light at the end of the dark tunnel of life. Some sunbeam dancing upon the bleak rooftop of existence, some . . . '

'All right, all right!' Omally said. 'That's enough, I've been kicked in the cobblers a few times myself, I know how much it hurts. Do you want to know how I can help you out or not?'

'I do,' said Neville wearily.

Omally peered furtively about the bar and gestured the barman closer. 'This is in the strictest confidence,' he whispered. 'Between you and me alone. Should you wish to express your gratitude in some way when the thing is accomplished, then that is a matter between the two of us.'

Neville nodded doubtfully. Whatever it was that Omally was about to say, he knew that it would as usual cost him dearly. 'Say your piece then, John,' he said.

'As I see it,' John continued, 'you have two big problems here. Five, if you wish to number your wounded parts. Firstly, we have the problem of the rapidly approaching darts tournament and the Swan's prospect of certain defeat, should Norman fail to captain the team.' Neville nodded gravely. 'Secondly, we have that.' Omally gestured towards the shrouded video machine, which was even now receiving the attention of a green-haired youth with a large nose and a pair of wire-cutters. Neville bared what was left of his teeth.

'If I was to tell you that I can solve both problems at a single stroke what would you say to me?'

'I would say free beer to you for a year,' said Neville, rising upon his elbows. 'But for now I must say, please get out of my pub and do not return. I am not able to assault you physically at present, but be assured that when I am fully restored to health I shall seek you out. You add insult to my injury and I will have no more of it.'

John tapped at his nose. 'We will let the matter drop

for now, as I can see that you are feeling a little under the weather. By the by, might I take the liberty of asking after the postcard.'

'You may,' said Neville, 'and I will give you that small part before you depart. It is from Archroy, he says that he has now removed the Ark of Noah from the peak of Ararat and is in the process of transporting it through Turkey to Istanbul. He hopes to have it here within a week or two.'

'Well, well, well,' said Omally, grinning hugely. 'We do live in interesting times, do we not?'

'Get out of my pub now,' growled Neville with restrained vehemence, 'or truly, despite my incapacitation, I shall visit upon you such a pestilence as was never known by any of your bog-trotting ancestors in all the hard times of Holy Ireland.'

'God save all here,' said Omally.

'Get out and stay out,' said Neville the part-time barman.

19

Professor Slocombe laid aside a scale model of the Great Pyramid and leant back in his chair. 'No,' he said to himself, 'it couldn't be, no, ludicrous, although . . . ' He rose from his desk and took himself over to the whisky decanter. 'No,' he said once more, 'out of the question.'

Partly filling an exquisite crystal tumbler, he pressed the prismed top back into the decanter's neck, and sank into one of the leathern fireside chairs. Idly he turned the tumbler between thumb and forefinger, watching the reflected firelight as it danced and twinkled in the clear amber liquid. His eyelids became hooded and heavy, and his old head nodded gently upon his equally aged shoulders. It was evident to the gaunt-faced figure who lurked in the darkness without the French windows, polluting the perfumed garden air with the acrid stench of creosote, that the old man was well set to take a quick forty.

Needless to say, this was far from being the case, and beneath the snowy lashes two glittering blue eyes watched as a flicker of movement close by the great velvet curtains announced the arrival of a most unwelcome guest. It was a flicker of movement and nothing more, for again the room appeared empty, but for an elderly gentleman, now snoring noisily in a fireside chair.

Professor Slocombe watched as the silent figure delved amongst the crowded papers of his desk and ran his hands over the bindings of the precious books. The Cerean, convinced of his invisibility, went about his evil business with a will, but naught was missed by the Professor, to whom the word 'hologram' meant little more than 'electronic party trick'.

At length, however, he could stand the defilement of his property no longer. Rising suddenly from his sham repose he addressed his uninvited visitor in no uncertain terms. 'Replace my papers and get out of my study at once,' said he, 'or know the consequences for your boorish behaviour.'

The Cerean stiffened and turned a startled face towards the Professor. He fingered the dials upon a small black box which hung at his belt.

'You can tinker with that piece of junk until the sun goes dim, but I can assure you that it will not work upon me.'

The Cerean opened his cruel mouth and spoke in an accent which was unlike any other that the Professor had ever heard. 'Who are you?' he asked.

Professor Slocombe smiled wanly. 'I am either your saviour or your nemesis.'

'I think not,' said the Cerean.

'If you are inclined to prolong your visit, might I offer you a drink?' the old man asked courteously.

The Cerean laughed loudly. 'Drink?' said he. 'Drink is the ruination of your species. Who do you think invented it for you in the first place?'

'Hm.' The old man nodded thoughtfully; it would be better to keep that piece of intelligence from Pooley and Omally. They might feel inclined to change sides. 'As you will,' he said blandly. 'May I inquire then why you have come here?'

'I have come to kill you,' said the Cerean, in such an off-hand manner that it quite unsettled the Professor's nerves. 'You are proving an annoyance, you and the pink-eyed man beneath. We shall deal with him shortly.'

'That may not be so easy as you might believe.'

The Cerean turned up the palms of his hands. 'You are old and decrepit. A single blow will cut the frail cord of your existence.'

'Appearances can sometimes be deceptive,' said the Professor. 'I for example happen to be a master of Dimac, the deadliest form of martial art known to mankind. My hands and feet are registered with the local constabulary as deadly weapons. They can . . . '

'Rip, maim, mutilate, disfigure and kill with little more than the application of a fingertip's pressure,' said the Cerean. 'I know. Who do you think invented Dimac in the first place?'

'I find your conversation tending towards the repetitious. Kindly take your leave now, I have much to do.'

'Such as plotting the downfall of the Cerean Empire?'

'Amongst other things – I do have more important business.'

The man from Ceres laughed hollowly. 'You have great courage, old man,' said he. 'We of Ceres hold courage and bravery above all other things.'

'I understand that you like a good fight, yes,' said the Professor. 'Although you do not always win. How's the armpit?'

The Cerean clutched at his tender parts. 'Shortly,' he snarled, 'your race will again know the might of Ceres. They will feel the jackboot upon their necks. You, however, will not be here to witness it.'

'I am expecting to enjoy a long and happy retirement,' said Professor Slocombe, noting to his satisfaction and relief that Gammon had now entered the French windows, wielding an antique warming-pan. 'I worry for *you*, though.'

'Do not waste your concern. When the battle fleet arrives and the true masters of Earth once more set foot upon the planet, they will have none to spare for your puny race.'

'Brave talk. When might we expect this happy event?'

'Two days from now. It is a pity you will miss it.'

'Oh, I won't miss it. I have a table booked at the Swan upon that evening. It is the darts tournament. We hold the challenge shield, you know.'

'Of course I know. Who do you think invented darts?'

'Are all your race such blatant liars?'

'Enough talk!' The Cerean pushed past the Professor's desk and crossed the room, to stand glaring, eye to eye with the old man. 'I know not who or what you are,' he said. 'Certainly you are unlike any human I have encountered hereabouts, although long ago I feel that I have met such men as you. But for the present know only this: as a race, you humans fear death, and you are staring yours in the face.'

Professor Slocombe met the Cerean's blazing glare with a cold, unblinking stare. 'I like you not,' he said mildly. 'It was my firm conviction that some compromise might have been reached between our peoples. I strongly disapprove of needless bloodshed, be the blood flowing from human veins or otherwise. There is yet time, if only you could persuade your race to reconsider. Be assured that if you go ahead with your plans you will meet with certain defeat. It is folly to attack Earth. We have been awaiting you for years and we are well prepared.'

'With the corner up, you have,' sneered the Cerean. 'You cannot stand against our battle fleet. We will crush you into submission. Slaves you were and slaves you shall yet become.'

'Is there no compassion then, no spark of what we call humanity?'

The Cerean curled his lip. 'None,' he said.

'Then at least it makes my task a little easier.'

'Prepare for death,' said the man from Ceres.

'Strike the blighter down,' said Professor Slocombe.

Gammon swung the antique warming-pan with a will and struck the Cerean a mighty blow to the back of the head. A sharp metallic clang announced the departure of a Cerean soul, bound for wherever those lads go to once parted from their unearthly bodies.

'He was surely lying about the darts, wasn't he, sir?' Gammon asked.

'I sincerely hope so,' the Professor replied. 'They might have got a team up.'

20

The editor of the *Brentford Mercury* screwed the cap back on to his fountain pen and wedged the thing behind his right ear. He leant back in his pockmarked swivel chair and gazed up at the fly-specked yellow ceiling of his grimy office. Before him, upon the overloaded desk, was a mountain of reports which, although being the very bread of life to the Fortean Society, could hardly be considered even food for thought to the simple folk of Brentford.

Certainly mystery and intrigue had been known to sell a few papers, but this stuff was silly season sensationalism and it wasn't the silly season for another month or more. The editor reached into his drawer for his bottle of Fleet Street Comfort. Tipping the pencils from a paper cup, he filled it to the brim.

It all seemed to have started with that riot in the Ealing Road. He had been receiving odd little reports prior to this, but they had been mainly of the lights in the sky and rumblings in the earth variety, and merited little consideration. The riot, strange enough in itself in peace-loving Brentford, had turned up the first of a flock of really weird ones, and this verified by the Brentford constabulary.

There was the long black limousine of American manufacture which had roared away from the scene of the crime pursued by two squad cars, and then simply vanished in a most improbable fashion up a cul-de-sac. The boys in blue had made a full-scale search of the area, which backed on to the allotment, but had come up with nothing. The car had simply ceased to exist.

There was this continuing sequence of power cuts the area had been experiencing. The local sub-station had denied any responsibility and their only comment had been that during their duration the entire power supply seemed literally to drain away, as if down a plughole.

If the disappearance of Brentford's electricity was weird, then the sudden appearance last week of a one-inch layer of sand completely blanketing Brentford's football ground was weirder still. The groundsman's claim that it was sabotage upon the part of a rival team seemed unlikely.

And then, of course, there was this lunatic craze for Jack Palance impersonation which was sweeping the borough. It seemed a localized vogue, as he had had no reports of it coming in from outside the area. But there they were in Brentford, lounging on corners or skulking about up alleyways. Nobody knew who they were, what they were up to, or why they did it, but all agreed that, whyever it was, they did it very well.

The editor sighed. What exactly was going on in Brentford? And whatever it was, was it news? He drained his cup and stared for a moment into its murky bottom for inspiration. He would adjourn to the Swan for a couple of pints of liquid lunch, that was the best thing. Get all this ludicrous stuff out of his mind. He flicked through the pages of his appointments diary, which were as ever blank. All except for tomorrow's date and this, surprisingly, was encircled thickly in red ink.

Now what might that be for? The editor drew his pen from behind his ear and scratched at his head with it.

Of course, how could he have forgotten? Tomorrow night was the most important night of Brentford's social calendar. The night which Brentford annually awaited with eagerness and anticipation. Tomorrow night was darts night at the Flying Swan. And it promised to be a night that all present would long remember.

21

Professor Slocombe drew together the great curtains and turned to address the small conclave gathered in his study.

The group, three in number, watched the old man warily. The first, Jim Pooley by name, leant against the marble mantelshelf, fingering the magnificent pair of moustachios he had chosen to cultivate. The second, a man of Irish extraction who had recently sold his razor at a handsome profit, lounged in a fireside chair almost unseen behind a forest of curly black beard. The third, a shopkeeper and a victim of circumstance, toyed nervously with his whisky tumbler and prayed desperately for an opportunity to slip away and feed his camel.

There was one last entity present at this gathering, but he was of ethereal stock and invisible to the naked eye. Edgar Allan Poe was maintaining the lowest of all low profiles.

'I have called you here, gentlemen,' said Professor Slocombe, 'because we have almost run out of time. We must act with some haste if we are to act at all.'

'You have reached a solution then?' asked Jim hopefully.

'Possibly.' The old gentleman made a so-so gesture with a pale right hand. 'Although I am backing a rank outsider.'

'I am not a man to favour long odds myself,' said Omally, 'unless, of course, I have a man on the inside.'

'Quite so. Believe me, I have given this matter a very great deal of thought. I have possibly expended more mental energy upon it than I have ever done upon any other problem. I feel that I might have come up with a solution, but the plan relies on a goodly number of factors working to our favour. It is, as you might reasonably expect, somewhat fraught with peril.'

'Tell us the worst then,' said Omally. 'I think you can call us committed.'

'Thank you, John. In essence it is simplicity itself. This worries me a little, possibly because it lacks any of those conceits of artistic expression which my vanity holds so dearly. It is, in fact, a very dull and uninspired plan.'

'But nevertheless fraught with peril?'

'Sadly yes. Under my instruction, Soap Distant has turned the allotments into a veritable minefield. The explosive used is of my own formulation, and I can vouch for its efficiency. I intend to detonate it as the first craft land. We may not be able to get all of the invading vessels, you understand, but if we can take out one or two of the lead ships then I think that it will give us the edge.'

'But what about the rest of them?' asked Pooley.

'That is where we must trust very much to psychology. These beings have travelled a very long way to return to their homeworld. As you are well aware, it no longer exists. When they discover this, they will logically be asking themselves the big "Why". They are being guided here by the communicating beacon in the Swan, but if the first craft to land are instantly destroyed, then I feel it reasonable to assume that they will draw their own conclusions. They will reason that the men of Earth have evolved into a superior force, which is capable of destroying entire planets, should it so wish.

I can only hope that they will hastily take themselves elsewhere. They have a long, long way to call for re-inforcements, should any actually exist.'

'I can accept that in theory,' said Omally, 'but with some reservations. There are a goodly number of ifs and buts to it.'

'I accept it wholeheartedly,' said Jim. 'My name has so far gone unmentioned and that suits me well enough.'

'There are one or two little matters to be cleared up,' said Professor Slocombe somewhat pointedly. 'That is where you come in.'

'This would be the fraught with peril side of it I expect,' said Jim dismally.

Professor Slocombe nodded. 'There is the small matter of the communicating beacon in the Swan. It will have to be switched off. We cannot afford to have the Cereans here giving the game away, now can we?'

Jim shook his head gloomily. 'I suppose not,' he said.

'We have only one opportunity to deal with the thing and that is tomorrow night.'

'I have to play in the finals tomorrow night,' Norman complained. 'Omally here promised I would do so.'

'You haven't fulfilled your side of the bargain yet,' said the voice behind the beard. 'The machine still hums, you have done nothing.'

'I haven't had a chance yet. I can't get in there, I'm barred, don't you remember?'

'Steady on now,' said Professor Slocombe, raising a pale hand. 'All can be reconciled.'

'The machine cannot be broken,' said Jim. 'Be assured of it. We are doomed.'

'I can vouch for the fact that it cannot be destroyed from within the Swan,' said the Professor, 'because I have already tried.'

'Come again?' said Pooley.

'Fair dos,' said Professor Slocombe. 'You surely do not believe that I have been idle?' All present shook their heads vigorously. 'My retainer, Gammon, despite his advanced years and decrepit appearance, is a master of disguise. Twice he has visited the Swan with a view to disabling the device. Firstly, he arrived in the guise of a brewery representative come to check the electrics. He assured me that the machine cannot be switched off in any manner whatever and also that Neville has no love whatever for brewery representatives. Later, he returned as an engineer come to service the device prior to switching it off. This time he received a three-course meal on the house, washed down with half a bottle of champagne, but still met with complete failure. Even a diamond-tipped drill could not penetrate the machine's shell.'

'I told you we were doomed,' said Pooley. 'I am for a Jack Palance mask and a dark suit, me.'

Norman shifted uneasily in his chair. 'I really think I must be going,' he said. 'I can't do anything if I cannot get inside the machine. Feel free to contact me at any time, but for now, goodbye.'

'Not so fast,' said Professor Slocombe. 'I have given the matter much thought, and feel that I have found the solution.'

'Can I go anyway?' Norman asked. 'I do have to be up early in the morning.'

'Test-driving your Morris?' Omally asked. The shopkeeper slumped back into his chair.

'We are dealing,' said Professor Slocombe, 'with beings who, although possessed of superior intelligence, are not altogether dissimilar to ourselves. They are of the opinion that we are a rising, but still inferior race. They might have your card marked, Pooley, but I doubt whether they have contemplated open sabotage. Certainly their machine is outwardly protected. But it might have its weakness if attacked from a different direction.'

'How so?' Pooley asked.

'From behind. The thing is faced against the wall of the Swan. My belief is that if we break through from behind we might find little resistance.'

'What, through the wall of Archie Karachi's Curry Garden? I can't see Kali's Curry King giving us the go-ahead on that one.'

'But Archie Karachi is a member of the Swan's darts team. I myself have seen the sign on his door, "Closed for Business All Day Thursday".'

Pooley tweaked the end of a moustachio whose length would have brought a jealous glance from Salvador Dali himself. 'With all the noise in the Swan,' said he, 'nobody is going to pay much attention to a bit of banging next door.'

'My thoughts entirely. We will need a spy on the inside though, just to keep an eye out. Gammon will take care of that side of it. When we have broken through to the machine it will be down to you, Norman, to deal with it appropriately.'

'No problem there,' said the shopkeeper, blowing on his fingertips. 'There is no machine built which I cannot get to grips with.'

'You might find a surprise or two when we open it.'

'Child's play,' said Norman with sudden bravado. He was quite warming to the idea of all this. He had never liked Archie Karachi very much, and the thought of knocking down his kitchen wall held great appeal. Also, if this machine was everything the Professor seemed to think it was, it was bound to contain a few serviceable components. 'Just lead me to it.'

Omally chuckled behind his whiskers. 'Bravo, Norman,' said the Professor, smiling profusely. 'Now, if you will pardon me, I suggest that we bring this meeting to a close, I have several loose ends still to tie up.'

The old man took a scrap of paper from his pocket and held it to each man in turn. 'We will meet tomorrow, seven-thirty p.m. sharp at this address. Please do not speak it aloud.'

The three men committed the thing to memory. With the briefest of goodbyes and no hand-shaking, they took their leave.

Professor Slocombe closed the French windows behind them and bolted the shutters. 'Now,' he said, turning upon the silent room, 'will you make yourself known to me of your own accord, Mr Poe, or must I summon you into visibility?'

'I should prefer that we did it the easy way,' said Edgar Allan Poe. 'We have much to speak of.'

22

Neville the part-time barman took up his mail from the mat and thrust it into his dressing-gown pocket. Amongst the bills and circulars were no less than three postcards sporting rooftop views of Brentford, but the barman did not give these even a cursory glance.

He had been up half the night trying to work out a deal with his pagan deity over his ill-considered blood oath, but was still far from certain that the matter would be allowed to rest. It was always a hairy business wheeling and dealing with the Elder Gods of Ancient Earth.

Neville drew the brass bolts and flung the door open to sniff the morning air. It smelt far from promising. He took a deep breath, scratched at his bony ribs, and gave the world a bit of first thing perusal. It had all the makings of a beautiful day but Neville could not find any joy to be had in the twinkling sunlight and precocious bird song.

Like others who had gone before him, Neville the part-time barman was a very worried man. The day he had been dreading had come to pass. All over Brentford, dartsmen were awakening, flexing their sensitive fingers, and preparing themselves for the biggest night of the year. The Swan's team had been growing surlier by the day. Where was Norman? they asked. Why was he not practising with them? Neville's excuses had been wearing thinner than the seat of his trousers. If Norman did not turn up for the tournament the consequences did not bear thinking about.

Neville looked thoughtfully up the road towards the

corner shop. Perhaps he should just slip along now and smooth the matter over. Throw himself on Norman's mercy if necessary, promise him anything. Omally had said that the shopkeeper would be present, but was he ever to be trusted?

Neville hovered upon his slippered toes. It would be but the work of a minute. Norman would be numbering up his papers, he could say he just called in for a box of matches, exchange a few niceties, then leave with a casual 'Look forward to seeing you tonight.' Something like that.

Neville took a step forward. At that moment, in the distance, a figure appeared from the shop doorway. Neville's heart rose; it was telepathy surely. The shopkeeper was coming to make his peace. All his troubles were over.

Nicholas Roger Raffles Rathbone hoisted his paperbag into the sunlight. Neville's heart fell. 'Bugger, bugger, bugger,' said the part-time barman, returning to the saloon-bar, and slamming the door behind him.

Parked close to the kerb in a side road opposite to the Swan, and lost for the most part in the shadow of one of the flatblocks, was a long sleek black automobile with high fins. In the front seat of this gleaming motor car sat a man of average height, with a slightly tanned complexion and high cheek-bones. He bore an uncanny resemblance to a young Jack Palance, as did his passenger, who lounged in a rear seat, smoking a green cheroot. The two watched the paperboy as he passed within a few feet of their highly polished front bumper and vanished into one of the flatblocks.

No words passed between these two individuals, but the driver glanced a moment into his rear-view mirror, and his passenger acknowledged the reflected eyes with a knowing nod.

The day passed in an agonizing fashion. Pooley and Omally took their lunchtime's pleasure in a neutral drinking house at Kew, where they sat huddled in an anonymous corner, speaking in hushed tones, bitterly bewailing the exorbitant prices, and casting suspicious glances at every opening of the saloon-bar door.

Norman closed up his shop at one and busied himself in his kitchenette. What he did there was strictly his own business, and he had no intention of letting anything, no matter how alien, interfere with his afternoon's work.

In his sewage outlet pipe, Small Dave paced up and down. His hair was combed forward across his forehead and his left hand was thrust into his shirt in a fashion much favoured by a diminutive French dictator of days gone by. As he paced he muttered, and the more he muttered the more apparent it became that he was plotting something which was to cause great ill to any camel owners in Brentford.

At intervals he ceased his frenzied pacing and peered up and down the hideous pipe, as if expecting the arrival of some fellow conspirator. None, however, made an appearance.

Professor Slocombe was not to be found at his desk that afternoon. He had pressing business elsewhere. Whilst the sun shone down upon Brentford and the Brentonians went about whatever business they had, he was conversing earnestly with a pink-eyed man of apparent albino extraction, who had given up such doubtful pleasures to dedicate himself to the search for far greater truths.

Even now, the Professor sat in what was to all appearances a normal Brentford front room, but which was, in fact, situated more than a mile beneath Penge; which I understand is a very nice place, although I have never been there myself.

At a little after three, Neville drew the bolts upon the Swan's door and retired to his chambers. He had been anaesthetizing himself with scotch since eleven and was now feeling less concerned about what was to happen during the coming evening. He was, however, having a great deal of trouble keeping the world in focus. He falteringly set his alarm clock for five and blissfully fell asleep upon his bed.

23

At long last the Memorial Library clock struck a meaningful seven-thirty. The Swan was already a-buzz with conversation. Pints were being pulled a-plenty and team members from the half-dozen pubs competing this year were already limbering up upon the row of dartboards arranged along the saloon-bar wall. The closed sign had long been up upon the Star of Bombay Curry Garden, and within the Swan, Gammon, in the unlikely guise of an Eastern swami, engaged Archie Karachi in fervent debate.

In the back room of number seven Mafeking Avenue four men held a council of war.

'The thing must be performed with all expediency,' said Professor Slocombe. 'We do not want Norman to miss the match. I have, as the colonials would have it, big bucks riding upon this year's competition.'

The shopkeeper grinned. 'Have no fear, Professor,' said he.

'Omally, do you have your tools?' John patted at the bulging plumber's bag he had commandeered during the afternoon from a dozing council worker. 'Then it is off down the alley and fingers crossed.'

Without further ado, the four men passed out into a small back yard and down a dustbin-crowded alleyway towards the rear of the Star of Bombay Curry Garden.

Norman was but a moment at the lock before the four found themselves within the ghastly kitchenette, their noses assailed by the horrendous odours of stale vindaloo and mouldy madras. Kali's face peered down from a garish wall-calendar, registering a look of some foreboding at the prospect of what was to be done to the premises of one of her followers.

'A moment please,' said Professor Slocombe. 'We must be certain that all is secure.'

Within the Swan, Gammon suddenly interrupted his conversation, excused himself momentarily from Archie's company, and thrust a handful of change into the Swan's jukebox. As the thing roared into unstoppable action, Neville, who had taken great pains to arrange for the disabling of that particular piece of pub paraphernalia years before, and had never actually heard it play, marvelled at its sudden return to life. The Professor had left nothing to chance.

'To the wall, John,' said Professor Slocombe.

'Whereabouts?'

'Just there.'

'Fair enough.' Omally swung his seven-pound club hammer and the cold chisel penetrated the gaudy wallpaper. The mouldy plasterwork fell away in great map chunks, and within a minute or two Omally had bared an area of brickwork roughly five feet in height and two in width.

'Better penetrate from the very centre,' the Professor advised. 'Take it easy and we will have a little checkabout, in case the thing is booby-trapped.' Omally belted the chisel into the brickwork.

Within the Swan the jukebox was belting out a deafening selection of hits from the early sixties. The sounds of demolition were swallowed up by the cacophony.

'Stop!' said the Professor suddenly.

'What is it?' The words came simultaneously from three death-white faces.

'Changing the record, that's all. You can go on again now.'

Pooley was skulking near to the back door. With every

blow to the brickwork his nerve was taking a similar hammering. His hand wavered above the door handle.

'If it goes up, Jim,' said the Professor without looking round, 'it will take most of Brentford with it. You have nowhere to run to.'

'I wasn't running,' said Jim. 'Just keeping an eye on the alleyway, that's all.' He peered over the net curtain into a yard which was a veritable munitions dump of spent curry tins. 'And not without cause. John, stop banging.'

'I'm getting nowhere with all these interruptions,' the Irishman complained. 'Look, I've nearly got this brick out.'

'No, stop, stop!' Pooley ducked down below window level. 'There's one of them out there.'

'Ah,' said Professor Slocombe, 'I had the feeling that they would not be very far from the Swan this night.'

The four men held their breath until they could do it no more. 'Is he still there?' the Professor asked.

Pooley lifted the corner of the net curtain. 'No, he's gone. Be at it, John, get a move on will you?'

'Perhaps you'd rather do the work yourself, Pooley?' said Omally, proffering his tools.

'I am the lookout,' said Pooley haughtily, 'you are the hammerman.'

'Oh, do get a move on,' sighed Norman. 'It's nearly a quarter to eight.'

Omally swung away with a vengeance, raising a fine cloud of brick dust, and dislodging chunks of masonry with every blow. When he had cleared a hole of sufficient size, the Professor stuck his head through and shone about with a small hand torch. 'I see no sign of touch plates or sensory activators. Have it down, John.'

Omally did the business. As Gammon's final selection came to an end and the jukebox switched itself off for another decade, the saboteurs stood before the exposed back plate of the Captain Laser Alien Attack Machine.

Norman opened his tool-box and took out a pair of rubber gloves, which he dusted with talcum powder, and drew over his sensitive digits. Taking up a long slim screwdriver, he teased out the locking screws. As the others crossed their fingers and held their breath, he gently eased away the back plate. The Professor shone his torch in through the crack and nodded. Norman yanked the plate off, exposing the machine's inner workings.

A great gasp went up from the company. 'Holy Mary,' said John Omally, 'would you look at all that lot?'

Norman whistled through his teeth. 'Magic,' said he. Upon the dashboard of a black Cadillac sedan parked in a nearby side-road a green light began to flash furiously.

The shopkeeper leant forward and stared into the machine's innards. 'It is wonderful,' he said. 'Beyond belief.'

'But can you break it up?' Omally demanded.

'Break it up? That would be a crime against God. Look at it, the precision, the design. It is beyond belief, beyond belief.'

'Yes, yes, but can you break it up?'

Norman shook his head, 'Given time, I suppose. But look here, the thing must serve at least a dozen functions. Each of these modules has a separate input and output.'

'Let me give it a welt with my hammer.'

'No, no, just a minute.' Norman traced the circuitry with his screwdriver, whistling all the while. 'Each module is fed by the main power supply, somewhere deep within the Earth, it appears. This is evidently some sort of communications apparatus. There is a signalling device here, obviously for some sort of guidance control. Here is the basic circuitry which powers the games centre. Here is a gravitational field device to draw down orbiting objects on to a preprogrammed landing site. The whole thing is here, complete tracking, guidance, communication and landing controls. There are various other subsidiary components: outward defence modifications, protecting the frontal circuitry, alarm systems, etcetera.'

The Professor nodded. 'Disconnect the guidance, communications, and landing systems, if you please, Norman.'

Norman delved into the works, skilfully removing certain intricate pieces of microcircuitry. 'It occurs to me,' he said, 'speaking purely as a layman, that as a protective measure we might reverse certain sections merely by changing over their positive and negative terminals.'

Professor Slocombe scratched at his snowy head. 'To what end?'

'Well, if this device is guiding the craft in by means of gravitational beams locked into their computer guidance systems, if we were to reverse the polarity, then as they punch in their coordinates on board the ships, the machine will short them out, and possibly destroy the descending craft.'

'Will it work?'

Norman tapped at his nose. 'Take it from me, it won't do them a lot of good. Come to think of it, it might even be possible to cross-link the guidance system with the actual games programme on the video machine. Pot the bastards right out of the sky as they fly in.'

'Can you do it?'

'Can I do it, Professor?' Norman unscrewed a series of terminals and reconnected them accordingly. He also removed a small unobtrusive portion of the contrivance, which appeared of importance only to himself, and secreted it within his toolbox.

'Are you all done?' the Professor asked, when the shopkeeper finally straightened up.

'All done,' said Norman, pulling off his gloves and

tossing them into his tool-box. 'A piece of cake.'

Professor Slocombe rose upon creaking knees and patted the brick dust from his tweeds. He put a hand upon the shopkeeper's shoulder and said, 'You have done very well, Norman, and we will be for ever in your debt. The night, however, is far from over. In fact it has just begun. Do you think that you might now pull off the double by winning the darts match?'

Norman nodded. He had every intention of pulling off the treble this night. But that was something he was keeping very much to himself.

The Swan was filling at a goodly pace. With seven local teams competing for the cherished shield, business was already becoming brisk. Neville had taken on extra barstaff, but these were of the finger-counting, change-confusing variety, and were already costing him money. The part-time barman was doing all he could, but his good eye wandered forever towards the Swan's door.

When at quarter past eight it swung open to herald the arrival of Omally, Pooley, Professor Slocombe and Norman, the barman breathed an almighty sigh of relief. Omally thrust his way through the crowd and ordered the drinks. 'As promised,' he announced, as the Swan's team enveloped Norman in their midst with a great cheer.

Neville pulled the pints. 'I am grateful, Omally,' said he, 'these are on the house.'

'And will be for a year, as soon as the other little matter is taken care of.'

'The machine?'

'You will have to bear with me just a little longer on that one. Whatever occurs tonight you must stand resolute and take no action.'

Neville's suspicions were immediately aroused. 'What is likely to occur?'

Omally held up his grimy hands. 'The matter is under the control of Professor Slocombe, a man who, I am sure you will agree, can be trusted without question.'

'If all is as you say, then I will turn a blind eye to that despoiler of my loins who has come skulking with you.' Omally grinned handsomely beneath his whiskers. Neville loaded the drinks on to a tray and Omally bore them away to the Professor's reserved table.

A bell rang and the darts tournament began. A hired Master of Ceremonies, acting as adjudicator and positive last word, clad in a glittering tuxedo and sporting an eyebrow-pencil moustache, announced the first game.

First on the oché were the teams from the Four Horsemen and the New Inn. Jack Lane, resident landlord at the Four Horsemen these forty-seven long years, struggled from his wheelchair and flung the very first dart of the evening.

'Double top, Four Horsemen away,' announced the adjudicator in a booming voice.

Outside in the street, two figures who closely resembled a pair of young Jack Palances, and who smelt strongly of creosote, were rapidly approaching the Swan. They walked with automaton precision, and their double footfalls echoed along the deserted Ealing Road.

'Double top,' boomed the adjudicator, 'New Inn away.'

Pooley and Omally sat in their grandstand seats, sipping their ale. 'Your man Jarvis there has a fine overarm swing,' said Omally.

'He is a little too showy for my liking,' Pooley replied. 'I will take five to four on the Horsemen if you're offering it.'

Omally, who had already opened his book and was now accepting bets from all comers, spat on his palm and smacked it down into that of his companion. 'We are away then,' said he.

Bitow bitow bitow went the Captain Laser Alien Attack Machine, suddenly jarring the two men from their appreciation of life's finer things, and causing them to leap from their chairs. Omally craned his neck above the crowd and peered towards the sinister contrivance. Through the swelling throng he could just make out the distinctive lime-green coiffure of Nicholas Roger Raffles Rathbone.

'It is the young ninny,' said John. 'Five to four you have then, I will draw up a page for you.'

Neville was by now moving up and down the bar, taking orders left, right, and centre. The till jangled like a fire alarm, and Croughton the pot-bellied potman was already in a lather.

No-one noticed as two men with high cheekbones and immaculate black suits entered the Swan and lost themselves in the crowds. No-one, that is, but for a single disembodied soul who lightly tapped the Professor upon the shoulder. 'All right,' said the old man, without drawing his eyes from the match in play. 'Kindly keep me informed.'

The Four Horsemen was faring rather badly. The lads from the New Inn had enlisted the support of one Thomas 'Squires' Trelawny, a flightsmaster from Chiswick. 'Who brought him in?' asked Pooley. 'His name is not on the card.'

'A late entry, I suppose, do I hear a change in the odds?'

'Treacherous to the end, Omally,' said Jim Pooley. 'I will not shorten the odds, who is the next man up?'

'Jack's son, Young Jack.'

Young Jack, who was enjoying his tenth year in retirement, and looked not a day over forty, put his toe to the line and sent his feathered missile upon its unerring course into the treble twenty.

A great cheer went up from the Horsemen's supporters. 'He once got three hundred and one in five darts,' Omally told Jim.

'He is in league with the devil though but.'

'True, that does give him an edge.'

Somehow Young Jack had already managed to score one hundred and eighty-one with three darts, and this pleased the lads from the Four Horsemen no end. To much applause, he concluded his performance by downing a pint of mild in less than four seconds.

'He is wearing very well considering his age,' said Omally.

'You should see the state of his portrait in the attic.'

'I'll get the round in then,' said Professor Slocombe, rising upon his cane.

'Make sure he doesn't charge you for mine,' called Omally, who could see a long and happy year ahead, should the weather hold. With no words spoken the crowd parted before the old man, allowing him immediate access to the bar.

Beneath his table Young Jack made a satanic gesture, but he knew he was well outclassed by the great scholar.

'Same again,' said Professor Slocombe. Neville did the honours. 'All is well with you, I trust, barman?' the old gentleman asked. 'You wear something of a hunted look.'

'I am sorely tried, Professor,' said Neville. 'I can smell disaster, and this very night. The scent is souring my nostrils even now as we speak. It smells like creosote, but I know it to be disaster. If we survive this night I am going to take a very long holiday.'

'You might try Penge, then,' said the old man brightly, 'I understand that it is very nice, although . . . ' His words were suddenly swallowed up by a battery of *Bitows* from the nearby games machine.

Neville scowled through the crowd at the hunched back of the paperboy. 'Perhaps I will simply slay him now and take my holiday in Dartmoor, they say the air is very healthy thereabouts.'

'Never fear,' said Professor Slocombe, but his eyes too had become fixed upon the green-haired youth. Speaking rapidly into Nick's ear was a man of average height, slightly tanned and with high cheek-bones. The Professor couldn't help thinking that he put him in mind of a young Jack Palance. The youth, however, appeared so engrossed in his play as to be oblivious to the urgent chatter of the darkly-clad stranger.

Neville chalked the bill on to the Professor's private account, and the old gentleman freighted his tray back to his table. 'How goes the state of play?' he asked Omally.

'Squires Trelawny is disputing Young Jack's score,' said John, unloading the tray on to the table. 'He is obviously not altogether *au fait* with Jack's technique.'

'Oh dear,' said Pooley pointing towards the dispute. 'Young Jack is not going to like that.'

Trelawny, a temperamental fellow of the limp-wristed brotherhood, frustrated by the apparent wall of indifference his objections ran up against, had poked one of the Horsemen's leading players in the eye with his finger.

'Trelawny is disqualified,' said the adjudicator.

'You what?' Squires turned upon the man in the rented tuxedo and stamped his feet in rage.

'Out, finished,' said the other. 'We brook no violence here.'

'You are all bloody mad,' screamed the disgruntled player, in a high piping voice. The crowd made hooting noises and somebody pinched his bum.

'Out of my way then!' Flinging down his set of Asprey's darts (the expensive ones with the roc-feather flights), he thrust his way through the guffawing crowd and departed the Swan. Young Jack, who numbered among his personal loathings a very special hatred for poofs, made an unnoticeable gesture beneath table level, and as he blustered into the street Trelawny slipped upon an imaginary banana skin and fell heavily to the pavement. As he did so, the front two tyres of his Morris Minor went simultaneously flat.

'This has all the makings of a most eventful evening,' said Jim Pooley. 'The first eliminator not yet over and blood already drawn.'

The adjudicator wiped away the New Inn's name from the board. With their best player disqualified, morale had suffered a devastating and irrevocable blow, and the New Inn had retired from the competition.

Next up were the North Star and the Princess Royal. The North Star's team never failed to raise eyebrows no matter where they travelled, being five stout brothers of almost identical appearance. They ranged from the youngest, Wee Tam, at five feet five, to the eldest, Big Bob, at six foot two, and had more the look of a set of Russian dolls about them than a darts team. Their presence in public always had a most sobering effect upon the more drunken clientele.

Their opponents, upon the other hand, could not have looked less alike had they set out to do so. They numbered among their incongruous ranks, two garage mechanic ne'er-do-wells, a bearded ex-vicar, a tall lift engineer with small ears, and a clerk of works with large ones. They also boasted the only Chinese player in Brentford. Tommy Lee was the grand master to the Brentford Temple of Dimac and was most highly danned, even amongst very danned people indeed. Few folk in the Borough ever chose to dispute with him over a doubtful throw.

However, Tommy, who had taken the Dimac oath which bound him never to use any of the horrendous, maiming, tearing, crippling and disfiguring techniques unless his back was really up against the wall, was a fair and honest man and very popular locally. He was also the only player known to throw underarm. He fared reasonably well, and as usual it took two strong lads to withdraw his hand-carved ivory darts from the board.

'I'll bet that took the remaining plaster off Archie's back parlour wall,' said Omally. 'By the way, Professor, I hope the man from Bombay is being well-catered for. We wouldn't want him popping next door to grill up a popadum, would we?'

Professor Slocombe tapped his sinuous nose. One or other of the North Star's men was throwing, but it was hard to tell which when they were detached from the set and you couldn't judge them by height.

'One hundred,' bawled the adjudicator.

'What odds are you offering at present upon the North Star?' the Professor asked. Out of professional etiquette John answered him tic-tac fashion. 'I will take your pony on that, then.'

'From your account?'

'Omally, you know I never carry money.'

'The Princess Royal need one hundred and fifty-six,' boomed the adjudicator, taking up the chalks.

The lift engineer, making much of his every movement, stepped on to the oché. There was a ripple amongst the crowd as his first dart entered the treble twenty. A whistle as his second joined it and a great cry of horror as his third skimmed the double eighteen by a hairbreadth. Crimson to the tips of his small and shell-likes, the lift engineer returned to his chair, and the obscurity from which he had momentarily emerged.

'Unfortunate,' said Professor Slocombe, rubbing his hands together, 'I have noticed in matches past that the lift engineer has a tendency to buckle under pressure.'

Omally made a sour face, he had noticed it also, but in the heat of the betting had neglected to note the running order of the players.

'The North Star needs eighty-seven.'

Amidst much cheering, this figure was easily accomplished, with a single nineteen, a double nineteen and a double fifteen.

'I am up already,' said Professor Slocombe to the scowling Irishman.

'And I,' said Pooley.

Now began the usual debate which always marred championship matches. A member of the Princess Royal's team accused the men from the Star of playing out of order. The adjudicator, who had not taken the obvious course of forcing them to sport name tags, found himself at a disadvantage.

Omally, who had spotted the omission early in the game, shook his head towards Professor Slocombe. 'I can see all betting on this one being null and void,' said he.

'I might possibly intervene.'

'That would hardly be sporting now, would it, Professor?'

'You are suggesting that I might have a bias?'

'Perish the thought. It is your round is it not, Jim?'

Pooley, who had been meaning to broach the subject of a loan, set against his potential winnings, began to pat at his pockets. 'You find me financially embarrassed at present,' he said.

'I think not,' said Professor Slocombe. 'I recall asking you for a pound's-worth of change from the Swan's cash register.'

'You did sir, yes.' Pooley shook his head at the Professor's foresight and fought his way towards the bar.

Neville faced his customer with a cold good eye. 'Come to kick me in the cobblers again, Pooley?' he asked. 'You are here on sufferance you know, as a guest of Omally and the Professor.'

Jim nodded humbly. 'What can I say?'

'Very little,' said Neville. 'Can you smell creosote?'

Pooley's moustachios shot towards the floor like a

dowser's rod. 'Where?' he asked in a tremulous voice.

'Somewhere close,' said Neville. 'Take my word, it bodes no good.'

'Be assured of that.' Pooley loaded the tray and cast a handful of coins on the counter.

'Keep the change,' he called, retreating fearfully to his table.

'We're up next,' said Omally, upon the shaky Jim's return. 'Will you wager a pound or two upon the home team?'

'Neville smells creosote,' said Jim.

'Take it easy.' Professor Slocombe patted the distraught Pooley's arm. 'I have no doubt that they must suspect something. Be assured that they are being watched.'

The Captain Laser Alien Attack machine rattled out another series of electronic explosions.

Norman stepped on to the mat amidst tumultuous applause. He licked the tips of his darts and nodded towards the adjudicator.

'Swan to throw,' said that man.

Norman's mastery of the game, his style and finesse, were legend in Brentford. Certain supporters who had moved away from the area travelled miles to witness his yearly display of skill. One pink-eyed man, who kept forever to the shadows, had actually travelled from as far afield as Penge.

'One hundred and eighty,' shouted the adjudicator, although his words were lost in the Wembley roar of the crowd.

'It is poetry,' said Omally.

'Perfect mastery,' said Pooley.

'I think it has something to do with the darts,' said Professor Slocombe, 'and possibly the board, which I understand he donated to the Swan.'

'You are not implying some sort of electronic duplicity upon the part of our captain, are you?' Omally asked.

'Would I dare? But you will notice that each time he throws, the Guinness clock stops. This might be nothing more than coincidence.'

'The whole world holds its breath when Norman throws,' said Omally, further shortening the already impossibly foreshortened odds upon the home team. 'Whose round is it?'

'I will go on to sherry now, if you please,' said the Professor. 'I have no wish to use the Swan's convenience tonight.'

'Quite so,' said John. 'We would all do well to stay in the crowd. Shorts all round then.' Rising from the table, he took up his book, and departed into the crowd.

Old Pete approached Professor Slocombe and greeted the scholar with much hand-wringing. 'My dog Chips tells me that we have a bogey in our midst,' said he.

'And a distinguished one of the literary persuasion,' the elder ancient replied. 'Tell your dog that he has nothing to fear, he is on our side.'

Old Pete nodded and turned the conversation towards the sad decline in the nation's morals and Professor Slocombe's opinion of the post office computer.

Omally found the boy Nick at the bar, ordering a half of light and lime. 'Have this one on me,' he said, handing the boy two florins. 'You are doing a grand job.'

Raffles Rathbone raised a manicured eyebrow. 'Don't tell me you now approve?' he asked.

'Each to his own. I have never been one to deny the pleasures of the flesh. Here, have a couple of games on me and don't miss now, will you?' He dropped several more coins into the boy's outstretched palm.

'I never miss,' Nick replied. 'I have the game mastered.'

'Good boy. Two gold watches and a small sweet sherry please, Neville.'

The part-time barman glared at Omally. 'You are paying for these,' he snarled. 'I still have my suspicions.'

'You can owe me later,' Omally replied, delving into his pockets. 'I am a man of my word.'

'And I mine, eighteen and six please.'

'Do you know something I don't?' Nick asked the Irishman.

'A good many things. Did you have anything specific in mind?'

'About the machine?'

'Nothing. Is something troubling you?'

Nick shook his limey head and turned his prodigious nose once more towards the unoccupied machine. 'I must be going now,' he said, 'the Captain awaits.'

'Buffoon,' said Omally beneath his breath. By the time he returned to the table, the Swan's team had disposed of their adversaries in no uncertain fashion.

'I am sure that I am up by at least two bob on that game,' said Pooley.

'Two and fourpence,' said Professor Slocombe. 'Don't let it go to your head.'

The final eliminating match lay between the Four Horsemen and the Albany Arms, whose team of old stalwarts, each a veteran of Gallipoli, had been faring remarkably well against spirited opposition.

'Albany Arms to throw,' boomed himself.

'Leave me out of this one,' said Pooley. 'Unless God chooses to intervene upon this occasion and despatch Young Jack into the bottomless pit, I feel it to be a foregone conclusion.'

'I will admit that you would have a wager at least one hundred pounds to win yourself another two and fourpence.'

'Don't you feel that one thousand to one against the Albany is a little cruel?'

'But nevertheless tempting to the outside better.'

'Taking money from children,' said Professor Slocombe. 'How can you live with yourself, John?'

Omally grinned beneath his beard. 'Please do not deny me my livelihood,' said he.

From their first dart onwards, the Albany began to experience inexplicable difficulties with their game. Several of the normally robust geriatrics became suddenly subject to unexpected bouts of incontinence at their moments of throwing. Others mislaid their darts or spilled their beer, one even locked himself in the gents' and refused to come out until the great grinning black goat was removed from in front of the dartboard.

It was remarkable the effect that Young Jack could have upon his team's opponents. The crowd, however, was not impressed. Being responsive only to the finer points of the game and ever alert to such blatant skulduggery, they viewed this degrading spectacle with outrage and turned their backs upon the board.

Young Jack could not have cared less. The Four Horsemen needed but a double thirteen to take the match and the Albany had yet to get away. The present-day Faust smirked over towards the Professor and made an obscene gesture.

Professor Slocombe shook his head and made clicking noises with his tongue. 'Most unsporting,' said he. 'I shall see to it that none of this occurs in the final.'

Without waiting to watch the inevitable outcome of the game, he rose from his chair and took himself off to where the Swan's team stood in a noisy scrum, ignoring the play.

'He has gone to bless the darts, I suspect,' said Omally. 'In his yearly battle of wits with Young Jack, the Professor leaves nothing to chance.'

'Do you believe it possible?' Pooley asked wistfully. 'That somewhere in this green and pleasant land of ours, this sceptred isle, this jewel set in a silver sea and whatever, that there might somewhere be a little darts team, based possibly in some obscure half-timbered country pub out in the sticks, which actually plays the game for the love of it alone, and without having recourse to some underhand jiggery-pokery?'

'Are you mad?' enquired Omally. 'Or merely drunk?'

Jim shook his head. 'I just wondered how such a game might look. If played by skill alone, I mean.'

'Jolly dull, I should think. Here, take this one-pound note, which you can owe to me, and get in another round.'

Jim watched a moment as Young Jack's hellish black dart cleaved the air, leaving a yellow vapour trail, and thrust its oily nose into the double thirteen. 'I should still like to see it,' he said. 'Just the once.'

'Naïve boy,' sighed Omally, running his pencil down endless columns of figures, and wondering by how many thousands of pounds he was up this particular evening.

Professor Slocombe finished muttering a Latin text over the table of laid-out darts and gave the benediction. 'This will not of course enable you to play any better,' he explained, 'but it will protect your darts from any mysterious deflections which might occur.'

The Swan's team nodded. They had defeated the Four Horsemen in the final five years on the trot now, which was, by way of coincidence, exactly the length of time that the Professor had been acting as honorary President. They took the old man's words strictly at their face value. None of the accidents which marred the play of the Horsemen's other opponents ever befell them, and although few of the team knew anything whatever about the occult, each blessed the day that Norman had suggested the elderly scholar's nomination.

'Be warned now,' Professor Slocombe continued, 'he does appear to be on superb form tonight. Look wherever you like, but avoid his eyes.'

Neville appeared through the crowd bearing a silver tray. On this rested a dozen twinkling champagne saucers and a Georgian silver wine cooler containing a chilled and vintage bottle of Pol Roger.

This little morale-booster was another of the Professor's inspirations.

'Good luck to you all,' said the part-time barman, patting Norman gingerly upon the shoulder. 'Good luck.'

A warlike conclave had formed at the other end of the bar. Young Jack and his demonic cohorts were clustered about Old Jack's wheelchair, speaking in hushed, if heated, tones. Neville sensed that above the smell of creosote, which so strongly assailed his sensitive nostrils, there was a definite whiff of brimstone emanating from the satanic conspirators. The part-time barman shuddered. Why did things always have to be so complicated?

The Swan now swelled with crowds literally to bursting point. It was almost impossible to move amongst the throng, and trayloads of drinks were being passed from the bar counter over the heads of patrons, generally to arrive at their destinations somewhat lighter of load. It was rapidly reaching the 'every man for himself' stage. The atmosphere was electric with anticipation and unbreathable with cigar smoke. The noise was deafening and even the Captain Laser Alien Attack machine rattled mutely, lost amidst the din. Croughton the pot-bellied potman had come down with a severe attack of no bottle and had taken himself off to the rear yard for a quiet fag.

'Ladies and gentlemen,' bellowed the adjudicator at the top of his voice, 'it is my pleasure to announce the final and deciding contest of the evening. The very climax of this evening's sport.' Omally noted that the word 'sport' appeared to stick slightly in the adjudicator's throat. 'The final for the much coveted Brentford District Darts Challenge Trophy Shield.'

Neville, who had taken this cherished item down from its cobwebby perch above the bar and had carefully polished its tarnished surface before secreting it away in a place known only to himself, held it aloft in both hands. A great cheer rang through the Swan.

'Between the present holders, five years' champions, the home team, the Flying Swan.' Another deafening cheer. 'And their challengers from the Four Horsemen.'

Absolute silence, but for the occasional *bitow* in the background.

'Gentlemen, let battle commence.'

The home team, as reigning champions, had call of the toss. As the adjudicator flipped a copper coin high into the unwholesome smoke-filled air, Professor Slocombe, who had taken up station slightly to the rear of Young Jack, whispered, 'The same coin had better come down and it had better not land upon its edge.'

Young Jack leered around at his adversary. 'As honorary President,' he said, 'I shall look forward to you personally handing me the shield upon your team's crushing defeat.'

Whether through the action of that fickle thing called fate, or through the influence of some force which the Professor had neglected to make allowance for, unlikely though that might seem, the coin fell tailside up and the Four Horsemen were first upon the oché.

Through merit of his advanced years and the ever-present possibility that he would not survive another championship game through to the end, Old Jack threw first.

Professor Slocombe did not trouble to watch the ancient as he struggled from his wheelchair, assisted by his two aides, and flung his darts. His eyes were glued to the hands of Young Jack, awaiting the slightest movement amongst the dark captain's metaphysical digits.

It was five hundred and one up and a five-game decision and each man playing was determined to give of his all or die in the giving. Old Jack gave a fair account of himself with an ample ton.

Norman took the mat. As he did so, both Pooley and Omally found their eyes wandering involuntarily over the heads of the crowd towards the electric Guinness clock.

Three times Norman threw and three times did those two pairs of eyes observe the fluctuation in the clock's hand.

'He cheats, you know,' whispered Pooley.

'I've heard it rumoured,' Omally replied.

'One hundred and eighty,' boomed the man in the rented tux.

On the outer rim of the solar system, where the planets roll, lax, dark and lifeless, appeared nine small white points of light which were definitely not registered upon any directory of the heavens. They moved upon a level trajectory and travelled at what appeared to be an even and leisurely pace. Given the vast distances which they were covering during the course of each single second, however, this was obviously far from being the case.

Upon the flight deck of the leading Cerean man o' war, the Starship *Sandra*, stood the Captain. One Lombard Omega by name, known to some as Lord of a Thousand Suns, Viceroy of the Galactic Empire and Crown Prince of Sirius, he was a man of average height with high cheekbones and a slightly tanned complexion. He bore an uncanny resemblance to a young Jack Palance and, even when travelling through the outer reaches of the cosmic infinite, smelt strongly of creosote.

'Set a course for home,' he said, affecting a noble stance and pointing proudly into space. 'We have conquered the galaxy and now return in triumph to our homeworld. Ceres, here we come.'

The navigator, who bore a striking resemblance to his Captain, but whose rank merited a far less heavily braided uniform and fewer campaign ribbons, tapped out a series of instructions into a console of advanced design. 'Goodness me,' said he, as the computer guidance system flashed up an unexpected reply to his instructions upon a three-dimensional screen. 'Now there's a funny thing.'

Lombard Omega leant over his shoulder and squinted into the glowing display of nine orbiting worlds. 'Where's the fucking planet gone?' he asked.

'One hundred and forty,' shouted the adjudicator, oblivious to what was going on at the outer edge of the solar system. 'The Horsemen needs ninety-seven.'

'If they aren't cheating,' said Pooley, 'they are playing a blinder of a game.'

'Oh, they're cheating all right,' Omally replied, 'although I don't think the Professor has worked out quite how yet.'

In truth the Professor had not; he had watched Young Jack like a hawk and was certain that he had observed no hint of trickery. Surely the Horsemen could not be winning by skill alone?

Billy 'Banjoed' Breton, the Horsemen's inebriate reserve, was suddenly up on the oché. The very idea of a team fielding a reserve in a championship match was totally unheard of, the role of reserve being by tradition filled by the pub's resident drunk, who acted more as mascot and comedy relief than player.

A rumble of disbelief and suspicion rolled through the crowd. Two of the Horsemen's team pointed Billy in the direction of the board. 'Over there,' they said. Billy aimed his dart, flight first.

'Young Jack is having a pop at the Professor,' said Omally. 'He is definitely working some kind of a flanker.'

A look of perplexity had crossed Professor Slocombe's

face. He cast about for a reason, but none was forthcoming. A gentle tap at his elbow suddenly marshalled his thoughts. 'There is one outside and one by the machine,' said Edgar Allan Poe.

Professor Slocombe nodded.

'May I ask the purpose of the game?'

'It is a challenge match between the hostelry known as the Four Horsemen and our own beloved Flying Swan,' Professor Slocombe replied telepathically.

'Then may I ask why you allow your opponents the edge by having their missiles guided by a spirit form?' A smile broke out upon Professor Slocombe's face which did not go unnoticed by John Omally.

'He's sussed it,' said John.

Professor Slocombe leant close to the ear of Young Jack. 'Have you ever heard me recite the rite of exorcism?' he asked. 'I have it down to something of a fine art.'

Young Jack cast the old man the kind of look which could deflower virgins and cause babies to fill their nappies. 'All right,' said he, 'we will play it straight.'

'That you will never do. But simply chalk that one up and be advised.'

'Forty-seven,' bawled the adjudicator, who was growing hoarse.

'Unlucky,' said Professor Slocombe.

'The Swan need sixty-eight.' The Swan got it with little difficulty.

Lombard Omega ran up and down the flight deck, peering through the plexiglass portholes and waving his fists in the air. 'Where's it gone?' he ranted at intervals. 'Where's it fucking gone?'

His navigator punched all he could into the console and shrugged repeatedly. 'It just isn't there,' he said. 'It's gone, caput, finito, gone.'

'It must be there! It was fucking there when we left it!'

The navigator covered his ears to the obscenity. 'It honestly isn't, now,' he said. 'There's a lot of debris about, though, a veritable asteroid belt.'

'You find something and find it quick,' growled his Commanding Officer, 'or you go down the shit chute into hyperspace.'

The navigator bashed away at the console like a mad thing. 'There's no trace,' he whispered despairingly, 'the entire system's dead.' He tapped at the macroscopic intensifier. 'Oh no it isn't, look, there's a signal.'

Lombard was at his side in an instant. 'Bring it up then, you wally. Bring the frigging thing up.'

The navigator enlarged the image upon the three-dimensional screen. 'It's on Planet Earth,' he said. 'A triangulation and a ley image, the constellation of the Plough surely, and look there.'

Lombard looked there.

'One third up from the base line of the triangulation, a beacon transmitting a signal. The coordinates of an approach run, that's where they are!'

'Hm.' Lombard stroked his Hollywood chin. 'The bastards have moved closer to the Sun. Wise move, wise bloody move. Take us in then. Earth full steam ahead. Lock into autopilot, the beacon will guide us in. Anybody got a roll-up?'

Omally rolled a cigarette as the Professor joined them at the table. 'You found them out, then?' he asked between licks.

'I don't think we've entirely got the better of him,' the old man replied. 'He's a trick or two up his sleeve yet, I believe.'

'I won't ask what that one turned out to be.'

'The Swan lead by one game to nil,' croaked the adjudicator. 'Second game on. Horsemen to throw.'

As this was a championship match, by local rules, the losing team threw first. Young Jack ran his forked tongue about the tip of his dart. 'Straight and true this time, Professor,' quoth he.

'With the corner up,' the old man replied.

Young Jack flung his darts in such rapid succession that they were nothing more than a triple blur. They each struck the board 'straight and true' within the wired boundaries of the treble twenty, which was nothing more nor less than anybody had expected. The grinning demonologist strode to the board and tore out his darts with a vengeance.

'I should like very much to see the fellow miss once in a while,' Pooley told the Professor. 'Just to give the impression that he isn't infallible.' Professor Slocombe whispered another Latin phrase and Young Jack knocked his pint of mild into his father's lap. 'Thank you,' said Jim, 'I appreciated that.'

Archie Karachi was throwing for the Swan. Dressed this evening in a stunning kaftan, oblivious to the damage wrought upon his kitchen, he was definitely on form. Archie had a most unique manner of play. As a singles man, his technique brought a tear to the eye of many a seasoned player. Scorning the beloved treble twenty, he went instead for bizarre combinations which generally had the chalksman in a panic of fingers and thumbs. On a good night with luck at his elbow he could tear away an apparent two hundred in three throws. Even when chalked up, this still had his opponents believing that he had thrown his shots away. Tonight he threw a stunning combination which had the appearance of being a treble nineteen, a double thirteen and a bullseye, although it was hard to be certain.

The degree of mental arithmetic involved in computing the final total was well beyond the man on the chalks and most of the patrons present. When the five hundred and one was scratched out and two hundred and fifty-seven appeared in its place nobody thought to argue.

'I admire that,' said Professor Slocombe. 'It is a form of negative psychology. I will swear that if the score does not come up in multiples of twenty, nobody can work it out.'

'I can,' said Omally, 'but he is on our side.'

'I can't,' said Pooley. 'He pulls his darts out so quickly I couldn't even see what he scored.'

'Ah,' said Omally, 'here is a man I like to watch.'

The Four Horsemen's most extraordinary player had to be the man Kelly. He was by no means a great dartsman, but for sheer entertainment value he stood alone. It must be understood that the wondrous scores previously recorded are not entirely typical of the play as a whole, and that not each member of the team was a specialist in his field. The high and impossible scores were the preserve of the very few and finest. Amongst each team, the Swan and the Horsemen being no exception, there were also able players, hard triers, and what might be accurately described as the downright desperate.

The man Kelly was one of the latter. When he flung a dart it was very much a case of stand aside lads, and women and children first. The man Kelly was more a fast bowler than a darts player.

The man Kelly bowled a first dart. It wasn't a bad one and it plunged wholeheartedly in the general direction of the board. Somewhere, however, during the course of its journey the lone projectile suddenly remembered that it had pressing business elsewhere. The man Kelly's dart was never seen again.

'A little off centre?' the player asked his fuming and speechless captain.

His second throw was a classic in every sense of the word. Glancing off the board with the sound of a ricocheting rifle bullet it tore back into the assembled crowd, scattering friend and foe alike and striking home through the lobe of Old Pete's right ear.

The crowd engulfed the ancient to offer assistance. 'Don't touch it,' bellowed the old one. 'By God, it has completely cured the rheumatism in my left kneecap.'

Lombard Omega scrutinized the instrument panel and swore between his teeth. 'I can't see this,' he said at length. 'This does not make any fucking sense. I mean, be reasonable, our good world Ceres cannot just vanish away like piss down a cesspit in the twinkling of a bleeding eyelid.'

The navigator whispered a silent prayer to his chosen deity. It was an honour to serve upon the flagship of the Cerean battle fleet, but it was a hard thing indeed to suffer the constant stream of obscenity which poured from his commander's mouth. 'We have been away for a very long time,' he ventured. 'More than six thousand years, Earth time.'

'Earth time? Earth bleeding time? What is Earth time?'

'Well, as target world, it must be considered to be standard solar time.'

Lombard Omega spat on the platinum-coated deck and ground the spittle in with a fibreglass heel. 'This doesn't half get my dander up,' said he.

Standard solar time was approaching ten-fifteen of the p.m. clock, and the Four Horsemen and the Flying Swan now stood even at two games all and one to play for the Shield. Tension, which had been reaching the proverbial breaking-point, had now passed far beyond that, and chaos, panic, and desperation had taken its place. Omally had ground seven Biros into oblivion and his book now resembled some nightmare of Einsteinian cross-calculation.

'I sincerely believe that the ultimate secrets of the

universe might well be found within this book,' said Pooley, leafing over the heavily-thumbed pages. For his outspokenness, he received a blow to the skull which sent him reeling. Omally was at present in no mood for the snappy rejoinder.

'For God's sake get another round in,' said Professor Slocombe. Omally left the table.

'Forgive me if you will,' said Pooley, when the Irishman was engaged in pummelling his way through the crowd towards the bar, 'but you do remember that we are under imminent threat of annihilation by these lads from Ceres. I mean, we are still taking it seriously, aren't we?'

Professor Slocombe patted Pooley's arm. 'Good show,' he said. 'I understand your concern. It is always easy to surround oneself with what is safe and comfortable and to ignore the *outré* threats which lurk upon the borderline. Please be assured that we have done everything that can be done.'

'Sorry,' said Jim, 'but strange as it may seem, I do get a little anxious once in a while.'

'Ladies and gentlemen,' croaked the adjudicator in a strangled voice, 'the end is near and we must face the final curtain.' There were some boos and a few cheers. 'The last match is to play, the decider for the Challenge Shield, and I will ask for silence whilst the two teams prepare themselves.'

A respectful hush fell upon the Swan. Even the boy Rathbone ceased his game. However, this was not through his being any respecter of darts tournaments, but rather that his last two-bob bit had run out, and he was forced up to the bar for more change.

'It is the playoff, five hundred and one to gain. By the toss, first darts to the Horsemen, good luck to all, and game on.'

Professor Slocombe's eyes swung towards the Horsemen's team. Something strange seemed to have occurred within their ranks. Old Jack had declined to take his darts and sat sullenly in his wheelchair. The man Kelly was nowhere to be seen, and the other disembodied members of the team had withdrawn to their places of perpetual night and were apparently taking no more interest in the outcome of the game.

Alone stood Young Jack, hollow-eyed and defiant.

'He means to play it alone,' said the Professor. 'I do not believe that it is against the rules.'

'By no means,' said Omally. 'A man can take on a regiment, should he so choose. As a bookmaker I find such a confrontation interesting, to say the least.'

The Swan's patrons found it similarly so and Omally was forced to open book upon his shirt sleeves.

Young Jack took the mat. He gave the Professor never a glance as he threw his stygian arrows. To say that he actually threw them, however, would be to give a false account of the matter, for at one moment the darts were in his hand, and in another, or possibly the same, they were plastered into the darts board. No-one saw them leave nor enter, but all agreed that the score was an unbeatable multiple of twenty.

'One hundred and eighty,' came a whispered voice.

Norman stepped to the fore. Although unnoticed by the throng, his darts gave off an electrical discharge which disabled television sets three streets away and spoiled telephonic communications a mile off.

'One hundred and eighty,' came a still small voice, when he had done his business.

Young Jack strode once more into the fray. His eyes shone like a pair of Cortina reversing lamps and a faint yellow fog rose from the corners of his mouth. He turned his head upon its axis and grinned back over his shoulders at the hushed crowd. With hardly a glance towards the board, he flung his darts The outcome was a matter for the Guinness Book of Records to take up at a later date.

'I don't like this,' said Professor Slocombe. 'I am missing something, but I do not know what it is.'

'We are scoring equal,' said Omally, 'he needs but one unfortunate error.'

'I am loath to intervene, John.'

'It might get desperate, Professor, say a few words in the old tongue, just to be on the safe side.'

'We will wait a bit and see.'

'He is closing for the kill,' said John.

Professor Slocombe shook his head. 'I still cannot see it, he appears to be winning by skill alone.'

'God bless him,' said Pooley.

Omally raised a fist towards his companion. 'We are talking about the Swan's trophy here,' he said, waggling the terror weapon towards Pooley. 'This is no joke.'

'One day,' said Jim calmly, 'I shall turn like the proverbial worm and take a terrible retribution upon you, Omally, for all the blows you have administered to my dear head.'

'*Sssh*,' went at least a dozen patrons. 'Uncle Ted is up.'

Uncle Ted, Brentford's jovial greengrocer, was possibly the most loved man in the entire district. His ready smile and merry wit, his recourse to a thousand cheersome and altruistic *bons mots*, of the 'laugh and the world laughs with you, snore and you sleep alone' variety, brought joy into the lives of even the most manic of depressives. It was said that he could turn a funeral procession into a conga line, and, although there is no evidence to show that he ever took advantage of this particular gift, he was never short of a jocular quip or two as he slipped a few duff sprouts into a customer's carrier-bag.

Omally, who could not find it within himself to trust any man who would actually deal in, let alone handle, a sprout, found the greengrocer nauseous to the extreme degree. 'That smile could make a Samaritan commit suicide,' he said.

Uncle Ted did a little limbering-up knee-work, made flexing motions with his shoulders, and held a wet finger into the air. 'Is the wind behind us?' he asked, amidst much laughter from his supporters. He waved at the smoke-filled air with a beermat. 'Which way's the board then? Anybody got a torch?'

Omally groaned deeply within the folds of his beard. 'Get on with it, you twerp,' he muttered.

Uncle Ted, who for all his inane clowning, was well aware that a wrong move now could cost him his livelihood, took a careful aim whose caution was disguised behind a bout of bum wriggling. His first dart creased into the treble twenty with very little to spare.

'Where did it land then?' he asked, cupping his hand to his forehead and squinting about. His supporters nudged one another, cheered and guffawed. 'What a good lad,' they said. 'Good old Uncle Ted.'

Ted looked towards the board and made a face of surprise upon sighting his dart. 'Who threw that?' he asked.

To cut a long and very tedious story short, Uncle Ted's second dart joined its fellow in the treble twenty, but his third, however, had ideas of its own and fastened its nose into the dreaded single one. The laughter and applause which followed this untimely blunder rang clearly and loudly, but not from any of those present who favoured the home team.

'What a good lad,' said Young Jack. 'Good old Uncle Ted.'

The greengrocer left the Flying Swan that night in disgrace. Some say that like Judas he went forth and hanged himself. Others, who are better informed, say that he moved to Chiswick where he now owns three shops and spends six months of the year abroad.

Omally was leafing frantically through the pages of his book. 'I am in big schtuck here,' he said suddenly, brushing away a bead of perspiration from his brow. 'In my haste to accept bets and my certainty of the Swan's ultimate victory, I have somewhat miscalculated. The fix is in and ruination is staring me in the beard.'

Professor Slocombe took the book from Omally's trembling fingers and examined it with care. 'I spy a little circle of treachery here,' he said.

'The Four Horsemen needs one hundred and forty-one,' gasped the adjudicator.

'I am finished,' said Omally. 'It is back to the old country for me. A boat at the dock and before the night is out.'

Professor Slocombe was staring at the dartboard and shaking his head, his face wearing an unreadable expression. Pooley was ashen and speechless. But for the occasional *bitow* to the rear of the crowd, the Swan was a vacuum of utter silence.

Young Jack squared up to the board as Omally hid his face in his hands and said a number of Hail Marys.

Jack's first dart pierced the treble twenty, his second the double, and his third the single one.

'One hundred and one,' mouthed the adjudicator in a manner which was perfectly understood by all deaf-mutes present.

Omally waved away a later punter proffering a wad of notes. 'Suck, boy,' was all that he could say.

The adjudicator retired to the bar. He would say no more this evening and would, in all probability, make himself known for the rest of his life through the medium of notepad and pencil.

Norman, who had sacked the rest of the team, took the floor. He threw another blinding one hundred and eighty but it really didn't seem to matter any more.

The Four Horsemen needed but a double top to take the Shield, and a child of three, or at a pinch four if he was born in Brentford, could surely have got that, given three darts.

Neville put the towels up and climbed on to the bar counter, knobkerry in hand. There was very likely to be a good deal of death and destruction within another minute or two and he meant to be a survivor at any cost.

Croughton the pot-bellied potman leant back in his beer crate refuge and puffed upon his cigarette. Up above, the night stars glittered eternally, and nothing there presaged the doom and desolation which was about to befall Brentford. 'Oh look,' he said suddenly to himself, as he peered up at the firmament. 'Shooting stars, that's lucky. I shall make a wish on them.'

Upon the allotment a tiny figure moved. He was ill-washed and stubble-chinned and he muttered beneath his breath. At intervals he raised his head and called, 'Edgar.' No reply came, and he continued upon his journey, driven by a compulsion impossible to resist.

'Four Horsemen to throw,' said some drunken good-time Charlie who had no idea of the gravity of the situation. 'The Four Horsemen needs forty.'

Young Jack appeared from the crowd, wielding his dreaded darts. He crossed the floor and approached the Professor. 'You will not enjoy this, St Germaine,' he spat. 'Be advised that I know you for what you are and accept your defeat like the gentleman you are not.'

Professor Slocombe was unmoved, his glittering eyes fixed upon Young Jack. 'If you want this to be sport,' said he, 'then so be it. If however you crave something more, then know that I am equal to the challenge.'

'Do your worst,' sneered Young Jack. 'I am master of you.'

'So be it,' said Professor Slocombe.

Young Jack took the oché. Again his head turned one hundred and eighty degrees upon his neck as he gazed at the crowd. 'The Swan is finished,' he announced. 'Five years have passed and you have grown weak and complacent. Prepare to bow to a superior force. Say goodbye to your trophy, you suckers.'

A murderous rumble rolled through the crowd. There was a great stamping of feet and squaring of shoulders. Ties were being slackened and top buttons undone. Cufflinks were being removed and dropped into inside pockets.

Young Jack raised his dart and lined up for a winner. Neville took a sharper hold upon his knobkerry and patted at his loins to ensure that the cricketer's box he had had the foresight to hire for the occasion was in place.

Omally smote the Professor, 'Save us, old man,' he implored. 'I will apologize later.'

Professor Slocombe rose upon his cane and stared at his adversary.

Young Jack drew back his hand and flung his dart.

The thing creased the air at speed, then suddenly slowed; to the utter dumbfoundment of the crowd, it hung suspended in time and space exactly six feet three inches above the deck and five feet from the board.

Professor Slocombe concentrated his gaze, Young Jack did likewise.

The dart moved forward a couple of inches, then stopped once more and took a twitch backwards.

The crowd were awestruck. Neville's knobkerry hung loose in his hand. Great forces were at work here, great forces that he would rather have no part in. But he was here at the killing, and as part-time barman would do little other than offer support.

Every eye, apart from one ill-matched pair, was upon that dart. Supporters of both Swan and Horsemen alike wrinkled their brows and strained their brains upon that dart. Beads of perspiration appeared a-plenty and fell, ruining many a good pint.

The dart eased forward another six inches. Professor Slocombe turned his stare towards the glowing red eyes of his opponent. The dart retreated.

Young Jack drew a deep breath and the dart edged once more towards its target.

'You wouldn't get this on the telly,' whispered Jim Pooley.

Old Jack suddenly put his wrinkled hands to the wheels of his chair and propelled himself towards the Professor.

'Restrain that man!' yelled Omally.

Pooley lurched from his seat, but, in his haste to halt the wheeling ancient, caught his foot upon a chair leg and tripped. He clutched at the table, overturning it, and blundered into Professor Slocombe, propelling him into the crowd. At this moment of truth the proverbial all hell was let loose.

The night-black dart set forth once more upon its journey and thundered towards the board. Young Jack stood grinning as Pooley upset his infirm father and brought down at least another four people in his desperation. Omally struggled up and struck the nearest man a vicious blow to the skull.

Before the eyes of those stunned patrons who were not yet engaged in the fracas the dart struck the board. As it did so a devastating explosion occurred overhead which shattered the bar optics, brought down great lumps of plaster from the ceiling and upset the part-time barman into the crowd.

'It is God!' shouted Omally, hitting with a will. 'He will stand no more!'

Nicholas Roger Raffles Rathbone fell away from the Captain Laser machine. 'It wasn't me,' he whimpered, 'I didn't do it.'

The lights of the Swan suddenly dimmed as the entire world which was Brentford proper went mad.

'It wasn't me, it wasn't me, I swear it.'

Nobody really cared. Outside something terrific was happening. Possibly it was the prelude to the long-awaited Armageddon, possibly earthquake, or tidal wave. Whatever it was, the darts fans were not going to be caught napping, and the stampede towards the door was all-consuming. A single darkly-clad figure wearing a brand of creosote aftershave was immediately trampled to oblivion beneath the rush.

As the patrons poured into the night the enormity of what had occurred became apparent. Shards of flaming metal were hurtling down upon Brentford. Great sheets of fire were rising from the tarmac of the Ealing Road as the surface met each blazing assault. Several front gardens were ablaze.

Pooley and Omally helped the fallen Professor to his feet. 'It has begun,' said John. 'What do we do?'

'To the machine,' yelled the old man. 'It would appear that Norman has served us right.'

Nicholas Roger Raffles Rathbone stood blankly staring at the screen. 'I didn't do it,' he said repeatedly.

Omally was at his side in an instant. 'Play it,' he roared. 'You are the kiddie, play it.'

Rathbone drew back in horror, 'No,' he shouted. 'Something is wrong. I will have no part of it.'

'Play it!' Omally grabbed at the green hair and drew the stinker close to the machine. 'You are the unbeatable master, play it.'

Nick drew up his head in a gesture of defiance. As he did so, he stumbled upon a chunk of fallen ceiling and fell backwards, leaving Omally clutching a bundle of green hair and what appeared to be an india-rubber face mask. The figure who collapsed to the Swan's floor, now bereft of his disguise, resembled nothing more nor less than a young Jack Palance.

'He's one of them,' screamed Omally, pointing to the fallen Cerean, and dancing up and down dementedly. 'He was never playing the machine, he was signalling with it. Get him, get him!'

Pooley hastened to obey. 'The left armpit, isn't it?' he growled.

The erstwhile paperboy backed away, covering his wedding tackle. 'Not the armpit,' he whimpered. 'Anything but the armpit.'

Professor Slocombe was at the machine. 'How does it work?' he cried. 'How does it work?'

'Leave him, Jim,' yelled Omally, 'play the machine, shoot the bastards down.'

Upon the allotments columns of pure white light were rising into the sky. The door of Soap Distant's hut was wide open and a great glow poured from it, silhouetting dozens of identical figures gliding through the opening.

When the first great explosion occurred, a small dwarf in a soiled postman's suit had flattened himself into a sprout bed, but now he arose to his full height and stared about in horror at the bizarre spectacle.

He danced up and down and flapped his arms, 'Edgar,' he shouted, 'Edgar, help me, help me.' The figures now pouring through the shed doorway were bearing down upon him, and the postman took to his tiny heels and fled. He plunged through the open allotment gates and paused only to assure himself that he still had a tight hold upon the pair of bolt-cutters he had been carrying. Without further ado he continued his journey, bound for a certain lock-up garage upon the Butts Estate, and destiny.

In the Swan, Pooley was at the controls. 'There's eight

of them,' he said, 'moving in a V formation.' His finger rattled upon the neutron bomb release button, and tiny beads of yellow light swept upwards towards the bobbing cones at the top of the screen.

'Get them, Jim,' screamed Omally. 'Come on now, you know how it's done.'

'I'm trying, aren't I? Get us a drink for God's sake.'

Neville, who had fallen rather heavily but happily not upon his tender parts, was on all fours in the middle of the floor. 'What the hell is going on?' he gasped. 'Get away from the counter, Omally.'

'We're breaking your machine,' said the breathless Irishman, 'don't knock it.'

'But what was that explosion? My God!' Neville pointed out through the Swan's front windows. 'Half the Ealing Road's on fire. Call the appliances.'

Pooley bashed at the button with his fist and jumped up and down. 'I've got one! I've got one!'

Overhead, but a little less loudly this time, there was another explosion, followed by the sound of faltering engines and a Messerschmitt dive-bomber scream.

Those present at the Swan ducked their heads as something thundered by at close quarters and whistled away into the distance. There was a moment's deadly silence followed by a muted but obviously powerful report.

Another Cerean craft had fallen to Earth upon Brentford; given its point of impact, it was unlikely that Jim Pooley would ever again receive a threatening letter regarding an overdue library book.

'There! There!' Neville was pointing and ranting. 'It is the third world war and we never got the four-minute warning. I am withholding my vote at the next election.'

Small Dave struggled up from the gutter and shrieked with pain. He had been rather nearer to the library's destruction and a sliver of shrapnel from the founder's plaque had caught him in the backside.

'Oh woe, oh woe, oh damn!' he wailed. A less determined man would by now have called it a day and dived for the nearest foxhole, but loathing and hatred overwhelmed the postman, and nothing would turn him from his vendetta. Feeling tenderly at his bleeding bum, he raised the bolt-cutter to the garage lock and applied all his strength. He strained and sweated as he fought with the steel clasp. Finally, with a sickening crunch the metal gave, and the garage door swung upwards.

Small Dave stood panting in the opening, his features shining pinkly by the light of ten thousand blazing dog-eared library books. Sweat poured from his face as he surveyed the object of his quest. Snorting and wriggling in the eaves of the lock-up garage was Simon. A camel far from home.

'Now that you have it,' said a voice which loosened Small Dave's bowels, 'what are you going to do with it?'

The postman swung upon his blakeys. 'Edgar,' he said, 'where in the holy blazes have you been?'

Norman had been almost the first man out of the Swan. As the explosion rang in his ears he had realized that big trouble was in store and that if he was to take his great quest to its ultimate conclusion, now was going to have to be the time.

Clutching his purloined microcircuit to his bosom he had braved the rain of fire and legged it back to his shop and his workroom. Now, as the explosions came thick and fast from all points of the compass, he fiddled with a screwdriver and slotted the thing into place.

'Power inductor,' he said to himself, 'will channel all the power from miles around directly into the apparatus. Wonderful, wonderful!'

Norman threw the much-loved 'we belong dead' switch and his equipment sprang into life.

In the Swan, the lights momentarily dimmed. 'Another power cut,' groaned Neville. 'All I bloody need, another power cut. Typical it is, bloody typical.'

Pooley thundered away at the machine, watched by the Professor and John Omally, who was feeding the lad with scotch.

'Go to it, Jim,' Omally bashed Pooley repeatedly upon the back. 'You've got them on the run. Here you missed that one, pay attention, will you?'

Pooley laboured away beneath the Irishman's assault. 'Lay off me, John,' he implored. 'They're firing back. Look at that.'

The skyline upon the screen had suddenly been translated into that of the immediate area. The silhouettes of the flatblocks and the gasometer were now clearly visible. As the three men stared in wonder, a shower of sparks descended upon the screen from one of the circling craft and struck the silhouette. Outside, a great roar signalled the demolition of one of the flatblocks.

'Get them, you fool, get them.'

Unnoticed, Raffles Rathbone edged towards the door and slipped through it, having it hastily away upon his toes towards the allotments.

The Swan's lights dimmed once more.

In Norman's kitchenette, lights were flashing, and a haze of smoke was rising from many a dodgy spot weld.

Norman sat at his console, punching coordinates into his computer, an ever-increasing hum informing him that the equipment was warming up nicely.

Clinging to the controls of a not altogether dissimilar console was a swarthy clone of a famous film star; Lombard Omega had taken the controls.

'Treachery,' he spat, from between his gritted and

expensively capped teeth. 'Fucking treachery! Those bastards have drawn us into a trap. Bleeding change of government, I shouldn't wonder. How many ships lost, Mr Navigator?'

The navigator shrank low over his guidance systems. 'Four now, sir,' he said, 'no, make that five.'

'Take us out of autopilot then, I shall fly this frigging ship manually.'

One of the remaining blips vanished from the video screen of the Captain Laser Alien Attack machine.

'Oh dear,' said the Professor. 'It had occurred to me that they might just twig it.'

'There's still another two,' said Omally. 'Get them, get them!'

There was now a good deal of Brentford which was only memory. The New Inn had gone, along with the library, and one of the gasometers was engulfed in flame. A falling craft had cut Uncle Ted's greengrocery business cleanly out of the Ealing Road, which, survivors of the holocaust were later to remark, was about the only good thing to come out of the whole affair. There had miraculously been no loss of life, possibly because Brentford boasts more well-stocked Anderson shelters per square mile than any other district in London, but probably because this is not that kind of book.

Pooley was faltering in his attack. 'My right arm's gone,' moaned he, 'and my bomb release button finger's got the cramp, I can play no more.'

Omally struck his companion the now legendary blow to the skull.

'That does it!' Pooley turned upon Omally. 'When trouble threatens, strike Jim Pooley. I will have no more.'

Pooley threw a suddenly uncramped fist towards Omally's chin. By virtue of its unexpected nature and unerring accuracy, he floored the Irishman for a good deal more than the count of ten.

Professor Slocombe looked down at the unconscious figure beneath the beard. 'If that score is settled, I would appreciate it if you would apply yourself once more to the machine before the other two craft catch wind of what is going on and switch to manual override.'

'Quite so,' said Pooley, spitting upon his palms and stepping once more to the video screen.

Small Dave backed away from Edgar Allan Poe, his tiny hands a flapping blur. 'What is all this?' he demanded. 'I don't like the look of you one bit.'

The Victorian author approached upon silent, transparent feet. 'You conjured me here,' he said, 'and I came willingly, thinking you to be a disciple. But now I find that I am drawn into a position from which I am unable to extricate myself. That I must serve you. That cannot be!'

'So leave it then,' whined Small Dave. 'I meant no offence to you, I only wanted a little assistance.'

'You realize who I am? I am Poe, the master of terror. The greatest novelist ever to live. Poe, the creator of Dupin, the world's original consulting detective. Dupin who was not, I repeat not, a dwarf. You mess me about with your trivial vendettas. I have spoken with Professor Slocombe, there is only one way I can find release. You vindictive grudge-bearing wee bastard!'

Small Dave backed towards the floating camel. Simon was floundering amongst the rafters, bawling now at the top of his voice, loosening slates and splintering woodwork.

'Stay away from me,' shrieked Small Dave.

'Stay away from me!' shrieked Simon in fluent dromedary.

Edgar Allan Poe stalked onwards, his patent leather pumps raising dust upon another plane, but leaving no footprint upon the Earth.

'Stay away from me!'

Simon gave a great lurch and burst out of the rafters

of the lock-up garage. As he rose through the shattered opening towards the stars, Edgar Allan Poe lunged forward and, in a single movement, bound the trailing halter line firmly about Small Dave's wrist.

'Oh no!' wailed the dwarf as he was dragged from his feet to follow the wayward camel through the open roof.

Edgar Allan Poe watched them go. 'I will be off now,' he said, and, like Small Dave, he was.

In Norman's kitchenette all sorts of exciting things were happening. Dials were registering overload to all points of the compass, lights were flashing, and buzzers buzzing.

The great brain-hammering hum had reached deafening point and a hideous pressure filled the room, driving Norman's head down between his shoulderblades and bursting every Corona bottle upon his shop shelves. With superhuman effort he thumped down another fist full of switches, clasped his hands across his ears, and sank to the floor.

Every light in Brentford, Chiswick, Hounslow, Ealing, Hanwell, Kew, and, for some reason, Penge went out.

Lombard Omega squinted through a porthole. 'Blackout!' he growled. 'Fucking blackout, the wily sods. Mr Navigator, how many of us left?'

The navigator looked up from his controls. 'We are it,' he said.

What Lombard Omega had to say about that cannot possibly be recorded. It must, however, be clearly stated in his defence that it was one of his ancestors who had invented the Anglo-Saxon tongue.

'Take us in low,' he said. 'We will strafe out the entire area. Stand by at the neutron bomb bays and make ready the Gamma weapon.'

'Not the Gamma weapon?' said all those present.

'The Gamma weapon!'

'Fuck me,' said the navigator.

Pooley, Neville, and Professor Slocombe peered around in the darkness. The only light available flickered through the Swan's front windows from a roaring inferno which had once been much of Brentford.

'What now?' Pooley asked. The Professor shook his head.

'You've done it, you've done it! Crack the champagne.' Neville performed a high-stepping dance before the now darkened and obviously defunct Captain Laser Alien Attack machine.

'Free beer for a year,' moaned a voice from the deck.

'For a century,' sang Neville. 'Oh bliss, oh heaven, oh no!'

From the distance came a faint whine of unearthly engines. Something large and deadly was approaching, and all means of confounding its destructive intent had vanished away.

'Oh dear,' said Professor Slocombe, 'anybody want the last rites?'

'Prepare the Gamma weapon,' ordered Lombard Omega.

'Gamma weapon prepared, sir.'

'Take out the entire quadrant, spare not an inch.'

'Not an inch, sir.'

'Fire the Gamma weapon.'

The navigator flinched and touched a lighted panel upon the master console. A broad beam of red raw energy leapt down from beneath the ship and struck home upon the Kew side of the river Thames.

The five-hundred-year-old oaks of the Royal Botanic Gardens took fire and half a millennium of history melted away in a single moment. The beam extended over a wider area and tore into the river. The waters thrashed and boiled, like a witches' cauldron, hissed and frothed beneath the unstoppable power of the deadly Gamma weapon.

And the beam moved forward.

The mother ship ground on over the river, a vast chromium blimp filling a quarter of the sky. Along the length of its mirrored sides, lights glittered and twinkled like oil beads. Above it, great dorsal spines rose sharklike and menacing.

The hideous beam moved up from the churning waters and ripped into the river bank, hewing out a broad and ragged channel into which the old Thames gushed in a billowing flood tide.

Ahead lay the Brentford Quadrant, the Ealing Road, and the Flying Swan.

Brentonians fled from their shelters out into the streets. They shielded their faces against the all-consuming heat and took to their heels. The world was coming to an end and now was not the time to take the old Lot's wife backward glance.

In the Swan the lads cowered in terror as the ghastly rumble of falling masonry and the death-cry of splintering glass drew ever nearer.

Outside, the Ealing Road, crammed with screaming humanity, pouring and tumbling in a mad lemming dash away from the approaching holocaust. Behind them the blinding red wall of fire pressed on, destroying everything which lay in its path.

Omally was upon his knees. 'Stop it!' he screamed at Professor Slocombe. 'Do something, in the name of our God. Only you can.'

The Professor stood immobile. The cries of terror rang in his ears and stung at his soul. The town he had for so very long cared for and protected was being razed to ashes and he was powerless to stop it. He turned a compassionate face towards the Irishman and tears welled in his eyes. 'What can I do?' he asked, in a choked voice. 'I am truly sorry, John.'

Lombard Omega stared down upon the carnage, with a face of hatred and contempt, 'Run, you bastards!' he shouted, as the antlike figures beneath scattered in all directions. 'I will have every last one of you, look at that, look at that.'

The crew of the mother ship craned their necks to the portholes. Below, the destruction was savage and sickening. The streets were being cleaved apart, the houses and shops, flatblocks and places of worship driven from existence.

More than thirty Morris Minors, some even priceless collectors' models with split windscreens, suicide doors and hand-clap wiper arms, had already been atomized, never again to sneak through the dodgy back street MOT.

Professor Slocombe closed his hands in prayer. As the wall of fire moved relentlessly forward and the buildings fell into twisted ruination, he knew that only a miracle could save Brentford.

'What's that, sir?' asked a Cerean deckhand, pointing through a porthole.

'What's what?'

'That, sir.'

Lombard Omega strained his eyes through the rising smokescreen of burning Brentford. 'Jesus Christ!' he screamed, catching sight of a floating object directly in the ship's path. 'It's a fucking camel! Hard to port! Hard to port!'

'You are at the controls,' the cringing navigator informed his captain.

Lombard swung the wheel and the craft veered sharply to the left, avoiding the drifting mammal by a hairbreadth.

Caught in the slipstream, a certain small postman let fly with a volley of obscenity which would have caused even the ship's captain to blush.

'That was fucking close,' said Lombard Omega, wiping creosote from his brow. 'Those bastards don't miss a trick, do they? Give me more power, Mr Navigator. More power!'

The navigator upped the ante and covered his eyes. A great vibration filled the air. A fearsome pressure driving everything downwards. The flood waters ceased their frenzied rush and hung suspended, as if touched by Moses's staff. The scattering Brentonians tumbled to the pavements, gasping at the super-heated air and clutching at their throats. The Captain Laser Alien Attack machine lurched from its mountings and toppled into the Swan, bringing down the side-wall and exposing the horrors of Archie Karachi's kitchen to Neville, who, borne by the terrible force, vanished backwards over the bar counter, losing the last of his fillings.

As Pooley and Omally struck the fag-scarred carpet, their last glimpse of anything approaching reality was of Professor Slocombe. The old man stood, the hell-fire painting his ancient features, hands raised towards the burning sky now visible through the Swan's shattered roof, his mouth reciting the syllables of a ritual which was old before the dawn of recorded history.

Above came the deadly whine of engines as Lombard Omega and the crew of the Starship *Sandra* moved in for the kill.

'Finish them!' screamed the Captain. 'Finish them!'

The ship rocked and shivered. Needles upon a thousand crystal dials rattled into the danger zone. A low pulsating hum set the Captain's teeth on edge and caused the navigator, who had suddenly found Christianity, to cross himself. 'Finish them!' screamed Lombard.

The ship's engines coughed and faltered. The air about the craft ionized as a vague image of something monstrous swam into view. It wavered, half-formed, and transparent, and then, amid a great maelstrom of tearing elements, became solid.

Lombard Omega stared in horror through the forward port. 'What's that?' he cried drawing up his hands. 'What in the name of F . . . '

His final words, however obscene, must remain unrecorded. For at one moment he was steering his craft through empty air above Brentford Football ground and at the next it was making violent and irreconcilable contact with the capping stone of the Great Pyramid of Cheops.

Whoosh, wham, crash, and *bitow* went the Starship *Sandra* as it lost a goodly amount of its undercarriage and slewed to one side. It plummeted downwards, a screaming ball of fire, narrowly missing the roof of the Flying Swan, cartwheeled over the Piano Museum, and tore down towards the allotments, the last men of Ceres, who were standing around looking rather bemused, a very great deal of carefully-laid explosive, and the few sparse and dismal remnants of a former postman's prize-winning cabbage patch.

There was a moment of terrible silence and then an explosion which rocked the seismographs at Greenwich and had the warlords of a dozen nations reaching towards the panic buttons.

A very great silence then fell upon what was left of the Brentford Triangle.

EPILOGUE

The sun rose the next morning at three a.m.

This came as a great surprise to those folk of Brentford who felt in the mood to enjoy the dawn chorus, but no more so than it did to the peoples of the Nile delta who, somewhat bewildered at the sudden disappearance of their greatest tourist attraction, noticed also that the nights were definitely drawing in a bit.

Had the Memorial Library clock been still extant, it would just have struck the hour when an impossibly long low-loader turned up the Ealing Road, demolishing Brentford's two remaining lampposts, and cracking a hundred paving-stones beneath its many-wheeled assault.

High in the cab, illuminated by the green dashlights and the first rays of the rising sun, sat a bald-headed man in a saffron robe. He puffed upon a Woodbine and stared through the tinted windscreen at the blackened wreckage which had once been the town of his birth.

There had been more than a few changes while he had been away, this was clear. Another council housing project, he assumed, or road-widening scheme, although it appeared a little drastic. He pulled the five-hundred-foot vehicle up through the gears and rolled it over the railway bridge, whose girders groaned beneath the strain. Where had the New Inn gone, and surely the council would not have demolished two of their cherished flatblocks?

The great vehicle's front wheels plunged into a pothole, dislodging the driver's Woodbine into his lap. He would have harsh words to say about all this and no mistake. Here he was, delivering the greatest archaeological discovery in the history of mankind, and they had let the roads go to ruin.

And what in Dante's name was that? Archroy brought the mammoth loader to a shuddering halt. Retrieving his fallen Woodbine, he climbed down from the cab.

In considerable awe he stared up at the vast structure which now stood upon the site formerly occupied by Brentford's football ground. That was the Great Pyramid of Giza or he was a clog-dancing Dutchman.

The man of bronze ground out his cigarette with a naked heel and scratched at his hairless pate. Whatever had been going on around here?

He climbed back into his cab and put the mighty vehicle into gear. He was rapidly losing his temper. Where was the reception committee? Where was the bunting and the Mayor? Had he not written to Neville detailing the time of his arrival? This was all a bit much.

Ahead, in the distance, faint lights showed in a window: the Flying Swan, surely, but candle-lit?

Archroy applied the brakes and brought the low-loader to a standstill outside the smoke-blackened and shrapnel-pocked drinking house. He fumbled in his dashboard for another packet of cigarettes, but could find nothing but a bundle of picture postcards displaying now inaccurate rooftop views of Brentford.

He climbed down from his cab, slammed shut the door and, kicking rubble to left and right of him, strode across the road to the Swan's doorway. With a single curling backward kick he applied his bare foot to the door, taking it from its hinges and propelling it forwards into the bar.

Four startled men looked up in horror from their drinks at the bar counter. Jim Pooley, John Omally, Professor Slocombe and Neville the part-time barman.

'Archroy?' gasped Neville, squinting towards the terrific figure framed in the Swan's doorway. 'Archroy, is that you?'

Archroy fixed the part-time barman with a baleful eye. 'I have the Ark of Noah outside on my lorry,' he roared. 'I don't suppose that any of you after-hours drinkers would care to step outside and give it the once-over?'

Omally struggled to his feet. 'The Ark of Noah, now, is it?' he said. 'Could I interest you at all in a guided tour around the Great Pyramid of Brentford?'

THE END

SPROUTLORE

The Now Official
ROBERT RANKIN
Fan Club

Members Will Receive:

Four Fabulous Issues of the *Brentford Mercury*, featuring previously unpublished stories by Robert Rankin. Also containing News, Reviews, Fiction and Fun.

A coveted Sproutlore Badge.

Special rates on exclusive T-shirts and merchandise.

'Amazing Stuff!' – Robert Rankin.

Annual Membership Costs £5 (Ireland), £7 (UK) or £11 (Rest of the World). Send a Cheque/PO to: **Sproutlore, 211 Blackhorse Avenue, Dublin 7, Ireland.** Email: sproutlore@lostcarpark.com WWW: http://www.lostcarpark.com/sproutlore

Sproutlore exists thanks to the permission of Robert Rankin and his publishers.

THE SPROUTS OF WRATH
by Robert Rankin

Amazing, but true: Brentford Town Council, in an act of supreme public-spiritedness (and a great big wodge of folding stuff from a mysterious benefactor) has agreed to host the next Olympic Games. The plans have been drawn up, contracts, money and promises are changing hands. Norman's designed some stunning kit for the home team, and even the Flying Swan's been threatened with a major refit (gasp!). But something is very wrong... primeval forces are stirring in ancient places...dark magic is afoot in Brentford and someone must save the world from overpowering evil...

... Jim Pooley and John Omally, come on down!

This must be the daring duo's toughest assignment yet. No longer can they weigh up the situation over a pint of lager at random moments during the day. No, this time, to save the world as we know it, the most horrible, the most terrifying, the heretofore untried – REGULAR EMPLOYMENT!!!

'A very funny book...a brilliant and exceedingly well written series'
Colin Munro, *Interzone*

The fourth novel in the now legendary *Brentford Trilogy*

0 552 13844 4

A SELECTED LIST OF FANTASY TITLES
AVAILABLE FROM CORGI AND BLACK SWAN

14802 4	MALLOREON 1: GUARDIANS OF THE WEST	David Eddings	£6.99
14807 5	BELGARIAD 1: PAWN OF PROPHECY	David Eddings	£6.99
14257 3	MIDNIGHT FALCON	David Gemmell	£6.99
14674 9	HERO IN THE SHADOWS	David Gemmell	£6.99
14274 3	THE MASTERHARPER OF PERN	Anne McCaffrey	£6.99
14615 3	CARPE JUGULUM	Terry Pratchett	£6.99
14616 1	THE FIFTH ELEPHANT	Terry Pratchett	£6.99
13681 6	ARMAGEDDON THE MUSICAL	Robert Rankin	£5.99
13832 0	THEY CAME AND ATE US, ARMAGEDDON II: THE B–MOVIE	Robert Rankin	£5.99
13923 8	THE SUBURBAN BOOK OF THE DEAD ARMAGEDDON III: THE REMAKE	Robert Rankin	£5.99
13841 X	THE ANTIPOPE	Robert Rankin	£5.99
13843 6	EAST OF EALING	Robert Rankin	£5.99
13844 4	THE SPROUTS OF WRATH	Robert Rankin	£5.99
14357 X	THE BRENTFORD CHAINSTORE MASSACRE	Robert Rankin	£5.99
13922 X	THE BOOK OF ULTIMATE TRUTHS	Robert Rankin	£5.99
13833 9	RAIDERS OF THE LOST CAR PARK	Robert Rankin	£5.99
13924 6	THE GREATEST SHOW OFF EARTH	Robert Rankin	£5.99
14212 3	THE GARDEN OF UNEARTHLY DELIGHTS	Robert Rankin	£5.99
14213 1	A DOG CALLED DEMOLITION	Robert Rankin	£5.99
14355 3	NOSTRADAMUS ATE MY HAMSTER	Robert Rankin	£5.99
14356 1	SPROUT MASK REPLICA	Robert Rankin	£5.99
14580 7	THE DANCE OF THE VOODOO HANDBAG	Robert Rankin	£5.99
14589 0	APOCALYPSO	Robert Rankin	£5.99
14590 4	SNUFF FICTION	Robert Rankin	£5.99
14741 9	SEX AND DRUGS AND SAUSAGE ROLLS	Robert Rankin	£5.99
14742 7	WAITING FOR GODALMING	Robert Rankin	£5.99
14743 5	WEB SITE STORY	Robert Rankin	£5.99
14897 0	THE FANDOM OF THE OPERATOR	Robert Rankin	£5.99
99777 3	THE SPARROW	Mary Doria Russell	£7.99
99811 7	CHILDREN OF GOD	Mary Doria Russell	£6.99